DATE DUE

BRADY'S REVENGE

Other books by L. W. Rogers:

The Twisted Trail

BRADY'S REVENGE

•

L. W. Rogers

AVALON BOOKS
NEW YORK

Published by Thomas Bouregy & Co., Inc.
160 Madison Avenue, New York, NY 10016

Library of Congress Cataloging-in-Publication Data

Rogers, L. W.
    Brady's revenge / L. W. Rogers.
        p. cm.
    ISBN 978-0-8034-9980-5 (hardcover : acid-free paper)
    I. Title.
    PS3618.O465B73   2009
    813'.6—dc22

                                        2009012578

PRINTED IN THE UNITED STATES OF AMERICA
ON ACID-FREE PAPER
BY HADDON CRAFTSMEN, BLOOMSBURG, PENNSYLVANIA

To my grandson, Brandon Ross,
who shares my love of horses and the old West.
And to my editor, Faith Black—thank you!

Chapter One

Kansas
1878

I swear this is my last job. Otherwise, I'll end up with a noose around my neck.

Sweat pooled in Brady Wilkes' armpits. The dusty blue wool uniform he wore made him even more uncomfortable. He knew from experience that odor told a lot about a man's composure.

From beneath the brim of his hat, Brady watched the craggy rancher finger the gold coins.

The old man shifted from one foot to the other as he met Brady's stare. He drawled slow and easy. "Figgered the Army would pay more'n forty dollars apiece for five head of prime horseflesh."

The rancher slipped the coins back into the canvas pouch and drew the leather straps shut with an audible snap. With his thumb he pushed his battered work hat back from his forehead. His eyes narrowed to slits. "What do you say about that, Lieutenant Hastings?" The rancher's legs spread a little farther apart, and his posture stiffened.

Brady read the challenge loud and clear. He kept his own voice steady and spoke with the confidence of his fictional rank. "I don't set the prices, Mr. Davis. My job is to select the best horses, pay whatever price the Army sets, then drive the horses to the fort."

Driblets of sweat trickled between Brady's shoulder blades. The deal was taking too long. What if the rancher decided to contact the post commander? What if he decided to ask Brady for credentials proving he was actually Lieutenant Hasting?

All the *what ifs* hummed like angry bees inside Brady's head. *This is the last swindle I'll pull for you, Lou Spearman.*

Silence hung heavy in the air. Brady extended a gloved hand, hoping to call a bluff. Ranch life was hard, he knew, and two hundred dollars would buy a lot of bacon and beans. "The pouch, Mr. Davis. It's obvious we don't have a deal."

Watching the indecisiveness on the old rancher's face, Brady knew he had to either push harder or walk away from the deal. He'd learned to read men and decided to try one more tactic. Pulling a slip of paper and a pencil nub from his uniform jacket, he licked the rounded lead point, allowing his hand to hover over the paper.

"Hold on there, young feller. What're you aiming to do?"

"Sir, my orders are to strike off the names of ranchers not interested in doing business with the United States Army."

"Hang on a minute. Never said I wasn't interested. Gotta pay my taxes, and winters are long and hard up here in the hills. I'd hoped to take my missus to visit her sister in Cheyenne, with money left over for a few niceties and such."

The rancher's voice rose a little as he jostled the pouch in his hand. "You tell that captain of your'n he's a swindlin' thief who oughta be horsewhipped." He gripped the money pouch tighter and turned to walk away.

"Mr. Davis. Sir?"

The old man turned back, a hard look on his face.

"The Army requires a bill of sale. If you'd be so kind as to write one out, my wranglers and I will be on our way."

Davis spat a stream of brown tobacco chaw. He dragged his sleeve across his mouth. His tone held no congeniality. "You write it out, Lieutenant, and I'll make my mark."

Tall and loose in the saddle, Brady nudged the horse to pick up its pace. Brady's sandy hair was wet under his black campaign hat. He wore Levis tucked inside his boots. Beads of sweat trickled down his sun-bronzed cheeks. Thick dust choked him and stung his eyes. He adjusted the dark blue bandana over his nose and felt as if he'd eaten every inch of dust between Colorado and Kansas while riding drag behind the herd.

Under him was a sturdy bay gelding, the kind of stock the Army preferred. Brady and the two wranglers pushed the herd hard. After a month on the trail playing nursemaid to a hundred head of horses, he was ready for a bath, a Kansas-sized steak, and a soft bed. After collecting his share of the money, he figured to cut his ties with Lou Spearman.

Then there was Kate. He'd thought a lot about his fiancée on this trip. Even though she had graduated from a fancy boarding school back East, was a fine cook, and he liked the way she always smelled of lilac water, he hadn't settled on his true feelings for her. There were times when he doubted Kate's commitment to him. As always, he pushed the thoughts aside.

By the time he and his wranglers reached the box canyon ten miles north of Willow Creek, the Kansas sun had dropped behind the horizon, and darkness was fast approaching.

"Push 'em in, Long Tom." Brady choked out the words through the haze of dust. With the last horse through a narrow slice between the rock walls, Brady dismounted. He motioned for Willie Moon to help him slide a sorry-looking tangle of tree limbs across the canyon's opening to act as a makeshift gate.

"Willie, you and Long Tom get 'em settled."

"Whar you goin'?" Long Tom's eyes spoke his dislike for Brady. He sneered. "I'm hungry enough to eat me a whole bear."

"You'll get to town soon enough. I'm riding to the shack to see if Pete's got orders from Spearman."

Brady gathered the reins, swung into the saddle, and rode the short distance to the canyon hideout.

Stan Peters, another of Lou Spearman's lackeys, slumped in the open doorway. The unshaven, middle-aged man in stained denims and run-down half boots lowered his rifle to his side. A genuine look of pleasure crossed his pocked face as he grinned. "Howdy, Brady. Didn't figger to see you for two or three weeks. Where's the fellers?"

Brady swung out of the saddle and dropped the reins, knowing the horse wouldn't wander off. He slapped the dust from his trousers. "Down in the canyon settling the herd."

He pointed toward the rifle at Stan's side. "You expecting trouble?"

"Never can tell when some coyote might come sniffing around." Stan propped the weapon against the building. "The two-legged kind, if'n you catch my drift."

When Stan looked back up at him, Brady caught the amusement in his face. "You see something funny, Stan?"

"I could use a loan—two hundred ought to do it."

Brady let out a sardonic chuckle. "Living out here for months at a time has addled your brain. Where would I get that kind of money?"

"Reckon you ain't heard." The fat man scratched his armpit.

"I'm saddle weary, Stan, and not much in the mood for cat-dancing around whatever you're busting at the seams to tell me."

Stan's laugh sounded almost like a girlish giggle. "You're a rich man, Brady."

Brady stiffened. "Speak plainer, Stan."

The aging teamster grabbed his rotund belly and bent double with laughter. "Somebody done found your pappy dead as a doornail."

Brady bunched a fist, stepped forward, and with the swiftness of a buzz-tailed rattler punched Stan Peters in the nose.

A wooden shingle clattered to the ground when the man landed against the shack's wall. He slid into a massive heap. Propping himself to a sitting position, he used the sleeve of his shirt to wipe away the blood oozing from his nose. "Now, what'd you go and do that for?"

Brady stood still, his legs braced wide apart. "Everybody between here and Willow Creek knows there wasn't any love lost between Hogue Wilkes and me, but his dying isn't a laughing matter. Who found him, and how'd it happen?"

Stan dabbed at his nose. "Don't matter—dead is dead. With Hogue out of the way, you're a rich man." He offered an innocuous look and released a long sigh. "Don't seem right, a snot-nosed, wet-behind-the-ears kid getting all that land and all that money."

His hands still bunched into tight fists, Brady glared down at the man. "Stand up."

"What for?"

The two men stared at each other in what amounted to a silent standoff.

"So I can bust you again."

Stan gingerly wiggled his nose between his thumb and forefinger. "Ah, come on, boy. I was only joshin'. 'Sides, I ain't bellied up to a bar in a coon's age. My bottles are all empty, and my gullet has worked up a powerful thirst." Stan wiped his nose again.

With a snort of disgust, Brady stepped around the man on the ground and entered the shack. "Hide the dun, and saddle my chestnut. Spearman is expecting me tonight."

A short time later he came out wearing a chambray shirt,

denim pants, and scuffed work boots, the soldier uniform folded and tucked under one arm.

A long-legged gelding stood saddled and tied outside the corral. Brady stuffed the uniform into one of the saddlebags. He gathered the reins in silence and stepped into the saddle.

"Now you've done gone and broke my nose, I need me a drink more'n ever," Stan whined.

"What you need is a bar of soap and a tub of scalding water." Brady rode away without looking back.

Chapter Two

Willow Creek was like a hundred other Kansas towns, born of a welcome source of water and nurtured by the sweat and backbreaking work of the men and women who had helped settle the region. Brady had lived there all his life, but it wasn't home—not really.

Darkness settled in as he rode across the last foothills. He stopped his horse on a high knoll above the town before pushing on. Lamps lit the buildings. From this height he heard the whoops of kids playing by the river after supper.

At the bottom of the grade, he turned his horse downriver, avoiding the main street. Across the road and past the last shabby hovel on the town's outskirts was a narrow frame building set beside a high gate, which bore a sign on its wide arch: LOU SPEARMAN—HORSES BOUGHT AND SOLD.

A high wooden fence began at the open gate and ran several hundred gray, sagging feet toward town. Behind it barns and sheds and corrals were scattered in an orderly maze down to the riverbank. The rich odor of manure filled the air, staining the sweetness of wild honeysuckle.

Brady was weary, sore, hungry, and bone dry as he rode his mount under the arch. He stopped in front of the lighted office, dismounted, and tied his horse to the hitch rail. He viewed his surroundings. Across the corrals he saw the dim flicker of the stable lanterns. A sudden anger welled inside him, anger at himself and more so toward Lou Spearman. Spearman was nothing more than a con man living off the weakness of others and then retiring behind a façade of respectability when pursued.

Opening a saddlebag, Brady collected the uniform that he'd rolled inside his rain slicker, and he tucked it under his arm.

Walking up the few steps to the open door leading into the front office, he entered and glanced at the empty desk behind the railing that acted as a barrier from the waiting area.

He noted the shabbiness of the room. A three-legged chair propped in a corner, and walls in need of a fresh coat of whitewash. He wondered why the lamps were still lit, and then he remembered Hannah Osterhaus.

He smiled when he spotted her kneeling in front of the safe, putting away a stack of ledgers. She looked up when she heard his footsteps. He thought he saw a flash of something— irritation?—surprise?—on her face when she glanced over her shoulder.

She reminded him of a long-legged, gangly colt when she stood. She was a slim, attractive girl with a straight nose, generous mouth, and high cheekbones, and the austere black office dress she wore exaggerated her creamy complexion. Her hair, pulled back in a neat chignon, reminded him of a new copper penny.

Despite her drab attire, she lent a kind of splendor to the office with her warm and honest amber eyes.

"Why are you working so late, Hannah?" He spoke politely and without banter.

"Why are teamsters always drunk when they unload their wagons?" Her voice was low and husky and held a hint of pleasure at the sight of him. "It's nice you're back, Brady."

He liked the merry spirit in her smile. Her lips were full and sweetly shaped, her eyes set wide apart, and in them was a lingering and friendly appraisal of him. She was a pleasure to see after the misery of his horse-buying trip.

"Back for good this time," he said. And because that reminded him of his errand, he asked, "Lou gone home, Hannah?"

She nodded toward the hall. "No. He's in the back."

Brady tipped his hat at her and lifted one long leg over the rail rather than walking through the opening and made his way down a long hall. Lamplight pooled in front of an open door. Not bothering to knock, he walked in.

The man sitting at the rolltop desk was tall with an immense frame rapidly turning to fat, but a bull-like vitality still shone from his ruddy face. A fringe of graying hair circled his shiny bald head. There was a tranquil shrewdness in his beady black eyes as he greeted Brady. His worn vest gaped open across his high belly.

He lifted a beefy hand a few inches off the desk in a lazy greeting. "Hello, boy." Lou Spearman's voice was quiet.

Brady's voice, equally quiet, said, "Lou." He sank into a chair, reared back on its legs, and leaned against the wall. He watched as Spearman surveyed him in silence.

Continuing in his same soft voice, Spearman said, "I tried to get word to you. I'm sorry about Hogue's death."

"You don't give a damn about Hogue, Lou, and we both know it." Brady fought to keep the malice out of his voice.

Lou Spearman eyed him without rancor and then answered with a crooked smile. "All right, I don't. No more than you."

Brady didn't bother to protest. He maintained the sober expression on his face. Pushing his worn Stetson off his forehead, he ran a hand idly through his hair where the hatband had pressed it down at his temples.

"I sent Billy Jack to find you." Spearman leaned forward and toyed with a pencil.

"He didn't look very hard." Brady set the legs of the chair down hard on the floorboards. Meeting the big man's eyes, he said, "Had to hear it from Stan Peters when we brought the herd in. What do you know about it?"

Spearman's massive left hand was lying palm down on the desk. "One of Hogue's ranch hands was bringing in some cattle over Rimrock Pass. Something spooked the herd—a cougar, maybe. Anyhow, when he rounded the peak, Hogue was there on the trail—facedown."

He shrugged one shoulder. "It looked as if he could've taken a spill from his horse and broken his back. From the condition of his body, he'd probably laid out there for weeks." He pursed his lips. "Too bad you missed the funeral. They buried him yesterday."

Brady stood. He opened the rain slicker and laid the

folded wool blue uniform on a corner of the desk. Spearman gave it little notice.

Brady settled slowly back into the chair again. The cubbyhole of an office was hot, and he felt sweat pooling in his eyelids. He drew a sack of tobacco from his shirt pocket and carefully rolled a cigarette, concentrating on it. When he'd finished, he scratched a match off the heel of one boot and lit the cigarette. Looking over the flame, he noticed Spearman eyeing him with a bland, bored patience.

Brady flipped the match to the floor, inhaled a long drag on the cigarette, and slowly exhaled the smoke. "I'm quitting, Lou."

The fat man nodded once, unperturbed.

"You'll have to get someone else in your crew to wear the soldier suit—somebody who'll pass for an Army officer and who won't get himself hog-drunk and behave like a public nuisance. You got anybody like that, Lou?"

Spearman thrummed his fingers on the desk, curiosity in his pale eyes. "You sore about something, Brady?"

"This last deal almost went bad. Rancher in Colorado questioned why the Army was paying so little for prime horseflesh . . . implied he might contact the post's commanding officer."

Spearman took his time answering. "Nope. You're sore about losing a daddy you hated and who hated you." Spearman's eyes narrowed shrewdly. "It couldn't be remorse, could it, Brady? After all, he didn't treat you well."

"No, he didn't." Brady kept his voice low and even. "I'm glad Hogue's dead."

"You should be," Spearman murmured in lazy contempt.

"Now that you own Anchor, you're practically rich. Anchor's a big ranch. It'll take you a long time to blow through all that dough."

"Do I detect a hint of envy, Lou?" Brady's tone was dry.

Spearman cocked his head to one side. "No, Brady, I don't begrudge you Anchor. I don't begrudge you anything. You know why?"

"I'm sure you're going to tell me."

Spearman's lips thinned as he smiled. "Because you'll lose it. You aren't man enough to hold on to Anchor. You won't ever marry Kate Parker and settle down. You'll get restless again, and you'll want to drift. Anchor will go through your fingers like sand, and you'll ride off to Mexico or California. And when you run out of money, just like always, you'll come skulking back."

"And beg you for the soldier suit?" Brady didn't try to hide his growing contempt for the man sitting behind the desk.

The flush on Spearman's face deepened perceptibly. "You'll come crawling for it, and when you do, you won't get it."

Brady flicked ash from the cigarette. "You're wrong. I'll never wear it again. I never liked wearing it."

"Naturally," Lou said with open malice. "I'm surprised you ever wore it at all—took some nerve."

"So am I."

Spearman's eyebrows lifted. "So, you admit it?"

Brady nodded. "Yes. Every time I'd go into a town and announce I was an Army officer buying horses for the cavalry, I expected someone to ask me for my credentials. Every time

I 'rejected' a good horse worth a hundred and twenty-five dollars, I expected a rancher to make me prove the phony reasons I gave him. And every time Fiske Cooper stepped out of the crowd and offered the seller forty dollars for the horse, I expected us both to be mobbed. I'll never know why those ranchers didn't connect me with Cooper, or both of us with you."

Spearman clapped his hands together as if applauding. "Well, now, you're quite a hero."

The two men's eyes leveled on each other. A slow puzzlement came into Spearman's face. "Why *did* you come here tonight?"

"I just told you. I make a poor crook, Lou. I don't enjoy cheating people. Like I said, I'm quitting." Brady leaned forward. He held Spearman with his eyes and in a low, even voice repeated, "I'm quitting."

"I heard you." Spearman regarded Brady for a long time and then sneered. "You think it's that easy to leave me? You're a coward, boy. I know it. You know it." Spearman's satirical laughter filled the stifling office. "And I'll bet my last dollar that your sweet Miss Kate Parker knows it too."

Brady dropped the cigarette to the floor and used the toe of one boot to grind it out. "When Stan Peters told me Hogue was dead, he asked for money."

It seemed as if Spearman mulled over that piece of news before he smiled. "Yeah, what's your point?"

"How did Stan know about Hogue's death before me?"

"I suppose it's because you were on the trail, buying horses." Spearman flicked at a piece of lint on his vest. "What'd you do when Stan asked for money?"

"I hit him. He changed his mind."

Still smiling, Spearman rose from his chair.

Brady stood as well. "Walk soft, Lou," he warned, and when Spearman didn't answer, Brady squared his shoulders and left the room.

The building was dark and empty as he went through it. Outside, the air was hot and humid. He walked to his horse and rode out the gate, turning toward town. It puzzled him that Lou Spearman's insults had the power to rankle. He had expected no less, because that was Spearman's opinion of him, which, in turn, was the town's opinion also. The thing that bothered him the most—he was certain it was Kate's too.

A man couldn't drift over a dozen states for five years, then come home and expect people not to bitterly envy him.

Nor should he inherit one of the biggest ranches in the country as a reward for his wanderlust. Brady shifted in his saddle, pondering that as he had the last four days coming in from Colorado.

As much as he needed to see Kate tonight, a part of him dreaded it just as much. There were words for men like him—*shiftless, good-for-nothing.*

Ahead of him, he spotted a figure vaguely outlined against lamplight. Walking in the road was Hannah Osterhaus. She was bareheaded, carrying her straw hat, and she hummed a soft tune that carried in the night.

He drew his horse alongside her, touching his hat, and said, "You too old to ride double, Hannah?"

Her laugh warmed him when she said, "Not too old, Brady, but I'd rather walk. I sit down all day."

He stepped out of the saddle and fell in beside the girl. Leading his horse, he held his peace, since she didn't seemed inclined to talk. The silence helped dull the sharpness of what had passed between him and Lou Spearman.

When their shoulders bumped, Hannah gave him a pleasant smile. "What's the country like where you were?"

"Most of it is dry like a big white bone."

He heard her sigh and guessed his answer wasn't what she'd wanted to hear.

"I started out to see it once when I was twelve." Her laughter warmed Brady.

"What happened?"

"My pa brought me back, because little girls didn't travel alone, he said." Her pleasant laugher came again, and he found himself trying to recall what he knew of this woman.

In the nine months he'd worked for Spearman, he had rarely returned to Willow Creek from buying trips and only passed her during normal working hours. He recalled someone's saying she was the daughter of one of Spearman's former teamsters who had died, and Spearman had given her a job running his small and unimportant freighting business, which Brady knew was a front for the shadier side of Spearman's enterprises.

"How far did you go?" Her voice interrupted his thoughts.

"Almost into Idaho."

"Did you and your men stick together, or did you split up?" Hannah asked.

Brady looked down at her in the dark. Caution caused his stomach to bunch into a knot. He wondered if Hannah was part of Spearman's dozen or more secretive schemes. Her curiosity made him wary.

"We split up. Too much territory to cover."

"Were you alone most of the time?"

Brady stopped in the road, and she halted too, facing him. "Sorry. I know I'm snooping, Brady." Her voice was quiet.

He tipped his hat and moved to step into the saddle.

She touched his arm, forestalling him. "Wait, Brady. Please."

"Why all the questions, Miss Osterhaus?"

"It's *Hannah,* and you know it."

"All right, Hannah, why all the questions?"

"Will you answer me honestly? Were you alone any of the time?"

"No, I wasn't alone," Brady lied.

"Can you prove it?"

"Is there a reason I should have to prove it?"

Hannah lowered her head, then looked up again and into his face. "So, Mr. Spearman didn't tell you?" She walked on a few paces.

Brady said nothing but again fell in beside her. Presently she said, "Bass Young's been in the office three times this week since they found your father."

"Bass is the sheriff. Is there a reason he shouldn't drop in on Spearman?"

"No. Except he keeps asking if you've come in yet."

Brady gripped Hannah's elbow. He kept his voice low. "What are you trying to tell me, Hannah?"

"Look, Brady. We live in a town where everybody for

miles around knows everyone else's business. There isn't a soul who doesn't know that Hogue Wilkes wasn't your real father. That he found you when you were a baby. So I guess that makes him more like a stepfather." She drew herself up into a tight sigh. "And people know that there was no love lost between the two of you."

"That's old news, Hannah. You might want to get to the point."

"Your stepfather had been dead at least three weeks before he was found."

"Yeah, so Spearman said." The thundercloud in the back of Brady's mind grew darker.

"You've been gone how long—two months?"

"Six weeks, this time."

"The whole town knows about the quarrel you and your stepfather had before you left town, Brady."

"We had a lot of quarrels." Brady tried to keep the bitterness from his voice. "More than I can possibly count."

"Yes, but don't you see? Now that Hogue is dead, you'll inherit Anchor. That alone has stirred up the sheriff's inquisitive nature."

Brady's sudden stop caused the horse to bump against his shoulder, almost knocking Brady into Hannah. He stood still, taking in her words. "That means Bass Young thinks my stepfather was murdered."

"And that you might have done it." Her words penetrated deep inside Brady.

He let his hand drop from Hannah's arm as they continued their walk. "It's odd Spearman didn't mention the sheriff's visits to me."

His stepfather's being murdered made little difference to Brady. It had been years since he felt anything for Hogue Wilkes except a quiet, controlled hatred.

"Hogue wasn't very well liked, was he?" Hannah wanted to know.

"He was a hard man, often cruel. I guess it would be generally accepted that he'd died a violent death."

A couple of riders from the Slash T ranch rode past and tipped their hats. A few of the town's stores were still open, their lamps casting a faint glow over the quiet main street. By their light Brady regarded the woman beside him, and he caught her watching him with an expression of earnestness mingled with curiosity.

"Where do you live, Hannah?"

"I have a room at the boardinghouse."

"I'll walk you there." He chose his next words with care. "I appreciate your telling me about the sheriff. Why did you?"

The faintest of smiles curled her wide mouth. "Maybe because you asked me to take a ride in the moonlight." She shrugged. "Maybe I like a man who laughs once in a while. Maybe I don't think it's a crime to want to see what's over the other side of the mountains." She spread her hands wide. "I don't know, Brady. Good night. Don't worry about walking me to the boardinghouse. I know the way."

He touched his hat and watched her step up onto the boardwalk, still carrying her hat in her hand, a straight girl with a proud walk.

A peculiar feeling stirred within him as he watched her, and for a moment his face lost its customary soberness.

Chapter Three

Judge Parker's two-story house sat high above the town. In the darkness, Kate Parker sat on the porch swing and, though two blocks away, listened to the sounds from Main Street—a buggy passing, hoofbeats muffled in the thick summer dust, and after that, quiet.

Aside from her father prowling about his upstairs study, it was too quiet.

After three years of waiting, she should have learned to curb her impatience. She pushed the toe of her shoe against the porch floor, giving motion to the swing. Patience was not one of her virtues.

Word had come that Brady was back in town. She knew he'd come to the house. She wanted to wait at the end of the steps. Pride kept her from it.

The pots of geraniums along the front steps had ceased gurgling and bubbling from the water she had given them.

Three times a week all the pots of flowers in the house were brought out, lined along the steps, and thoroughly drenched. This summer ritual stretched all the way back to her childhood days, when her mother needed an activity to curb Kate's restless energy.

She glanced at the watering can on the porch, and she heard hoofbeats. Rising quickly, she squinted into the darkness to make out the dim shape of a rider as he reached the walkway, passed the stepping block, and dismounted.

Excitement almost choked her. Dignity held her still. At last, by the faint lamplight of the hall shining through the front door, she watched him tramp up the walk.

She came slowly to the steps and said in a voice that almost shook, "Be careful of those steps, Brady. I've got all the geraniums on them."

She saw him stop and peer down, then heard him swear mildly as he stumbled against a pot, knocking it over in his haste to reach her.

He opened his arms, and she walked into them and kissed him lingeringly. Seconds ticked by. She forgot herself, forgot her resolve and her promises to herself, and savored the kiss.

Brady pulled her gently to the doorway and into the light. She stood there while he leaned against the doorjamb and looked at her hungrily. She stirred with pleasure while he drank in her heart-shaped face.

Kate's lips always reminded Brady of rosebuds waiting to open. Her blue eyes danced with excitement now, and he especially liked the rounded softness of her small body demurely hidden under a pale yellow dress adorned with a stiffly starched white collar embroidered with tiny pink flow-ers. He watched her in the half light until Kate laughed.

"Say something, you fool. All I've heard you utter is a swear word."

Brady drew her to him again and kissed the tip of her nose. "All right. I'm hungry."

She hugged him impulsively, grabbed his hand, and pulled him through the front door. "Follow me."

Inside the kitchen, she stood on tiptoe to turn up the ceil-ing lamp. When his hands circled her tiny waist, she looked at him over her shoulder.

"Too bad about Hogue's death."

"He and I were never close. We had our differences—" Brady broke off when Kate snorted rudely.

"That's an understatement."

Brady drew her close and nuzzled the nape of her neck. "I'd rather not talk about my stepfather."

The bitterness in Brady's voice didn't seem to surprise Kate. "All right, how about, you need a shave." Turning to face him, she tousled his curly hair. "And a haircut wouldn't hurt, either."

Brady ran a hand through his mop of unruly hair and grinned. He walked to the counter and lifted the lid of the cookie crock. His movements reminded Kate of an animal on the prowl. His restlessness worried her. When he caught her watching him, he grinned and winked. His friendly, impu-dent handsomeness could melt stone.

Swallowing the last of an oatmeal cookie, he grabbed her in his arms and lifted her off the floor, kissing her neck at the hairline.

"Put me down, Brady," she scolded, her voice sharper than she'd intended. "Can't you ever be serious?"

She was supposed to marry this man, and she wondered why sadness filled her. If she were honest with herself, she knew she'd have to admit that part of her didn't like his reckless, insouciant attitude.

"Sit down while I serve your plate." She ladled out a bowl of stew and set it on the table. Brady dragged one of the chairs out and sat down. He scrubbed his hands over his face and yawned.

"Bad trip?" Kate hadn't missed the troubled expression in his eyes.

"Could've been better." He broke off a piece of bread and sopped it in the bowl of thick stew. "How's the judge?"

"You know Father, always the same." She kept her back to Brady. "Before I forget, he'll want to see you, Brady."

Brady loaded his mouth with a forkful of beef. "Anything important?"

He stopped chewing when she said, "It's about Anchor. You own it now."

Brady grimaced while he toyed with a piece of bread. "I suppose everyone will expect me to grow a handlebar mustache and strut around in a pair of hand-tooled, silver-inlaid boots."

Her smile trembled a bit. "With a jelly belly too. Fat, rich, and happy." As soon as it was out, she regretted saying it. She rose and walked to the cooler and lifted out a pie plate and a bowl of fresh clabber.

Brady watched her. "Is that what you want of me, Kate?"

Without replying, she set a generous slice of apple pie on

a plate and slid it across the table to him. She gathered her skirts and sat facing him.

His eyes were serious, and he ate in silence.

Kate's cheeks flushed. "More pie?" she said quickly, exasperated with herself. *Fat, rich, and happy* had been her words—a terrible comparison between Brady and his stepfather. Though a man of rotund stature, Hogue Wilkes had never acted rich or happy.

"I didn't mean . . ." She fiddled with the hem of the tablecloth. "What I meant to say is, now maybe you'll be happy to put down roots."

"Yeah. Sure." Brady scowled as he looked at his plate.

He looked miserable, and Kate could imagine what was going through his mind. Her words had described what she bitterly knew was his opinion of men who stayed in the same place for a lifetime.

She felt the old skepticism, the old disbelief that he would ever settle down, and she hated it.

"Hogue wasn't all that bad, was he, Brady?"

"You know the answer to that, Kate."

"Let's not argue. He'd dead now."

"We always argue, Kate. What's new?"

She saw the way he clenched his jaw before he reached across the table and lifted her hand. His eyes were without humor or mockery. A tenseness gathered within her. She knew that look in him.

"I have a lot of things to say tonight, Kate. And I'm going to try to say them, if you won't jump down my throat."

She held her peace and nodded.

A kind of shadow crawled up into Brady's eyes. "Don't

ever expect me to be sorry about Hogue's dying or even to say that I am. Dead dogs are mourned more than my stepfather ever will be. I know it, and you know it."

Kate nodded again.

A swift smile came and went across his handsome face, and he was once again serious. "Hogue never had a kind word for me, never expressed the smallest bit of affection. It's always been a puzzle as to why he took me in and gave me his name. But now that I've inherited Anchor, I'm riding out to the ranch, and I'm going to stay and work it."

He looked at Kate as if willing her to believe him. She sat there, afraid to breathe.

"So I think we should get married." Brady kissed the palm of her hand while he waited for her answer.

Kate regarded him for a few bleak seconds. She withdrew her hand and rose from the table. Trying to collect her thoughts, she gathered the dishes from the table, carried them to the washbasin, and pumped water over them.

With her back to him, she stood there, her fists clenched, fighting the turmoil inside her. She had waited for this, halfgladly, half-fearfully, and now it was here.

She could answer with a simple yes. That's what she had ached to do for several years. But something inside her had changed.

She turned and kept her face void of expression.

Brady sat at the table, rolling a cigarette. Looking up, he left the unrolled cigarette where it lay, pushed himself away from the table, and came to her. He placed a finger under her chin and forced her to look up at him. "Kate?" His voice was quiet.

Kate reached up, removed his hand, and held it between hers. "I like fairy tales, Brady, but I don't believe in them."

"And you think this is a fairy tale?"

She dipped her head in affirmation.

"I'm a simple man. Maybe you'd better explain." He leaned against the counter and crossed his arms over his chest.

Kate took in his tall, lanky frame. Eyes the color of slate looked almost black against his chiseled, tanned features. She hoped her face didn't show the turmoil she felt.

"There once was a young prince who often quarreled with the king, and every time there was an argument, the prince saddled his horse and left the kingdom for months without ever sending word to anyone. Then one day the king died, and the prince returned to marry the princess, expecting to live happily every after." Her grin was quick and insincere.

"I'm not a prince, Kate, and this is no fairy tale. If you marry me, I'll do everything within my power to make you happy."

When she didn't answer, he said, "You love me. You can't hide that from me."

"And if you think about it long enough, *maybe* you love me." Kate's voice was almost a whisper. "Though I'm not convinced you really know the meaning of the word."

He put both hands on her arms and gave her a gentle shake. "Don't think so much, Kate. We've got Anchor. I'll settle down and work it. We'll have a good life. We'll—"

He paused when Kate once again disengaged his hands. She backed off a step and met his questioning eyes.

"You almost make me believe you, Brady. Almost."

She watched his eyes darken with confusion and pain and

knew that they matched her own. "I've waited for you for three years. Now I'll wait a little longer—until my heart and my head make sense of each other."

Brady didn't bother keeping the anger from his voice. "And your head says what, Kate?"

She caught her bottom lip between her teeth and nibbled. "You wouldn't want to know."

"Try me."

She knew it would hurt, because it was the truth she had learned about him all the years she'd known him. She sighed. "You're only a born drifter, Brady, and maybe even a bit of a coward. You've never dared try to prove yourself as a real man the way a man must."

"And what way is that, Kate?"

They stared at each other, both confused and unsure, which didn't bode well for a future together. But she'd started this, and now she had to finish it.

"To find out what he can bear, what he can fight, what he can break, and what he can save. You run—you hide or dodge from any trouble that doesn't lie down on its back and roll over when you smile so handsomely." She hesitated. "I-I guess I've said enough."

Brady only nodded.

Kate was appalled at what she had said. She watched all the life go out of Brady's face; all the careless, easy vitality had vanished.

She came to him, wrapping her arms around his chest and burying her face in his shirt. "Oh, Brady, don't you see? I've got to know. I guess I'm a bit of a coward too—I'd rather eat my heart out here at home than have you break it out at

Anchor. You've . . . you've got to earn me. You've got to prove you won't run away every time the chips don't fall the way you think they should."

She felt him twirl one of the ringlets in her hair. Whatever he was about to say was lost in the sound of footsteps on the stairs. She knew her father was coming down for his evening walk.

She pulled back from Brady and looked up at him. He gave her his old, quick, careless smile before he moved around the table and out into the hall.

A bleakness settled over Kate. *The truth didn't stick. It never will.*

Before moving over to the lamp and blowing it out, she heard Brady and her father exchange greetings. She walked into the hall in time to hear her father say, "Had something to eat, Brady?"

"I fed him, Dad." Kate walked to her father and kissed his cheek.

Judge Parker was a spare, graying man with a taciturnity in his face that was belied by the mildness of his eyes. He wore a rumpled black suit that was seldom pressed, yet there was an unbending dignity about him that clothes couldn't alter.

He had never by word or gesture been anything but courteous to Brady, but Kate saw the brief, measuring glance he gave the younger man and read the distrust in his gaze.

"Brady and I were about to say good night, Dad, if you wish to speak to him." She gathered her skirts as she stepped onto the staircase.

"No, my business can wait. It's pretty dull." To Brady he said, "I suppose Kate told you that you're Anchor's sole owner now. Hogue appointed me his executor some time ago. There are papers that need signing."

Brady nodded. He flicked a quick look of appreciation at the judge. "Who . . . who saw Hogue . . . afterward, Judge?"

Judge Parker looked at him sharply. "I didn't hear. The usual people, I suppose—coroner, sheriff."

When Brady said nothing else, her father glanced at Kate and cleared his throat. "Well, uh, yes, I'm going for my walk. Good night, Brady."

"Careful of the flower pots," Kate reminded her father.

"I know. I've been tripping over the blasted things for years."

Kate smiled and looked at Brady, but he was watching the judge's disappearing back with a sober thoughtfulness. When her father was out of sight, Kate said, "Why did you ask him about Hogue?"

Brady shrugged. She noticed that when he looked at her, the old impudence and fun were back in his face.

"Practicing," he murmured. "I'll have to talk to my future father-in-law about our marriage." He came over and kissed her. "I'm riding out to Anchor tonight. I'll be back as soon as I can."

She walked to the door with him and watched him pick his way through the geraniums, and then she leaned against a porch post until he mounted his horse and rode away.

Afterward, as she lay in bed staring up at the ceiling, she sorted out the promises he had made her tonight, weighing them against promises he had made in the past.

Where did she go from here?

Chapter Four

A short way down the street, Brady turned in the saddle and saw Kate outlined against the light shining from the living room. He disliked the troubling thoughts brewing within him.

How could he explain to her that the kind of promise given and broken ten times before could be kept the eleventh?

No, he reasoned, he'd used that coin with her until it had lost its value. If he wanted to win her trust, he'd have to start over.

In the middle of the next block he spotted the figure of Judge Parker standing on the boardwalk in the dim moonlight. The judge came out to the road and called in a firm voice, "Brady?"

Brady kneed the gelding to the edge of the street. In the almost unbroken darkness, Brady was unable to see the expression on the judge's face.

"Judge?"

"Why did you ask that question about Hogue?" Judge Parker asked him.

"Somebody said Bass Young isn't sure Hogue's death was an accident."

"What else did that somebody say?"

Brady hesitated, reluctant to answer. "That Bass might suspect me of Hogue's murder."

A long silence passed before the judge spoke. "Brady, what did you and Hogue quarrel about before you left this last time?"

"Same as usual—my general uselessness." Brady spoke in a flat voice. He sighed heavily, groping for words. "One thing led to another."

"Fists?"

"No." Brady bit back his temper. "Hogue hit me, and I let him." Brady remembered that night all too well. "He said he was sorry he'd ever gone near the wagon train and found me. Said he was sorry the Pawnee didn't kill me along with my ma. Said they must have known I was worthless and that's why they let me live. He said . . ." Brady hesitated.

"Yes?" Judge Parker prompted.

Brady shifted in the saddle. Then he continued in a matter-of-fact voice. "He said that before he buried my mother, he looked for a wedding ring and couldn't find it. She wore other rings but no wedding ring. He said she looked as if she'd come out of a pleasure palace—a stinking, cheap bawdy house."

"Ah." Judge Parker's voice held faint disgust. "I don't suppose anyone else heard this testimonial about your mother."

Edginess tempered Brady's sarcastic chuckle. "Hogue said

it in the bunkhouse in front of the whole crew. That's when I gathered my gear and left."

Only the sound of the horse swishing its tail to ward off a fly broke the silence.

"Why didn't you stay away, Brady?"

"Kate." Brady's answer was sharp.

"She's the reason you *should* have stayed gone."

"I suppose you've felt this way all along, haven't you, Judge?"

"No father likes to see his child unhappy," the judge said quietly. "He'll do something about it if he can."

"You can't do anything about me."

"There'll be land speculators, other ranchers—no doubt there'll be a lot of offers for Anchor," Judge Parker went on. "That always happens when a man like Hogue Wilkes dies. Take the best offer, and get gone, Brady. This is a big country—as I think you've proved to yourself."

"And run away once more." It was more of a statement than a question.

"Yes. I won't have my daughter's emotions tampered with."

Brady squinted through the darkness, wanting to see the judge's face. He measured each word. "It's not my intention to cause Kate any grief."

"That's not good enough, Brady. Kate's heart would eventually heal if you left for good. And what I'm really referring to is her standing in this community."

Brady scowled. "Speak plainer, Judge."

"All right. What if the sheriff decides, rightly or wrongly, that you murdered Hogue? It could happen. You've got a reputation around here for being good-natured, good-looking, and good-for-nothing. Folks will envy your getting a ranch almost the size of Kansas. What if you end up in jail, waiting for a trial? The verdict won't matter. What about Kate then?"

Brady heard the bitter truth in the judge's words. "If I sell the ranch and leave, isn't that admitting I'm afraid of what the sheriff will turn up in his investigation? Isn't it admitting I'm not worth much as a man?"

"I'm not interested in any of that."

"Even if I'm innocent?"

Judge Parker remained silent for a long moment, as if he were searching his mind for the most honest of answers. "No." A strange implacability filled his voice as he said, "Not even then. Because you really aren't worth that much, Brady—not even an hour's unhappiness for my Kate."

With an audible sigh, Brady said, "I'm sorry you feel that way, Judge," and he touched a spur to the gelding's flanks, setting the horse into a gallop down the quiet street.

Brady's thoughts were bitter. *I've gone a long way down the road if the judge thinks that poorly of me.* He knew it would take time to prove he was a different man.

He paused at the crossroads of town, looking at the Four Corners Saloon in the middle of the block. Chances were that Bass Young would be there. Brady understood now that his business with the sheriff was urgent.

He angled his horse toward the saloon. Before dismounting, he perused the line of ponies tied to the hitch rail. Several bore Lou Spearman's Trident brand, and one of them was Willie Moon's unshod Indian paint. The crew was back. He figured to use the men to allay the sheriff's suspicions.

Shouldering his way through the swinging doors, he strode to the scarred mahogany bar. Poker players occupied several tables in the rear. A dice game beyond the bar had drawn a small crowd. Brady spotted the drooped shoulders of Bass Young.

Beyond that he saw Spearman's bunch—Stan Peters, Long Tom, Willie Moon, and "One-Eyed Lester" Galt, whose broad back was to the door.

The Bjorn brothers stood at the bar, and Brady halted next to Sven, the younger of the two. Sven was a tall, work-worn man in the rough clothes of a ranch hand. Gunnar, the older brother, wore a neat black suit. His mild, cheerful face made him look years younger than his sibling. With stubborn skill they operated a growing freighting company. To keep their business going and the overhead low, the brothers worked at everything from hauling freight to bookkeeping.

Sven's usually morose face broke into a smile when he spotted Brady. "Vhere you been, Brady?" He shoved a hand the size of a bear paw toward Brady. "Ve haf need of some new horses."

Brady felt as if his hand was being crushed. "See Lou." He asked the bartender for a beer.

Gunnar leaned around Sven. "To hell vit Spearman. Der last horse ve buy from him died of sand colic in less than a veek."

Brady smiled to take the edge off his refusal. "Don't work for Lou anymore. I quit. You're on your own to buy horses."

He took his beer and made his way through the crowd to the back of the room, hearing Sven's mild frustration. Just as he'd anticipated, Bass Young broke away from the craps game and intercepted him.

"In a hurry, Brady?"

Brady halted. Bass Young was a man of fifty, pleasant with the meaningless affability of an elected public servant, but his eyes were alert and searching. He was coatless, his blue plaid shirt buttoned at the neck. He wore no badge.

The two men shook hands. "Let's sit down, Brady. Thought you might want to know about Hogue."

"Reckon I've got some questions, Bass." Brady noticed Spearman's crew eyeing him. Only one concerned him. Willie Moon, Spearman's half-blooded Kiowa wrangler, leaned across his cards to speak in a low voice to Long Tom, whose pocked face turned toward Brady.

The sheriff offered Brady a cigar. "Smoke?"

Brady waved it away. "Never acquired the taste."

Sheriff Young struck a match against the tabletop. After drawing several puffs from the cigar, he said, "I know how you feel about this, Brady. I know—"

"How do I feel?" Brady cut in.

Bass Young's affable look altered into hardness. "No need for sarcasm. All right, how *do* you feel?"

"I'm glad he's dead, Bass." Brady all but sneered the words. "You can make anything out of that you want."

"What would I make out of it?"

"Lots of things. That I murdered Hogue, so I hear."

Keeping his voice mild, the sheriff said, "People talk too much." He never ceased watching Brady, though, noting each change of expression, weighing what he saw.

"How did he die, Bass?"

That question seemed to surprise the sheriff. "Why, his back was broken, and somebody stuck a knife between his ribs a couple of times."

Brady made no comment. He kept his face contained and noncommittal until the sheriff gave a weak chuckle. "So, you're glad?"

"Stop beating around the bush, Bass." Brady had forgotten about his beer. Noticing it, he drew a long draught and used the back of his hand to wipe foam from his mouth. "What do you want to know? That we fought? That when I left, I was down to my last dollar? That Anchor is the biggest outfit east of the Colorado? And now I own it?"

The sheriff puffed on his cigar, blowing a few smoke rings into the air. He tamped ash from the end of the stogie against the heel of his boot. "Reckon I know all that. What I want to know is, where you been this last month?"

Brady lifted the mug of warm beer to his mouth and drained the glass. "Come with me." He rose and led the way to the table where Spearman's crew sat.

One-Eyed Lester nodded as Brady halted beside him. Lester Galt was a short, stocky man who'd lost an eye during a knife fight. Not yet thirty, he yet had a sleepy indolence about his every movement. He was Spearman's first man, a born horse trader with an astute knowledge of the four-legged beasts, a nerveless gall, and a devious mind, all smothered skillfully by a slow smile and the one steady, guileless eye of a simple and satisfied man.

Of the twenty-five men Spearman worked on and off his horse lot, Lester was absolute boss, the key figure in all of

Spearman's countless deals, from the sly sucker's game from which he and Brady had just returned to the hiring and paying of the silent, furtive men who passed into Spearman's office, talked behind closed doors, then quietly slipped away.

Lester wore a stained calico shirt. His beard stubble—the same pale color as the red hair tucked under his tattered hat—gave him the air of an amiable if unwashed line rider.

He nodded again and grinned at Brady.

Brady's face screwed up in thought. "Bass here wants to know where I've been this last month."

Lester regarded Brady with a lazy look. He shifted his body to accommodate his vision toward the sheriff. "Everywhere, Bass. Hell, when you buy horses, you cover a lot of ground."

The sheriff seemed to ponder the answer. "I'm specifically asking about who Brady's been traveling with that'll vouch for him and the places he's been."

Lester chewed the toothpick in his mouth. He spat on the floor. "Damned if I know, Bass."

He turned his good eye toward Brady. "Where were you, Brady?"

A cold premonition stirred within Brady. Lou Spearman and One-Eyed Lester, just as much as he himself, had to hide the facts of the Army-officer swindles Spearman had concocted. While Brady needed proof that Willie Moon and Long Tom were with him in the three months he'd been gone, he knew why Lester was hesitating.

A kind of wary panic pooled in the pit of Brady's stomach. If he was on his own, he'd need to tread with caution. "I wasn't always with a wrangler, Bass. Can't rightly say when

I was alone or with someone." To name names, to point fingers, might mean a sudden end to his young life.

Lester spoke up. "We were all over the country, Bass—singly and in pairs and with the whole bunch. We'd hear of a ranch with a good string of horses, and one of us would go to look 'em over. If it was a big bunch and they looked good, we'd buy and send for help to drive 'em to the main herd." He scrubbed a hand over his stubble, then scratched behind one ear. "What's this all about, Bass?"

The sheriff persisted with his questions. "Was Brady alone long enough for him to ride back to Anchor without the rest of you knowing it?

Here it is. Brady shifted his weight from one leg to the other. The faint mocking glance from Lester's one eye caused Brady to flinch.

Lester's voice was thoughtful. "Why, I don't know, Bass. He might have been. I never kept track of him much. He knows a good horse and what Lou'd pay for one. Brady'd get money from me and bring in the horses. I knew about where he was, and that's all."

He repeated, and in a more demanding voice, "What's this all about, anyway? We just got back into town."

Brady saw the chagrin mount in Bass Young's eyes. "In other words," the sheriff said, "you didn't pay any attention. You didn't know where he was."

Lester shrugged to indicate his innocence. "Why should I?"

Bass didn't answer him. Lester looked speculatively at Brady. "Ask Brady."

The sheriff turned on his heel and, before walking out of

the saloon, said, "There's a smell of rot in the air. If I were you, Brady, I wouldn't be leaving on no more horse-buying trips until the business of Hogue's death is settled."

A white heat tightened Brady's chest and spread through his body while he glared at Lester.

The smugness in Lester's voice was unmistakable. "Yeah, Brady. Tell us."

Brady balled his hands into hard fists. His voice was thin with anger. "Let's go where we can talk, Lester—in private."

The one-eyed man's laugh sounded hollow. "I've got something to say to you too, but let's wait till you cool off."

"You'll come now or I'll drag you out." Brady spoke through gritted teeth.

Lester's face hardened. He narrowed his one good eye to a slit and offered Brady a hard look. "Maybe I will, at that."

Willie Moon pushed back his chair and started to rise. Brady put a hand on his shoulder and pushed him back down. "Stay out of this Willie."

Brady shifted his look to the men seated around the table. "That goes for the rest of you too." He said impatiently, "I'm waiting, Lester."

The two of them tramped toward the rear of the room. Passing two cubbyholes that were reserved for cards, they stepped out the back door to the loading platform that ran the length of the building and was stacked with empty beer barrels at its far end.

Brady moved away from the door and halted. Lester stopped too. He stood with legs apart, hands on hips, every line of his blocky form exuding pugnacious arrogance.

Brady didn't try to rein in the hard recklessness rippling

through his body. He matched Lester's stance, and his voice was deadly. "What the hell was that all about?"

Lester answered with a glare.

"You could've pulled the sheriff off my neck in there, Lester. Why didn't you?"

"Because Spearman wants you back in your soldier suit, boy." Lester's voice held an unspoken threat. "You're very convincing as young Lieutenant Hastings. Got those honest eyes. Without you, we'd lose money."

"I told Lou I'd quit. Sooner or later it's my neck that'll be in a noose."

"Looks like your neck's about to be in a noose anyway, what with your stepdaddy dead and all." Lester slapped his thigh and guffawed. "Face it, Brady, you're licked. Bass won't drop this because I left it open—on purpose. I don't want him dogging me and the boys. One way to put an end to his questions is for you to come back to Lou, and I'll account to Bass for every day you were out on the trail."

Lester jabbed a finger into Brady's chest. "Be stubborn, and me and the boys will start remembering the days when nobody saw you." He paused. "And you can tell Bass what you were really doing."

"And who I was working *for*?" Brady rose to the challenge.

"And who wore the uniform?" Lester countered. "Federal offense."

A dismal hopelessness took hold of Brady and shook him like a dog gnawing a bone. "Looks like I'm in a damned-if-I-do and a damned-if-I-don't situation."

He knew as long as he kept his mouth shut, Lou Spearman would protect him about the Army uniform, because if their scheme became known, they'd both be neck-high in trouble.

"This is blackmail, and you know it, Lester."

"So?"

The man's insolence grated on Brady. Hogue's death and the sheriff's suspicions had opened the door for Spearman to blackmail him into keeping quiet about swindling ranchers by paying lesser prices for their horses and then selling the horses to the Army at an exorbitant profit.

The alternative was to tell Bass Young the truth, and when that became known, he would lose Kate as surely as if she had died. Her trust in him was tenuous at best. She'd made that clear.

And so had her father.

A savage stubbornness and black rage wouldn't let him return to Lou Spearman's fold of con men and cutthroats.

He'd remained silent for so long, Lester finally said, "Well, Brady, figure it out?"

"Yeah." It was Brady's turn to poke Lester in the chest. "I told Spearman I've quit, and I have."

"Ain't nothing worse than a fool, and you're the biggest one I've seen in a long time, Brady Wilkes." The contempt in One-Eyed Lester's voice was evident. "Listen up, and hear me good. We all know how you feel about Miss Kate Parker. Do you want to be tried by her pappy and hanged by the neck with your eyes buggin' out and your legs a-kickin' in front of your li'l darlin'?"

Brady hissed through his teeth, "For killing you, sure."

It took Lester several seconds to register those four words. He stepped forward and slapped Brady with his open palm. "You ain't tough enough, friend. Never were."

On the heels of Lester's last word, Brady's blow caught Lester on the jaw. The punch took the one-eyed man by surprise. He reeled backward before catching his balance. Motionless for a moment, he then lunged.

Like two bulls, the impact of their bodies shook the platform, causing one of the empty beer barrels to topple over. Lester wrapped his huge arms around Brady in a bear hug. Brady slugged viciously at the man's back.

The punishment forced Lester to break away, and Brady took a step backward. Without warning his arms were grabbed from behind and pinned in an iron grip. He wrestled savagely, smelling the fetid odor of Willie Moon against him, and he cursed himself for not having remembered Willie's blind loyalty to Spearman.

It didn't take him long to realize that his struggles were useless. Willie slammed Brady facedown on the platform. His knee gouged into the small of Brady's back. He whipped out his skinning knife.

"Let him up, Willie. I ain't finished with this snot-nosed kid." Lester huffed out the words.

Willie hauled Brady to his feet. Wheeling, Brady turned and with a smashing right blow caught the Indian flush in the throat.

Willie clasped his throat with both hands, stumbled over the edge of the platform, and, clawing at the air, landed solidly on his back in the dirt below.

A wild rage had gripped Brady. He jumped from the platform to the ground. He dropped to his knees and pummeled Willie with his fists.

Acting quickly, Lester vaulted to the ground. He pulled his revolver and brought it crashing down on Brady's head.

Brady crumpled, and he fell forward, covering the Kiowa's body.

"Get him off me," Willie gasped.

Wedging the toe of a boot between Brady's chest and the Indian, Lester shoved Brady's limp body aside.

Willie untied and pulled the bandana from around his neck and wiped the blood from his nose. "Damn fool near kilt me. Him drunk?"

"Naw. Stone sober." Lester adjusted the patch that had slipped from the hole that once was his eye. "He's feeling a bit pious right now, claiming to quit Spearman." He huffed a chuckle. "Reckon he's wrong."

Willie slid his knife back into the scabbard at his waist. "Yeah, me reckon too. Maybe when Lou is finished with this cur pup, I cut off his ears."

One-Eyed Lester and Willie Moon's raspy laughter filled the night air.

Chapter Five

Brady pointed his chestnut toward the wagon road out of town. His head throbbed where Lester's pistol had landed, leaving a sizeable lump, and last night's beer seemed to sit cold and unwanted in his gut.

The moon lit his way until he reached Blackbuck Creek. Brady stepped out of the saddle, letting his horse drink. Squatting at the creek's edge, Brady splashed water over his face and head. He inhaled the scent of black, moist earth.

As he snugged his boot back in the stirrup, he reached forward and patted the gelding's neck. "Gonna rain, ol' son. I can smell it."

The horse pricked its ears as if he understood. At Brady's urging, the animal broke into a lope and crossed a meadow. Brady spoke again. "We're home." They had reached the edge of Anchor land.

Man and horse rode through wild hay. A breeze almost

chilled the air. Brady heard cattle moving away from him in the night.

A little later he made out the scattering of Anchor's out-buildings abutting the tall pine trees. The entire place was dark, sleeping, and for that he was thankful.

One of the yard dogs picked up on Brady's presence and yapped. "Dammit, Jack. Shut up," Brady scolded. The dog settled at the sound of Brady's voice.

At the corral next to the barn he unsaddled his horse. Opening the gate, he gave the horse a gentle slap on the rump. "We're home, Pye," he repeated.

The horse whinnied and galloped toward the meadow.

The first sprinkles of rain dropped on Brady's Stetson and shoulders. He hunched his shoulders and sprinted past the bunkhouse and the cookhouse. As he approached the porch of the cabin reserved for Anchor's ranch foreman, the moon cast enough light for him to spy the figure of a man standing in the darkened doorway.

A voice called out, "Who's there?"

"Me, Clem . . . Brady."

"Oh."

Brady wondered if it was his imagination or he had heard an undertone of resignation and disappointment.

"Wait'll I get a light, Brady."

"Go back to sleep." Brady was in no mood for the company of Anchor's foreman and ranch manager. "I'll talk to you in the morning."

Clem grunted his assent. Rain fell hard, pelting Brady as he ran across the yard and up the porch of the two-story log house that loomed in the dark.

He knew that likely no one at the ranch would welcome his homecoming. Long ago Clem Garret and the crew had written him off as worthless. He didn't blame them. At the first sign of trouble between him and his stepfather, Brady would pack his saddlebags and ride out, staying gone until he ran out of money.

The crew considered him a drifter who usually brought trouble when he returned.

A gust of wind caused a lower branch of a cottonwood tree to scrub against the weathered shingles of the house. Brady removed his hat and beat it against his leg to get rid of any raindrops that might have collected in its crown.

He let himself in through the unlocked front door. Hogue Wilkes had believed that locks were only good for keeping honest thieves out. Brady chuckled at the memory.

He struck a match and lit a lamp, carrying it to the office. He set the lamp on the rolltop desk pushed against the back wall. He looked around. Nothing had changed, from the dusty set of longhorns mounted over the desk, to the litter of newspapers, bridles, odd bits of leather, guns, traps, and chaps that lay scattered about the leather sofa, the deep armchair, and the unswept floor.

This was Clem Garret's domain, the ranch office where the daily operations of the ranch were recorded in journals— from the breeding dates of bulls to heifers, stallions to mares, and the hiring and firing of men.

Brady picked up the lamp and opened the door at the rear of the room that led into the hall. Turning left, he walked to the living room. Lifting the lamp high above his head, he looked around. The sight of the gilt trashiness brought a score of ancient and unwelcome memories to him.

Here were the tastes of a dozen of Hogue Wilkes' women recorded in tarnished gilt mirrors, in fluffy pillows trimmed in ostrich feathers, and ornate lamps purchased in New Orleans.

He moved slowly across the room toward another hallway, tag ends of memory once again made vivid. Where had the women gone?

Some of their names and faces were part of his childhood; some were pretty, some drunken, some cruel; all were indifferent to the growing waif Hogue Wilkes tolerated around the house.

He remembered their carousing, the nights made hideous and wakeful by singing and shouting and fighting. Those were the times he ate at the cookhouse and rode with the crew, and often when he came back, the house was empty and Hogue was gone without a word or a note to the boy he called son.

There were months on end when Brady never saw school, when he ran in the brush with half-wild Pawnee kids, and nobody knew where he was, or cared.

There were times, too, when Hogue returned, sometimes with a new woman, sometimes alone, issuing beatings and threats and a harshly policed life.

Oftentimes there were only Hogue's black silences, his obvious indifference, and his savage discipline. The only thing that had stayed constant throughout the years was Anchor itself, its vaulting mountain ranges, its meadows, and its cattle. And Hogue's greed to own all of Kansas.

Brady walked on down the hall, past two closed doors and into his own room. It had been his since the first day Hogue brought him to the ranch as a toddler of three.

Moving across the floor, he set the lamp on the nightstand, then opened the outside door, letting the fresh night air drive out the musty scent of disuse.

An iron bed and a single chair beside the washstand comprised the furniture. He pulled off his boots and peeled off his shirt. When he tossed his boots across the room, he spotted the bullet hole in the wall.

He regarded it for a moment, remembering the day long ago when, a few days after his ninth birthday, he had stolen Hogue's new Sharp's rifle, hiding it under his covers until nighttime, when he could try it.

In the darkness he had fondled it, admiring it, and finally he had sighted at the wall. He hadn't meant to pull the trigger, but somehow it fired. Hogue had raged, baffled by the boy he had never tried to raise until it was too late.

Brady rolled a cigarette and lit it. He stretched out on the bed and let the bitterness wash over him. *Is it so wrong for a boy to want to be loved by his father—even if the man is a stepfather?*

The only thing Hogue had given Brady was his name. On Brady's thirteenth birthday, Hogue had given him a piece of paper signed by Judge Parker stating that Brady's name was legally Brady Wilkes.

Hogue had spoken that night at the bunkhouse. *"I've given this foundling boy my name. It's all legal. But just because he now carries the Wilkes name doesn't mean he'll get special treatment. No, siree. He'll become a man the only way there is, and that's the hard way."*

He'd never treated Brady as a son and often reminded him that he was a foundling who should be grateful for all Hogue did for him.

Lying there, he recalled their last argument, the demeaning words about his mother. All the self-doubt he had known in his life with Hogue had been confirmed by those words—he was the unwanted son of a cheap woman and an anonymous father.

It had taken him three weary months to accept that, to reason away the shame and the hopelessness, but those three months had done more harm than he'd expected.

He knew Kate might accept his irresponsibility with a patient hope that in time she could change him. But he also knew that she would never accept his scandalous involvement with Lou Spearman's con games.

And he knew he would stand trial for Hogue's murder before he would rat on Spearman and his crew.

This house, the cattle, and these acres were his, and he was beyond rich for his twenty-three years. Still, he would give it all up to wipe out the last three months of his past.

He took a final deep drag on the cigarette before mashing out its fire. He let his eyes close.

He didn't know how long he'd slept. A thought had awakened him, and the strength of it brought him to a sitting position.

I'm between a rock and a hard place. Can't rightly accept

the ranch with Hogue's murder hanging over my head. Maybe that's the answer—not taking legal possession of the ranch until I find a way to clear my name. Maybe I should ask the judge to hold off on the legal documents for a while.

He lay back, his hands behind his head.

Brady knew that his hatred for Hogue was shared by half a hundred people in Willow Creek and the surrounding areas. Hogue had bullied and swindled and trampled over people until he eventually gained what he wanted.

As for losing Anchor, Brady didn't much care. He had nearly a hundred head of horses in the hills, the only things he could call his own.

He'd start from scratch and show Kate he was dead serious about planting roots and settling down. Minutes later he felt a tenuous peace.

The clanging of the triangle and the cook's call to breakfast awakened Brady the next morning. By the time he'd tucked in his shirt, pulled on his boots, and reached the cookhouse, the last ranch hand had gone in. Brady stopped at the washbasin and splashed water over his face and ran his hands through his hair.

A subtle change came over him when he entered the building. The men were the same men who had witnessed his exit three months ago, and while they had remained aloof and silent that evening, he knew they'd thought that Hogue was at least half right about his mother and him.

Then there was Clem Garrett, who'd taught him how to fatten a steer, how to judge a horse, and how to keep simple books, grooming him for the job he'd contemptuously thrown in Hogue's face that last night.

Harsh memories of the last words that had passed between him and his stepfather caused Brady's heart to quicken.

"You filthy-minded old man. With all the women who pass through this house, how can you judge my mother? You met her once, and that was after she was dead, with half her scalp taken by the Pawnee."

Hogue had sneered. "Boy, I've had plenty of experience with soiled doves, and your mama was one, sure as I'm standing here."

Raucous laughter drew Brady back to the present.

The men who made up Anchor's crew lined the benches on both sides of the long table in the center of the room. A clamor of tinware and idle chatter filled the air. That is, until he entered. Conversations and good-natured guffawing trailed off into silence.

Clem Garrett rose from his place at the end of the table. A tall man in his sixties, slow-moving and with blue eyes made stark against a sun-darkened, leathery face, the ranch foreman offered his hand to Brady. Clem's gaze was reserved and held no particular emotion. "Figured your belly would tell you when to wake up. Grab yourself a plate."

Brady held himself tight, wondering how the ranch hands would react to his return. He chose a place halfway down the table. He touched the broad shoulder of the smithy. "Howdy, Rube." His greeting was returned with a simple nod. He glanced around the table, quietly speaking names. Some of the men grunted responses; others stared at their plates. These were proud men, competent, loyal to the brand, and hostile to him.

Brady stepped over the bench into the vacant place between the blacksmith and a new face to Anchor.

"Howdy. Name's Wally Sims." Wally passed a tin plate of biscuits. His voice held quiet indifference. "Don't believe we've met."

Brady laid two fist-sized biscuits on his plate and slathered them with molasses. "Brady Wilkes. I've been away."

Rube, the blacksmith, didn't try to hide the dislike in his eyes. "Make any money for yourself while you were gone, Brady?"

"Made more for Spearman."

Wally Sims observed good-naturedly, "That's one thing you can quit worrying about now."

"Never was too worried about it, Wally."

A ruddy-faced man with thinning hair slammed his cup onto the table. "That's right. You never worried about it. Like you never worried about Anchor."

Brady was aware that every man at the table, while still eating, had his ears tuned. He was further aware that the hands were understandably uneasy about the change of ownership of the ranch. While Hogue Wilkes might have been a savage tyrant, he was smart enough to leave the men and the running of the ranch to Clem Garrett.

Ready for a sharp retort, Brady checked himself, recalling the words Clem had told him when he was a cocky kid of eighteen and had sported a busted lip for spouting off to Hogue. *"A wise man chews on his words before he spits them out."* He set about eating.

Rube pushed harder. "When you plan on selling out, Brady?"

Anger seared Brady's insides. He wrapped his hand around his tin cup, allowing the heat from the coffee to burn his fingers. He spoke through clenched teeth. "Clem is foreman. Ask him."

There was a deep and mounting resentment in Rube's voice. "Yeah, foreman for who? The bank? One of them big associations back East?" The bulbous-nosed blacksmith rose and stepped away from the table. "Or any stranger who skunked you in a poker game?"

"Rube." Clem's voice held a sharp reprimand.

Brady set his cup down. "You talk too much." Half turned in his seat and from the corner of his eye, he spotted the smithy's beefy hands bunched into fists.

"I can do a lot more than talk, *Mr. Wilkes.* I pull my weight around here. That's more than any of us can say about you."

All eyes were centered on Brady, and he knew that the blacksmith spoke what the men were thinking. The time had come to prove himself not only as the new owner of Anchor, but as a man.

He came boiling out of his seat. He mounted the bench and dived at the burly blacksmith.

As if by prearranged signal, the entire room exploded into action. Wally Sims grabbed a handful of biscuits and made for the other side of the room. The cook, fat Amos Tucker, jumped onto Brady's back and wrapped pudgy hands under his chin. Jim Eagle came across the table to land a few punches to Brady's belly.

Brady staggered back against a wall to rid himself of the

hefty cook's choke hold. Bracing himself, he put his head down and fought blindly, savagely, and the crew fought among themselves to take their turn at him. He knew with gray despair that this was their revenge for his undeserved luck, for the years they thought he had idled away while they worked in blistering heat, freezing cold, and drenching rain. And for their backbreaking efforts they earned fifteen dollars a month and room and board.

The rain of blows on his chest, belly, and face drove the breath from him, and the pain was numbing. He fought stubbornly, ferociously, a feral anger twisting inside him.

Just when certain he was ready to collapse in defeat, a shotgun boomed, filling the room with a deafening roar, and Clem Garrett's voice followed on the heels of it. "Back off, all of you, or I'll fill your sorry hides with lead."

Amos sat sprawled in a corner, rubbing the back of his bald head. The others backed off. Brady sat slumped on his knees on the dusty floor. His hands at his sides, head hung low, dragging in great gusts of breath, he heard rather than saw Clem Garrett roughly shoving his way through the crowd of the wranglers.

Clem's gravelly voice bellowed with disgust. "Have the whole bunch of you gone plumb loco?"

Amos Tucker mumbled, "Hell, a body don't have to be crazy to want to hit Brady." Amos used the hem of his apron to swipe at the beads of sweat on his forehead. "He ain't nothing but a cocky pup. I been wantin' to take him on for years."

Rube pointed a beefy fist toward Brady. "Yeah, Amos, I'm

glad you got a few licks in before Anchor's new owner fires the lot of us."

Brady sucked in a painful breath, wiping blood from his nose with his sleeve. His torn shirt hung from one shoulder, and his chest was livid with bruises.

He brushed away Clem's offer to help him to his feet. "I've got to do this on my own," he said quietly to the man.

When Clem nodded, he knew the old foreman understood. Staggering to his feet with a grunt, Brady held his ribs. He braced his legs to keep from crumpling to the floor.

The men stood lined against a wall, arms crossed over their chests. Looking at them, Brady saw the residue of anger in the faces, and a perverse pleasure too.

His throat ached from the cook's crushing grip. Words failed to come out when he tried to speak. When at last he did speak, his voice rasped. "If you want to draw your time, see Clem. He's running this outfit, and he'll keep running it."

Breathing hard, he stood a little taller. "I admit to getting Anchor the easy way. To set the record straight, I'm not taking legal possession of the ranch until Hogue's killer is found. Until then you'll continue taking orders from Clem."

He paused, considering the men's silence their agreement. Pulling the torn shirt from his body, he wiped it across his face. "Until Bass Young finds who murdered Hogue or decides to charge me with his death, I'll be trading horses, and I'll live in my room at the house."

Casting a challenge, he looked directly at each man. "I'll

be around here a lot, and if you think to break me, then be done with it now. I've taken all I'm going to take—and that includes from you, Rube."

The blacksmith moved past Clem and out the door, leaving the room as quiet as the church graveyard.

Chapter Six

Hannah Osterhaus sat with her head bent, making out a waybill for a waiting teamster, when old Sam Copeland paused by her desk in the late afternoon and said in a dry and worried voice, "Mr. Spearman said for you to come to his office."

"In a minute." Hannah continued writing.

The brittle and withered man cleared his throat to get her attention. "He said, right now."

"Go to your own desk, Sam. I'm busy."

Copeland sniffed and shuffled over to his desk. Hannah finished the waybill and handed it to the teamster, a man with dangerous eyes and a sulking face. She said in a matter-of-fact voice, "If you hadn't come in drunk this morning, Hank, you'd be ten hours on your way by now."

The corners of the teamster's lips drew into a sneer. He

jammed the waybill into his pocket. "Only had a drop, Hannah. Nothin' wrong with that, is there?"

"Not if it isn't a drop too much," Hannah said, "and with you, it always is." She stood and bunched her hands on her hips. "One more thing, Hank: you will address me as Miss Osterhaus. Is that clear?"

The teamster tramped out, and Hannah sat down at her desk. She stretched luxuriously. All the teamsters were out, her bills of lading were filed, and her desk was cleaned up for the day. She was aware that Sam Copeland watched her with a disapproving frown, looking almost fearful. The boss had spoken, and she hadn't jumped.

Sam Copeland was a little gray man with a little gray mind. Out of some perverse wish to agitate him, Hannah rose, walked through the gate in the railing, and, instead of turning down the corridor to Spearman's office, she strolled to the outside door. There she paused, looking out over the yard, watching Hank Tillman climb up onto the high-sided freight wagon's seat. She listened to the sharp crack of the whip as he lashed it over the team of six horses, spurring them into action.

When he passed the office, he waved and called out, "Good-bye, li'l darlin'," and he guffawed loudly.

Hannah regarded him with a cold frown, not moving until his back was to her and his team had clopped out of the yard. It was then that she went down the corridor and stepped into Spearman's office.

Her boss stood at the open window, his back to her. Without turning, he said, "That happen often?"

"Often enough. Doesn't matter. I can handle it."

He settled into the oversized leather chair behind his desk. "There'll be no more of that. I'll have Lester speak to the men." Spearman's voice was grim. "Sit down, please."

Hannah pulled a straight chair up to his desk and sat. She folded her hands in the lap of her drab office dress and noted without interest that the sleeves were getting shiny and that her fingers were ink-stained.

She watched her employer as he laid a massive hand on top of a stack of papers on his desk. "I've finished with these." Though his voice was pleasant, he frowned a little. "Are you sure your figures are right?"

Hannah smiled. "The money's in the bank, sir."

"I can't believe it," Spearman said, his voice slow and easy. "Frankly, when I gave over the freighting end of the business to you, I'd have been satisfied if it made enough to pay your salary. The thing was a pocket-draining nuisance."

"And now?"

"And now"—his laughter was genuine—"it's a money-making nuisance. I don't know how've you done it." Spearman's voice was kindly, almost fatherly.

For a moment he concentrated on forming his fingers into a pyramid. He flexed them back and forth, as if he were playing a game. "What's happened to the Bjorn bothers? I dare say you've taken a bite out of their business, haven't you?"

"Oh, no, sir, Mr. Spearman. We can do one thing best, and we do it," Hannah assured her boss. "You see, we haul freight downriver at a rate the Bjorn brothers can't touch, and they don't even try. But from Dodge City to here, we can't buck them. We each go our own way."

Spearman's eyes sharpened. "Why can we beat them downriver but not upriver?"

"We're hauling feed for the stockyards downriver all the time," Hannah explained. "Our wagons used to go down full and come back empty. Now I load them with freight, so we're full coming and going, and we can offer a lower rate. The Bjorns' wagons have to come back empty, and it doesn't pay them."

Spearman smiled and nodded his appreciation. "What about upriver?"

Hannah pursed her lips. "The Bjorns have us there. They've got good wagons and good teamsters, and they keep tight schedules."

"And we don't?"

Hannah laughed out loud. "Hank's an example of the teamsters Lester got me. Anybody half-drunk or sick or too lazy to hold a regular job is a teamster. For wagons we use anything lying around the lot. For teams I've been given half-wild range horses that aren't properly broken to harness." She shrugged. "As for a schedule, we couldn't keep one at the point of a gun."

Spearman leaned back in his chair and laughed, and Hannah smiled in turn. She had never complained before, and now that the opportunity had arisen, she wondered if it would do any good. She was a woman in a man's world, she knew, yet Lou Spearmen suddenly seemed interested.

She watched his eyes rake over her—not like a man looking for passion, rather like a man assessing a good horse and wondering if he could make a profitable deal.

He said, "What do you need, Hannah?"

Without hesitation, she named the items. "Sound freight wagons, real working teamsters instead of saloon bums, and strong horses broken to harness."

"Think you could give the Bjorns a run for their money?"

"I wouldn't try, sir."

Spearman frowned, puzzled, and Hannah leaned forward a little. "Look, Mr. Spearman, plenty of freight outfits in Danforth and Dodge City book freight on through to points in Colorado and up to Utah. The Bjorns don't.

Spearman nodded. "And?"

"Well, the Bjorns have an agent in Danforth. Why not work with Sven and Gunnar? Let them book freight on through to Salt Lake City too. They can haul it from Dodge City to Willow Creek and then transfer to our wagons. We can haul it to the Utah points and still bring back all our feed. With our low rates tacked onto the Bjorns' rates, we could haul cheaper than other outfits, and both of us would make more money than we do now."

Spearman scowled and swung his swivel chair around to look out the window. His big hands lay on his massive thighs, and a thick finger tapped his frayed trousers.

Hannah wondered about his worn clothes and guessed that a shrewd horse trader such as Lou Spearman could never afford to seem too prosperous.

Spearman scrubbed his chin thoughtfully and turned to regard her. "I like the way you think, Hannah. You're smart for a gal who didn't have the opportunity to attend finishing school for young ladies. But I'm wondering, why make money for the Bjorns? Why don't we do it all?"

With infinite patience she repeated, "They've got the good equipment, drivers who keep to schedules, and reliable horses. Unless you're willing to spend a lot of money, we can't compete."

Tapping his fingers together, he said, "What would happen if we hauled freight from Danforth to points in Utah for ninety cents a hundred?"

"You'd lose money."

"But I'd get the business. What else would happen? Could the Bjorns match that rate?"

"Not and stay in business." Hannah didn't like the direction of this conversation.

"Exactly." Spearman spoke almost as if he were the only person in the room. "I've made a little money this summer that I'd like to gamble with." His eyes seemed to snap with energy when he looked at her. "Do you think the Bjorns have money behind them or . . . could get it?"

Hannah frowned. "They've gotten where they are with hard work and little money. About getting funds"—she hesitated—"I couldn't say."

Spearman rose from his chair and paced about the room, his hands clasped behind his back. "What would happen if I invested a few thousand dollars into cutting rates until the Bjorns couldn't match mine?"

Staring wide-eyed, Hannah quietly said, "You'd ruin them."

Spearman detected the censure in her words, and he raised his eyebrows. "And if I do?"

She kept her words simple. "I like Sven and Gunnar Bjorn. They are good men. Hardworking and honest."

Spearman's voice took on a satirical tone. "It's your privilege to like them—after working hours."

Appalled at what was shaping up, she said in a quick and curious voice, "You mean you'd break them for . . . for money, Mr. Spearman?"

He smiled at her naivete and nodded. "I'll throw away as much money as it takes to cut rates. By that time they'll be out of business, and we can pick up their wagons cheap. Hell, maybe the entire outfit. After that, I can jack up the rates and make back my losses."

Hannah sat rigid and motionless. She was picturing Sven Bjorn, a big, loose-framed, gangling man who had spent scores of evenings telling her about Sweden and how he missed his mother, of his deep ambitions since coming to America, watching to see if he stirred affection or love in her, and finally being content with her friendship. He was a good man, simple and kind and tolerant, and all his hopes, along with his brother's, were doomed now by Lou Spearman, who certainly seemed to live up to his reputation as a shrewd businessman. His plan was greedy and heartless, and it frightened her.

Why would he want to drive Sven and Gunnar out of business, to ruin them? Watching Spearman pace the room, she felt as if she'd glimpsed something black and evil and nameless that she wasn't meant to look upon. Instinctively, she glanced away.

"Well?" Spearman said. "What's wrong with my idea?"

She controlled the shudder that threatened to ripple through her. "I . . . I . . . What do you want me to do?" Pleating a fold of her skirt, she refused to look at him.

He sat at his desk and took a cigar from its humidor. After lighting it, he leaned back and propped his feet on the desk. Drawing a few puffs, he said, "Go see the Bjorns. Tell them what we're going to do. Get their offer on the whole outfit, bring it to me, and we'll see how it looks. Only fools won't know when they're licked."

Hannah stood up, looking at a point beyond Spearman's head. "Isn't this a job for a man?"

Spearman disagreed. "You, my dear, are running the freighting end of this business. I'm only the backer, supplying the money and the plans."

"If you say so, Mr. Spearman." She nodded. "Good night."

After she returned to her desk, Sam Copeland said, "Sure took a long time with the boss."

In a crisp and businesslike tone she said, "I'm certain that if Mr. Spearman had wanted you involved in our conversation, Mr. Copeland, he would have requested your presence."

The old man gathered his books and shoved them into the safe. He grabbed his hat off the rack and thrust it onto his head. He bade her good night and left as quickly as his arthritic legs would carry him.

Hannah sat down slowly at her desk and stared at the dingy walls. Why did there have to be a price on everything? Her thoughts were bitter. Now there was a price on her job. A high price. An impossible price. It was her responsibility to ruin the two brothers who were her friends.

She remembered that Gunnar had come in just yesterday to rent four teams of horses for a special hauling job, carting machinery to the mining camp back in the mountains. He and Sven would be home tomorrow, and tomorrow night, she knew, she would have to face them.

Footsteps interrupted her thoughts. She turned to see who was entering the office so late. One-Eyed Lester gave her a lazy grin. "You've put in a full day, Hannah. Go on home."

"On my way." As an afterthought, she said, "Mr. Spearman is still in his office."

Lester nodded and went on through to the office, and Hannah stared at the doorway. It seemed to her that it was no longer a plain doorway in a shabby, ill-lit office anymore. Now it was the entrance to a dark cave where a cunning monster wove his secret schemes and spared no pity for anyone.

She wasted no time tidying her desk while controlling the urge to race out of the office and as far away as her legs would take her. How dare Spearman make her an accomplice in his avaricious scheme?

I've got to think of a plan. I've just got to.

Chapter Seven

Serious about proving his worth to Anchor's ranch hands, Brady was up before dawn, saddled and ready to ride out of the ranch yard. Deciding to work the draw north of the ranch, he nudged the sturdy blue roan beneath him into an easy gallop.

The day was cloudy and warm, the breeze off the river was sweet smelling, and a profusion of wildflowers was everywhere. Brady took little time to notice as he pushed the gelding to Anchor's highest range until he came to a secluded glen. Relief filled him when he spotted the small herd of horses.

The gelding beneath him quivered and whinnied. "Yeah, I know, ol' son, it wasn't too long ago that you were running free."

He dismounted and hobbled the gelding, knowing the horse was eager to join the herd.

After washing down a cold biscuit and jerky with water from his canteen, Brady stepped back into the saddle and urged the gelding forward. "Okay, boy, let's head 'em home."

Two hours before dusk twenty mustangs broke out of the cottonwoods and into the meadow. Brady reined in at the edge of the timber, letting the band lope toward the creek. Removing his hat and rubbing an arm over his sweaty brow, he noted the remnants of slate-colored clouds. If rain came again, it would be after dark, and he had a good hour of working daylight left.

As he rode past where he'd made camp under three stunted cottonwoods along the creek, he noticed how the tarp covering his gear was pooled with water from the same rain that had soaked him earlier in the day.

Pushing the horses toward a makeshift corral, he rode to the gate and lifted the braided rawhide loop from the post. He swung the gate wide, then kneed his gelding around and behind the milling band. The horses moved into the corral, and Brady secured the gate.

Stiff and sore from strenuous riding and yesterday's beating, he unsaddled and turned the blue roan loose to graze. At camp he built up a fire, filled a coffeepot from the creek, and set it to boil. Afterward he rummaged in his saddlebag and found a cold biscuit to chew on.

Later he grabbed his rope and headed for the corral. His step was slow, a grinding weariness dragging at him. His ribs ached so much that breathing was an effort, and every movement reminded him of the welcome he had received at the hands of the crew.

Inside the corral, he stubbornly set about the laborious

task of cutting out horses from the general bunch and pushing them back into the rope corral, where a dozen or so other mustangs stood with ears alert as if assessing the possibility of escape.

At deep dusk he was finished, and he turned out the unwanted horses. He looked at the fifteen he had kept. He had no certain plans, but he knew that these horses represented his fortune and his future.

Back at camp he made a quick supper of bacon and beans and coffee and afterward sat under the tarp, his back against a tree trunk. He watched night come to the meadows. Tomorrow he would drive this bunch down to the main ranch and then return to the secret stronghold at Mt. Sunflower for the twenty-five head corralled there, also driving them to the ranch.

He sat back, enjoying the smoke he'd rolled. In the darkness he concentrated on the cigarette's flare of red ash and wondered what Kate would say when he rode into town to tell her of his decision to give up Anchor.

While pondering this, he heard the soft clop of hooves in damp earth. He crushed the cigarette into the dirt and eased his six-shooter from its holster, then scooted farther into the shadows of the tarp and waited for the rider to come out of the cottonwood grove.

Brady squinted through the darkness, wishing the campfire provided more light. Presently a voice rang out. "Hullo, the camp."

Not recognizing the voice, Brady responded, "State your business, friend."

"Brady? Brady Wilkes? It's me, Wally Sims, from Anchor."

Brady felt caution gather in him. "Show yourself."

The cowhand crossed the creek, his horse kicking up ribbons of water that the moonlight turned to silver as they rose and fell. He reined in by the fire, and Brady said, "Light and eat, Wally."

"Sure you want me?"

Brady approached the fire. At his nod, Wally stepped down out of the saddle and looked about. His glance settled on the corral, and in bright shafts of moonlight he spotted the small herd of horses. "Man, that's a backbreaking job. Why didn't you ask Clem for the loan of a couple hands?"

Brady filled two tin cups with coffee and handed one to the sinewy figure. "Seems like you'd know that answer without asking."

"Yeah," Wally said in a slow drawl. "Like you said, Rube talks too much." He sat by the fire and crossed his long legs Indian style. "The men should've waited before they waded in on you like that." He blew to cool the scalding coffee before taking a sip.

"Noticed you didn't take part," Brady said. "How come you didn't try to get in a few licks?"

"Hired on right after you left. Oh, I've heard all the bunkhouse rabble about the argument between you and Hogue and about your reputation for running off every time your steppaw rankled you." Wally poured himself another cup and offered to fill Brady's.

"Still didn't answer my question. You could've gotten in your share."

"Ten against one ain't my way. I'll square off toe-to-toe, but ganging up? Nope."

The two men sat in silence as if sizing up each other. "Mind if I ask why you'd give up a prize like Anchor?"

"Wasn't any love lost between me and Hogue. That's reason enough." Brady didn't offer more. "Mind if I ask how a cowpoke came to be named Wally?"

The answer followed after a lighthearted guffaw. "My full handle is Elvoy Wallace Sims. Answer your question?"

"Reckon it does." Brady drank the rest of his coffee and stoked the embers, sending up sparks to float and die on the breeze. "Who killed Hogue?"

Wally almost smiled. "I wouldn't have picked you," he said mildly. "Not even after what Hogue said about your mother. After you left, he didn't have a kind word for you, either."

Brady didn't comment. Wally searched inside his pocket, drew out a tobacco pouch, and rolled a smoke. Pinching the resulting cigarette ends, he reached toward the edge of the fire, picked up a twig, and used the tip as a match.

Brady observed the man's rope-callused hands and figured he'd had decades of punching cows and wrangling horses. "Is there anyone at the ranch willing to back me if need be?" he asked.

"Me . . . and Clem." Wally closed his eyes for a moment as if enjoying his smoke. When he stubbed out the butt, he said, "The way I figure it, you had every right to kill Hogue that *night*. But you didn't. That's why Bass Young's wrong to suspect you."

"How do you know he does?"

"Said so," Wally replied. "He was at the ranch yesterday."

Brady felt a faint chill of premonition. *Lou Spearman.*

"He wants you to come in and see him," Wally added

while he watched the younger man's face. "That why you're set on giving up Anchor?"

Brady nodded. The tall cowhand stood and said offhandedly, "The way Rube figured a week ago, you'd come back and rooster around, maybe pension Clem off, and fire the whole bunch of us."

"How do you know I wouldn't have, if the sheriff had let me alone?"

"Guess you still could, couldn't you?"

Brady remained silent, wondering what this was leading up to.

Wally seemed satisfied. He said almost shyly, "Clem saw some of your ponies tucked in over by the Silver Creek line shack. He'll drive 'em in for you tomorrow. Said to tell you to go on in and see Bass, then him and me will bring down your string."

Brady stared at him uncomprehendingly, and Wally met his glance. Finally Brady asked, "Why, Wally?"

"Got helped out once or twice myself. Figure it's time I pass on the favor."

"Why didn't Clem ride out and tell me himself?"

"Don't know. Reckon that's between him and you." The answer came soft and honest.

Daybreak came with the answering calls of two meadowlarks. Brady turned his string of horses out of the corral, and he and Wally ran them for a couple of miles until the morning friskiness was off them. By midday they drove the bunch toward the ranch. Wally rode ahead to open the corral gates.

Turning the horses into the big corral, Brady unsaddled his roan, roped a broad-chested bay, and shifted his saddle to the fresh horse. In thanks to Wally, he tipped a forefinger to the brim of his hat.

Riding past the cookshack, he got a reluctant wave from fat Amos standing in the doorway, and that was all.

He made the ride to Willow Creek at a mile-eating trot, and now he speculated on what the sheriff, prompted by Lou Spearman's fabrications, might have to say. He didn't know, and that frustrated him. In late afternoon he came to the rise above the town. Halting his horse, he watched the activity along the main street.

Beyond the town he heard faint shouts and whistles. Rising in the stirrups, he saw a band of horses being hazed out of Spearman's lot and down toward the creek by a trio of riders. The unvarying solid color of every horse told him what he needed to know. This was part of the bunch he, Long Tom, and Willie had brought in from Colorado—all solid color, all under sixteen hands high, all flat-backed and close-coupled geldings between five and seven years old. They met the requirements of the United States Cavalry and were now being driven one hundred thirty miles to Fort McClaren. He remembered the long, hot drive to Dodge City and was glad he wasn't with them.

He angled his pony down the town's busy central street and tied up in front of the saddle shop on the corner opposite the bank. The usual row of idlers lined the sidewalks. Some regarded him with curiosity, and others nodded a cursory greeting. He walked past the hotel to the sheriff's office.

Bass Young sat in a swivel chair, his head bent over a stack of WANTED posters. A faint smile appeared on Brady's mouth when in aggravation the sheriff reached out and swatted at a pesky fly.

In clear agitation, Bass rolled the posters into a cylinder, took aim, and came down heavily on the desk, only to send the fly flitting off in another direction.

"How's the hunting, Bass?"

The sheriff looked up, a cold cigar between his teeth. He swatted again. "It's like trying to kill a buffalo with a slingshot filled with watermelon seeds." He regarded Brady for a moment. "Who pasted that shiner on you?"

"Nobody to worry yourself about, Bass." Brady sat in the chair across the desk from young. "Heard you wanted to see me."

"Worried?"

Brady nodded. "Some. I'd like to know where I stand."

Bass rose and walked to the potbellied stove. "Coffee?"

Brady waved off the offer.

Bass poured a cup of the thick brew and walked back to his desk. He answered Brady's concern. "You're a little closer to trial than you were a couple days ago." He chewed thoughtfully on his cigar before he said, "I suppose you've developed a weak memory."

"Memory of what?"

"Hmm." Bass grimaced as he sipped the coffee. He walked to the door and tossed it out. He spoke as he seated himself. "You wouldn't, let's say, know where you were the five days between May first and May ninth, would you? Like, recollect anybody at a May Day dance or at a church social or playing horseshoes?"

Brady's face went bland and blank. "Can't say I remember."

"Uh-huh. I thought so. You remember a man named Jones?"

"Should I?"

"You bought four horses from him on the second. You remember a man name of Smith? No, of course you don't. You bought ten horses from him on the ninth."

"Who said I did?"

"Lou Spearman," Bass said. "I've been checking dates on bills of sale with him. He claims you bought horses from both Jones and Smith on those dates and turned the bills of sale over to him. Funny thing, though—he can't recollect your buying any horses in between those dates. Can you?"

Brady took his time answering. Almost imperceptibly Spearman was drawing the noose tighter, and there was nothing he could do to stop it. If he contradicted Spearman's story, Bass would make him prove the contradiction. He drummed his fingers on his knee. "Where did I run across Jones and Smith?"

"Around Bristol."

"That would give me time to leave Jones, ride back here, track down Hogue's whereabouts on a range of over ten thousand acres, kill him, and get back to buy Smith's horses on the ninth. That what you're thinking, Bass?"

The sheriff observed Brady. In a sardonic voice, he said, "You said it. I didn't."

Brady shifted in the chair. "Have you and Doc decided when Hogue was killed?"

"The last time he was seen was on the third. He picked up a drunken Slash T rider that night and put him back on his horse, or so the rider says."

"And why did I kill Hogue?" Brady didn't flinch when he met the sheriff's stare.

"You hated him."

"Did *you* like him? Brady countered.

"That's different."

"Right." Brady's voice was flat. "Ever since I was knee-high, I've been mad enough to kill Hogue. Lots of times. But I never even tried. Why would I sneak back all the way from Colorado to do it now?"

"From what I hear, he said some pretty rotten things about your mother the night you left."

Brady nodded. "Hard enough things that I could have choked the life out of his miserable hide with my bare hands right then and there in the bunkhouse, and no one would have blamed me. But I didn't."

The sheriff said nothing, only studied Brady's face.

"Since you're not talking, I guess that reason's no good, is it, Bass? What others have you got?"

"The largest and most profitable ranch in Kansas."

"So you think I killed Hogue to inherit Anchor." Brady emphasized each word. "All the more reason I shouldn't claim my inheritance."

Bass sighed. "Yeah, I heard about that yesterday at the ranch." He reached into a desk drawer and pulled out another cigar, then clipped the end with his pocketknife. "What happens to Anchor and to the men who call it home if you don't claim it?"

"What do you think will happen?"

Bass twirled the cigar between his fingers before lighting it. "You got me there, Brady."

"Then leave me alone."

Something in Brady's voice caused the sheriff to look up, and Brady rose.

"I mean it, Bass."

The sheriff sighed again and rubbed his chin. "I know you do." One bushy eyebrow rose. "Listen, son, one thing to ponder on. If you can't prove your innocence, you might want to consider what'll happen to Anchor when a noose is placed around your neck."

"Yeah. I'll do that."

Brady stepped out of the hot office and walked a short distance down the boardwalk. When he stopped to roll a cigarette, he noticed that his hands trembled. How well had he succeeded in curbing Bass Young's suspicions? There was no way of telling.

Taking a deep drag on the cigarette, Brady contemplated his next move and decided he might as well see Judge Parker and settle the business about Anchor. He waited until Sven Bjorn, driving a freight team, passed by.

The man called out a cheerful, "*Güt morgen.*"

Brady nodded an acknowledgment.

He took the courthouse steps by twos and walked through the double lead-glass–paned doors and down the hall to the judge's chambers. He lifted a hand to knock, then hesitated. Voices behind the door stopped him. Then Kate's voice drew him inside.

Dressed in a short-sleeved blue street dress with a matching shawl, Kate left her chair and rushed to him when she saw him. "Who've you been fighting with?"

Brady offered only a sheepish grin when he kissed her

forehead. Judge Parker regarded him without any cordiality in his expression. He gestured toward a chair. Brady removed his hat and hung it on the rack next to the door. There was a look of silent reproof in Kate's face when she tenderly touched his eye.

Judge Parker said, "Come about the business?"

At Brady's nod the judge rose, opened the cabinet beside his desk, and removed several papers, which he laid on the desk. "Kate . . ."

She wrinkled her nose, "I know, Dad—you want me out."

As she moved toward the door, Brady grasped her hand. "Don't go, Kate. It'll save me having to tell you later." He looked at the judge and drew a sizeable breath. "I'm not taking Anchor, at least not right now, Judge. Can you draw up a paper stating that I won't assume rightful ownership of the ranch until I've fully cleared myself of Hogue's murder?"

A long silence passed before Kate said, "You don't want Anchor?"

Brady nodded, avoiding her questioning stare. "Bass seems to think I killed Hogue. He thinks I did it because I wanted the ranch." He ran a hand through his hair. "I'd like to hold off on ownership until I've cleared my name."

Kate managed to collect herself and sputtered, "But what if you don't?"

He said with a half chuckle, "Then I won't need Anchor, will I?"

Kate uttered an unladylike oath. "Bass Young is an old, incompetent fool. Why, I should go over there and give him a piece of my mind."

"You'll do no such thing, young lady," her father admonished.

"Dad, it's blackmail." Hot tears brimmed in her eyes.

Judge Parker looked at Brady. "Don't be absurd, Brady. Like it or not, the property is legally yours. Let Bass try to make a case against you."

"According to Bass, hatred is enough cause." A note of dejection filled Brady's voice.

Kate's voice rose an indignant octave. "But why would you give up a ranch the size of most of Kansas?"

The judge seconded her question. "Exactly. You're doing it all backward, Brady. The law is founded on the assumption that a man is innocent until proven guilty, not that he's guilty until proven innocent. Let Bass try to prove your guilt."

Brady's shoulders slumped forward. How could he make them understand? "What if he can make a good case against me?"

"He can't if you can account for your time. You can, can't you?"

"No," Brady lied.

"I thought you were traveling with Spearman's men."

"Not all the time," he lied again. *Everyone thinks Lou Spearman is an honest, upstanding citizen. Oh, Kate, you'd never understand why I let him talk me into wearing a cavalry uniform. If they don't hang me for killing Hogue, the Army will hang me for impersonating a cavalry officer and cheating honest ranchers. Who's going to believe me over Spearman?*

A look of accusation spilled into Judge Parker's eyes, and

Brady knew what the man was thinking. This was the hurt he'd mentioned that night in the quiet darkness, the disgrace that would break Kate's heart, and Brady accepted it.

The judge's face remained stony. "It's yours to dispose of, Brady. I'm Hogue's executor. I suppose I could arrange to hold Anchor under any terms you wish."

Kate's gaze shifted from Brady to her father, and the protest rose in her blue eyes when she leveled them on Brady. "So, everything you said the other night was a bald-faced lie. You promised you'd run Anchor and prove to me you weren't a shiftless drifter, that you were ready to settle down and accept the responsibility of running the ranch, didn't you?"

If felt as if she'd ripped his heart from his chest. All Brady did was nod.

"And now you won't. You've found another way to dodge responsibility."

Weary to the depths of his soul, Brady said, "That's what you think?"

"At long last you have a chance to prove yourself." Kate spoke with passion. "You've got a ranch to run, a crew to pay, cattle to raise, and you've . . . you've even got my heart to win."

Brady looked down at his hands for a long moment, and he tasted the full bitterness of his situation. The one thing that could free him he couldn't tell her, because telling Kate about his involvement with Spearman's scams would cause him to lose her.

Miserable, he rose and said, "You've got to let me work this out my way, Kate."

"Of course." She managed a faint and unenthusiastic

smile. "As if a few more months added on to these past three years will make me grow any younger." Then, like a petulant child, she stamped her foot. "Waiting on you has made me an old maid, Brady Wilkes."

"Twenty is hardly old, Kate." He hadn't meant it the way it came out.

Swishing her skirts, she pushed past him, and without saying good-bye to her father or Brady, Kate stormed from the office.

Chapter Eight

One-Eyed Lester drifted into Ma Smalley's Boarding-House and Restaurant. He sidled up to the counter. "Two of your finest cee-gars, Miz Smalley."

"Twenty-five cents." She reached under the counter and brought out two cigars.

He counted out the coins and then strolled over to one of the deep leather chairs in the lobby and sat down. Passing the dining room, he didn't bother to look in. He already knew Brady was there.

Lighting a cigar, he stretched out his legs and settled comfortably in the chair. He lazily counted the people who passed through the lobby. Some he acknowledged, and others he ignored. Except for waiting for Brady to show up, there was nothing much on his mind.

He slouched lower in the chair and, leaning his head back,

shut his one good eye to a mere slit, pretending to doze. When he spotted Brady emerging from the dining room, Lester merely watched him, noting the black eye, bruised cheek, and the sober set to his expression. An indolent smile touched the corners of Lester's mouth as Brady headed outside.

Through the front window, he watched Brady light a cigarette. Lester reached the door just as Brady untied the reins of his horse. Lester strolled across the boardwalk to lean against a porch pillar.

"Nice horse, Brady," he observed. "Want to sell him?"

Brady met One-Eyed Lester's smile with a hard scowl. "Not to you."

Lester countered with, "Well, now, that's too bad." Keeping his voice pleasant, he said, "Lou'd like to see you."

A foot in the stirrup, Brady paused and looked sharply at Spearman's head toady.

Thinking to bait the one-eyed man, Brady kept his voice calm and even. "Now that you're a big man, Lester, don't you think it's time to stop running Spearman's errands?"

Lester shrugged in response. "I don't mind. You comin'?"

When Brady flipped the reins over the horse's head, Lester said, "Leave him tied. Lou's over at the barbershop taking his Saturday bath."

Brady paused, his eyes meeting Lester's challenge. There was a faintly amused expression on Brady's face when he retied his horse and fell in beside the slack-hipped gunman. They crossed the street, passed the bank, and entered Elmer Johnson's barbershop. Johnson was seated in the one barber chair reading a dime novel. At their entrance he lifted his thumb, pointed over his shoulder toward the rear, and resumed his reading.

Brady followed Lester down the hall. The smile on the one-eyed man's face concerned Brady. Lester palmed open the knob of the second door and stepped into a spacious, dimly lit room.

An oversized galvanized tub sat in a corner. Spearman lay submerged in its soapy water, a half-smoked cigar in his mouth, a folded newspaper in one hand. A paraffin lamp provided light for the windowless room.

Spearman's massive arms and chest almost filled the width of the tub. Next to him on the floor stood a brace of buckets filled with hot water.

Brady crossed the room to lean against a wall and to face the man he'd grown to loathe.

"Hello, son."

Where Spearman's voice sounded almost affectionate, Brady's mocked. "Hello, Uncle Lou."

One-Eyed Lester seated himself in a straight-backed chair, looking perversely pleased at Brady's cockiness. Doubtless he thought it would make what was about to happen much more entertaining. He reared the chair onto its two hind legs so that the back rested against the wall. He crossed his arms over his chest and looked over at Spearman in time to see him glowering.

"Is it the light, or have you got a black eye?" Spearman inquired with mild indifference.

Lester shifted his gaze to Brady's casual stance, one boot heel propped against the wall, thumbs tucked into the pockets of his pants.

"Get down to business, Louis," Brady knew Spearman didn't like his given name.

Spearman chuckled. "You were at the sheriff's office today."

"You spying on me?"

Spearman lazily splashed water over his hairy chest. "Think Bass is convinced you bought horses from Jones and Smith?"

"You're the one who supplied him with the information. You tell me."

"Ah, young lad . . . young and foolish. Seems you've got yourself into a fine fiddle of a fix. I don't see how you can beat the trouble you're in." Spearman motioned for Brady to add more hot water to the tub.

"Looks like I'm already beat."

Spearman released an exaggerated sigh as he soaped under his arms. "Yes, so I've heard." Smugness crept into his voice. "Won't do you much good, I'm afraid, Brady."

"Not sure I know what you're referring to, Uncle Lou. What won't do me much good?" Brady spared a glance at Lester, who looked faintly amused. Was Spearman privy to his decision not to take immediate ownership of the ranch?

Brady touched a match to a cigarette and inhaled, studying the blue-white smoke that lingered in the air. "How far are you going to push this, Spearman?"

A belly-busting laugh rose up from Spearman before his eyes squinted into a deadly warning. "Right up to the finish."

"I won't hang for Hogue's murder. The finish will be my telling Bass about the Army uniform and my using the moniker Lieutenant Hastings, so he can prove where I was."

Lester cut in softly, "You're lying." He was watching Brady. Keeping his voice low and even, Lester said, "You want Judge Parker's daughter too much to rat us out. You know she won't have you if you squeal."

"You want to bet on that, Lester?"

"It's a bet you'll lose, but sure, I'll take your money."

"That's a bet I'll also take." Spearman raised a foot from the water and scrubbed the bottom of it with a bristle brush. "I have the uniform, remember, Brady? That's why I'm willing to bet that you'll never tell Bass anything about our little— ah, shall we say—enterprise."

Lester watched stubbornness come into Brady's face, darkening it, and felt a perverse pleasure. The boy reminded him of trout struggling to get off the hook.

"I'm done with your crooked dealings, Spearman. I won't work for you, and I won't wear that uniform again."

"Who said anything about your putting on the uniform?"

Brady glanced across the room. "Lester suggested as much."

Spearman looked reprovingly at his one-eyed minion, who was studying the floor as if he had no part in this.

"Lester only has my best interests at heart." Spearman managed to sound forgiving. He puffed on his cigar long enough to find that it had gone out, then tossed it carelessly to the floor. In an almost casual voice he said, "You still owe me, boy, and what I want, Brady, is a partnership."

"Partnership?" Brady echoed. "In what?"

"In Anchor, of course." Spearman settled back into the tub a little, laced his fingers together behind his head, studied the ceiling a moment, and then frowned. Looking at Lester, he said, "Get me a cigar, and warm the water again, will you?"

The one-eyed man went to the chair where Spearman's clothes where, removed a cigar from the breast pocket of his vest, gave it to him, held a match for the cigar, then dumped a bucket of hot water into the tub. He went back to his chair and sat down.

With a gentle persuasiveness, Spearman said, "Here's how it is, Brady. I've got money and plenty of horse buyers, but every time the Army needs a big shipment of horses, I have to send men around the country on buying trips. Now that you've inherited Anchor and all that goes with it—grass, buildings, corrals—*you* need a partner. Together we'll raise horses, buy horses, train them, trade them, and sell them. We'll be the biggest horse dealers in the West. I can see it now, boy. We'll make a fortune."

Brady pushed away from the wall, his hands clenched into tight fists with realization as he regarded Spearman. His words came out in a choked whisper. "*You* killed Hogue, didn't you, Lou?"

Spearman's voice filled with exaggerated awe. "Why, yes, of course, I did."

Lester gently slipped his pistol from its holster and held it at his side. He watched Brady standing completely motionless, his lean restlessness stilled, hands at his sides, legs apart, his face hard and unforgiving and wild.

When Brady glanced in his direction, Lester said, "Admit it. Part of you doesn't care that Hogue is dead, right?"

Brady stared at the floor.

Presently Spearman spoke, "Now, now, Brady. Don't take

it so hard. I want you to listen to me carefully. The way I've figured it, there are three things you can do." He leaned both arms on the edge of the tub. Water sloshed over the edges and spilled onto the floor at the big man's motion.

"Look at me, boy." Spearman's tone was that of a father admonishing a wayward son. "As I was saying, you can get reckless and walk out of here and straight to Bass Young and tell him I've admitted to killing Hogue. If you do, I won't even have to deny it. I'll simply tell Bass that you came to me with the proposition to split Anchor with me if I would dig up a man who could prove you were with him between May first and ninth." He pointed to the man in the corner. "Lester will be my witness. Furthermore, after Bass throws you in jail, I'll dig up another man who'll testify to seeing you here in Willow Creek between the first and ninth."

Spearman paused, nodding as if to nail this down. He held up his left hand and used the right to tick each item off on his fingers. "Or, he said, "you can play it your way by telling Bass about wearing the Army uniform on those dates, thereby freeing yourself of all suspicion of Hogue's murder." He made a *tsk-tsk* sound. "Of course, you'd still have to answer to the Army."

He ticked another finger. "Or, you can take over Anchor and throw in with me, and I'll have Fiske Cooper swear you were with him between the first and ninth. And we'll both make money . . . lots of money."

Spearman settled back in the tub.

Brady knew what he would do. He crossed the room, but the moment his hand touched the doorknob, Lou straightened up and commanded, "What'll it be, Brady?"

"I'm going to Bass." Brady turned the doorknob.

Spearman scrubbed up and down an arm. "You've got plenty of gall, boy, but very little sand."

Brady swore under his breath.

Lester tipped up his pistol. "Hand off the knob, Brady." He motioned with the weapon for Brady to move away from the door.

Brady halted. Lester moved over to him, lifted the gun from Brady's holster, and stepped back.

Spearman sounded indifferent when he spoke. "Are you sure, Brady?"

Brady didn't answer. Lester glanced at Spearman, and when he saw his nod, he hefted Brady's gun in his hand, thumbing back the hammer. He pointed it at the floor and pulled the trigger. The sound ricocheted through the room, and Lester quickly opened the door, shouting, "Elmer! Quick, get Bass Young!"

He heard the slapping of the barber's feet. Lester grinned. "Things beginning to take shape for you?"

Unsmiling, Brady nodded.

Spearman's voice held a measure of pity. "I never believed Hogue's theory about your being shiftless, Brady, but I do believe you're a naïve fool."

They waited, the three of them, and bitter resignation replaced the anger in Brady's gut.

After several minutes passed, Bass Young burst through the door. The three men hadn't moved from their positions. The sheriff halted just inside the room and glanced from one to the other. Elmer Johnson and a couple of locals poked their heads around the door to peek inside the room.

Spearman stormed, "Get out, you fools! I'm taking a bath."

Bass closed the door on the curiosity seekers. He addressed the man in the tub. "What's the trouble, Spearman?"

The sheriff eyed Brady with cold suspicion. Lester handed him Brady's gun. Spearman spoke in a half-angry tone. "Bass, this boy has gone plumb loco." He pointed a soapy finger at Brady. "You've got to keep him away from me."

Bass squinted at Brady. "Sure. What happened?"

"He shot at me," Spearman said. "That is, he was going to, if Lester hadn't knocked his gun away."

"Why?" Bass wanted to know.

Spearman leveled his eyes on Brady. "You gonna tell him?" His voice held an undertone of irony.

Brady remained stony-faced. He said nothing, didn't even nod his head.

"I ain't got all day. One of you gonna tell me what this is about, or leave me to guess?" Annoyance sounded in the sheriff's voice.

"All right." Spearman managed to sound resigned. "Lester brought Brady here because he asked to see me. He barged in and said he'd heard that Fiske Cooper was coming in from Colorado. He told me to keep Cooper out of town."

"Who's Fiske Cooper?" Bass was quick to ask.

"One of my crew," Spearman said patiently. "I'd already sent for him, but Brady didn't like it. When I told him I couldn't stop Fiske from coming, Brady said Fiske would lie about where he was between the first and ninth, and the young fool pulled a gun on me. Lester jumped him, and the gun went off."

Bass raised the revolver's barrel and smelled it. His voice held the cold authority of his badge. "That what happened, Brady?"

Brady laughed bitterly.

"Speak up, boy. Cat got your tongue?" Lester's hand rested easy on the butt of his Colt revolver.

Brady smirked as he looked at the three of them. His words were dry and brittle. "Anything they say."

Keeping his eyes on Brady, the sheriff said, "For a man who swears he didn't kill his stepdaddy, you seem plenty damn jumpy." He glanced at Spearman. "What do you want me to do, Lou? If you want him arrested for attempted murder, you'll have to come by the office and swear out a complaint first."

"What about a peace bond?" Lester suggested.

"No," Spearman protested. "Hell, I don't want to prosecute the boy. The kid's worried, and I don't blame him. Maybe Fiske *will* lie. Even so, I can't have Brady shooting at me."

"Make up your mind, Spearman. You want me to arrest him or not?"

Spearman motioned for Lester to bring him a towel. "Oh, hell, forget it, Bass. I was scared for a moment, that's all."

In a savage voice Lester said, "Give me ten minutes alone with Brady, okay?" He tried to grab Brady's shirt, but the sheriff stepped between the two men.

Again the sheriff asked, "Brady?"

His question was met with a shrug.

"I don't know what's going on here, but my gut tells me it's something more than meets the eye." Bass strode to the door and yanked it open. He sent a hard look toward Lou Spearman. "When Fiske Cooper rides in, send him straight to me."

He went out, taking Brady's gun with him.

When Bass was gone, Lester grinned broadly at Spearman.

Spearman's faced dropped its geniality. He pierced Brady with a look of malicious evil. "You had your chance, boy. Where was your big story to the sheriff?"

A slow flush crept into Brady's face, and the anger in his eyes stirred Spearman into irritation.

"You see, Brady, I can do anything with you I want now, can't I? Tell any story I want, can't I, as long as you're afraid of that soldier suit?"

When Brady didn't answer, Spearman continued. "Fiske will arrive in less than a week. You'd better decide about our partnership and see me before he rides into Willow Creek."

Spearman wrapped the towel around his massive body and stepped from the tub. In disgust he said, "Now get out of my sight."

Chapter Nine

Hannah turned the key and let herself into the second-story room she rented from Ma Smalley. She skirted around the bed and opened the floor-to-ceiling window. Afternoon sun streamed into the room, filtering through bright yellow curtains.

She stood looking out over the back lots and rooftops of the town and could not rid herself of the despondency that had been with her all day. She stared out, trying to imagine this as a different town, wishing desperately that she were far away from Willow Creek and did not have to go through with carrying Lou Spearman's business proposal to Sven and Gunnar Bjorn.

She bit down on her lower lip and walked to the mirror above the washstand. She spoke to the reflection frowning back at her. "I feel like an executioner."

Unbuttoning her drab office dress, she stepped out of it

and, with a grimace of distaste, hung it in her tiny closet, exchanging it for a simple green dress starched so stiffly, it rustled when she moved.

She lifted the hatbox from the closet shelf and removed a small straw hat adorned with yellow daisies and situated it on top of her red hair.

Taking a last look in the mirror, she left the room and took the stairs down to the lobby, leaving the key at the desk. The usual bunch of lobby loafers eyed her approvingly.

Outside, she followed the boardwalk toward the river. At the end of the walkway she stepped onto the weed-grown cinder path along the road until she could see the Bjorns' wagon yard.

Surrounding the yard was a new split-rail fence, and the sight of it had a strange effect on her. Split rails were cheap. Miller's sawmill gave them away for a few cents a hundred feet, and the Bjorns, with seldom a spare dollar, had used them for all their buildings and fences.

While walking along the back road toward the office, Hannah heard a hostler in one of the lots cursing a horse with passionate profanity. She knew by the voice that it was neither of the Bjorn brothers, whose normal tendencies leaned toward shyness.

She walked through the open door of the office and spotted Sven Bjorn looking out the window, his elbows resting on the sill. Neat as always in his black suit, Gunnar Bjorn came to his feet the moment she entered the building.

Sven called out the window to a man below, "Kick him in der belly, Abe."

Hannah's laughter caused a crimsoned-faced Sven to

bump his head on the window as he turned to face her. He bowed from the waist. "Beg your pardon, Miss Hannah. Such language is no güt for a lady's ears."

A broad grin spread across her face at the big Swede's obvious discomfort. "Believe me, I've heard worse coming from Mr. Spearman's men."

His face covered in a sheepish grin, Gunnar said, "I guess ve're not used to having a voman around, Hannah."

He shoved his chair toward Hannah, and she sat down. Catching the worried look in his round face, she hastened to clear up the reason for her visit. "Don't worry, I'm not here about money."

Sven glanced at his brother and laughed. "It's a good thing, Hannah, 'cause ve don't collect on der job ve do yesterday for another ten days."

Sven pulled up a homemade three-legged stool while his brother chose to sit behind the desk. Hannah gave the office area a quick appraisal. "I wish I had this much room and a pair of scales too. Sure would make weighing freight a lot easier."

Gunnar scratched his head. "I don't know if that vould be güt for our business. Vit a brain like yours, ve'd be out of business in no time."

They smiled at this, and Hannah's heart sank. How was she going to break the news? These men respected her, and she liked them, and there was no way to sugarcoat this bitter pill.

She toyed with one of the pleats in her skirt until Gunnar said, "Vat's on your mind, Hannah? Vat's bothering you?"

She began by telling them about her monthly report to

Spearman and how he'd complimented her for making a profit for the lesser side of his business.

As the story unfolded, Gunnar gave a puzzled look at his brother, who returned a confounded glance and a slight shrug of his shoulders. Both turned their full attention to her.

She twisted her hands together and felt a hot flush creeping up her neck. "Now comes the difficult part. Mr. Spearman practically ordered me to come here tonight to tell you that he wants to buy your whole outfit—all of it, right down to your last horse and wagon. He wants you to name a price."

Gunnar sat in silence, a frown deepening the furrows in his forehead. He pushed away from his desk, taking his time rising from the chair. He rubbed the back of his neck with the palm of one hand while he circled the room.

When he stopped pacing, he stood in front of her, and his voice was quiet. "You know how Sven and I are fixed, Hannah. Ve can't beat you."

"Not *her,* Gunnar. Spearman." Sven's voice sounded as desolate as his brother's.

"My apologies, Hannah. I did not mean—" Gunnar offered a polite smile, and Hannah felt a pang of remorse. The two brothers stared at each other in silence, and she sensed they wanted to be alone to talk this over. She refused to allow Lou Spearman to railroad these two honest men. She had to think of something—anything—to help them.

"Then why buck Spearman?"

Gunnar frowned. "You mean ve should sell out to dat *sniken ratte* at his price?" He raked a hand through his hair. "I am sorry for such language, Hannah."

Although he'd spoken the expletive in his native Swedish,

it didn't take much to figure out what he'd said. She spoke with no emotion. "Never would I imply such a thing. Spearman is counting on your selling out to him without a fight." She stood and squared her shoulders. "Stop thinking about yourselves for a moment, and clear your heads. I've written to an agent in Danforth with instructions to advertise Spearman's new low rates. What do you think will happen next?"

Sven spoke up. "Shippers vill leave us for Spearman."

"Exactly. And we can't handle the business," Hannah said. "We haven't the wagons or the teams or the teamsters, and our equipment is pretty much in decay. Which means we'll have to pay top dollar to replace what we have."

"So, vat if Spearman does that?" Gunnar said. "Vat then?"

"I'm not sure he will." Hannah pursed her lips in concentration. "He's counting on your selling to him lock, stock, and down to the last wagon. If he has to buy all new equipment and then operate at low rates, he'll lose money. But if you're willing to wait him out, he'll eventually give up on his plan."

"Are you sure, Hannah?" Gunnar's voice was sober and filled with uncertainty.

She *wasn't* sure. She shrugged her shoulders. "No, I'm not, Gunnar. I'm just counting on his greed."

With a long sigh, Sven looked at his brother. When he spoke, he didn't try to keep the contempt from his voice. "Counting on his greed, Hannah, von't pay our bills or put food in our bellies." The big Swede scrubbed his hands over his face while expelling an agitated growl. He turned his eyes toward his brother. "Gunnar?"

Gunnar's frown was a knowing one. "Ve come to this country vith only our strong backs and der hope of making our fortune. Sven and me, ve have sacrificed and vorked hard." He spread his arms wide. "I don't know how long ve can last, vaiting for Spearman to quit."

Hearing their recitations, Hannah felt anger build inside her. Her words were laced with vehemence. "Then force his hand. Put your heads together and come up with an outrageously ridiculous price for me to quote to Spearman."

As if they were of one mind, the brothers said in unison, "Seventy-five thousand dollars."

"Okay, ve haf der price. Now what?" The expression on Gunnar's face spoke his apprehension.

Hannah's voice was uncharacteristically tentative. "Board up your windows, lock your gate, go to the bank, insure your wagons, and drive your horses into the mountains."

"Sounds like you have given this a lot of thought, Hannah," Gunnar said.

In spite of the urgency she felt building inside her, she simply nodded. "There's more. Spearman is smart. He'll smell a rat. You must be convincing." She drew a breath, measuring her next suggestion. "Go to one of the ranches and get jobs—go on a roundup, or go hunting. Live on beans or deer meat, and don't come back until the snow drives you in."

Sven scrubbed a fist across his mouth. "Und when ve do dis, Hannah?"

"The sooner you get started, the better." A wry smile touched her lips. "By that time, Spearman's wagons will be wrecked, he'll have a dozen lawsuits for nondelivery of freight, and I'll be taking up all his time with complaints.

Either that, or he'll have new wagons, and rates will have gone up so high, the two of you can undercut us."

The brothers stood quietly. Sven walked to the window and gazed out over the horse lots. Gunnar cleared his throat. "Dis is much to tink about, Hannah. You mind if Sven and me step outside and talk this over?"

With a gentle touch that belied his massive hand, he patted Hannah's shoulder when she stood. "No, please stay. Ve vill only take a minute."

She settled back in her chair while Sven followed his brother outside the door. She heard low, indistinct murmurings. She concentrated on her hands. *I've done all I can. I just hope it's enough.* And somehow her heart and soul felt a little lighter for helping her friends.

Making this decision had been difficult for her. By nature she was a loyal person, and she knew that by coming to the Bjorn brothers, she was showing disloyalty to Spearman. He had befriended her after her father's death and given her work, and for this she was greatly appreciative. But what he now planned went against every grain of morality her father had instilled in her.

She was smart enough to know that Spearman was counting on her feelings of obligation to him, but what he had ordered her to do had no bearing on her sense of duty for what he'd done for her.

She would continue to work faithfully and carry out her daily duties for him, and if the Bjorns were not successful in defeating Spearman's plot against them, then what more could she do?

A small doubt intruded into her thoughts when she heard footsteps and turned to look over her shoulder. Thinking the brothers were returning with their decision, she was surprised when Brady Wilkes entered the office.

The sight of her halted him. A wide grin came on the wings of a deep restlessness within him, but his voice held disapproval at her presence. "What are you doing in enemy territory, Hannah?"

He watched her cheeks glow with color and liked the way she met his eyes with her own. She kept her voice low. "It's just business."

Whatever he was about to say died on his lips when Sven and Gunnar came in. Hannah noticed an odd but subtle change in their faces. They liked Brady and seemed to trust him. After what she'd laid out on the table, she'd wondered how they'd feel about a man who worked for their enemy.

The brothers exchanged handshakes with Brady and commented on his black eye. Hannah stood in front of him and chastised him in a concerned voice. "Didn't you think to put a steak over your eye to draw out the swelling?

Brady laughed. "Tell you the truth, Hannah, at the time, a steak was the last thing on my mind." He laughed again. "Besides, why waste a good slab of beef?"

"Who did this to you?" Hannah asked with wide-eyed curiosity.

"Doesn't matter. What's done is done."

An awkward moment passed before Brady said, "I've got those two teams you asked for, Sven."

"Dis is gut. How much?"

"Have you got a buckboard?"

Seemingly taken aback, Sven said, "You vant a buckboard instead of money?"

With a wide grin on his face, Brady nodded.

"Okay, then, Brady. Ja, ve haf a buckboard—a gut, sturdy one."

"I'll take it," Brady said without hesitation. "I've got to get it to Anchor tonight, though." He concentrated on the tips of his boots for a moment. "Hate to ask, but I'd like to borrow one of the teams. I'll return them tomorrow."

"Sure." Sven glanced at his brother, who answered with a quick nod.

"About those teams, Brady." Gunnar shoulders rose and fell. "Ve von't need them back." And then, as if he did not want his refusal to sound unkind, he added, "Sven and me, ve're closing up der yard at der end of der veek."

Hannah held herself tight. A sobering pride filled her, for the brothers trusted her good faith enough to take her advice. She didn't miss the look of puzzlement on Brady's face.

And now it was Sven's turn to speak. His voice held no bitterness. "It seems Lou Spearman has decided my brother and I should retire."

Brady cleared his throat when he glanced at Hannah. "You run the freighting end of Spearman's business, Hannah. I hope you aren't taking on his *enterprising* traits." He har-rumphed in disgust.

Gunnar came to her defense. "You've got it all wrong, Brady. Hannah is our friend. She came to help us." He walked to the window and called out to a hostler to hitch up the buckboard, and then he came back to Hannah. "Our price"—his voice filled with wry solemnity—"seventy-five thousand dollars. And if you please, ve vould like two checks."

Hannah smiled a little. A transaction like this was nothing to joke about. She liked Brady more than she'd admit. Still, she wasn't sure how he might react to her small conspiracy against Spearman.

Gunnar touched her shoulder lightly, his voice a mere whisper, "If dis got out, Hannah, it could get rough for you, ja?" When she nodded, he said, "If you're vorried about Brady, don't. He didn't hear nothing. No one knows 'cept der three of us."

Gunnar backed away. Hannah watched Brady walk to the window to look out into the yard and was surprised to see a faraway expression of bitterness on his face. A strange new emotion filled her. Adjusting the little hat atop her head, then brushing the pleats in her skirt, she drew in a sigh. Her job here was done. "I'll take your price to Mr. Spearman, and I wish both you and Sven well."

With two quick steps, she went to stand next to Brady. She brushed her hand against his arm as if it were the most natural thing, and from the look on his face, her innocent touch did not go unnoticed. "There's no moon, and I know you aren't asking me"—she hesitated—"but I would like a short ride in your new buckboard, Brady."

When his face lit with a slow, quizzical smile, she knew he remembered. "All right, Hannah."

Her thoughts were her own when she bade the Bjorn brothers a good night.

Chapter Ten

Sven held the team while Brady placed his hand on Hannah's elbow and helped her up onto the buckboard's seat. He waited while she slid over to make room for him.

She said a sober good-bye to the brothers, while Brady flapped the reins, urging the two horses into motion. He turned an apprehensive gaze to Hannah. "Got someplace particular in mind?"

Her mind was spinning with doubt. She drew in a breath and let it out slowly, the way she did when she was dealing with a difficult decision. *What if everything goes wrong? What if my plan backfires? What if Sven and Gunnar lose all they've worked for?*

Lost in thought, she hadn't heard Brady's question.

"Hannah, you look as if you're trying to hold up the world on your shoulders. What's bothering you?"

To avoid his question, she said, "Let's drive down by the river."

Brady pointed the team toward the dusty road and in the direction of the river. Although they only were a short distance from town, Hannah found the road along the river and through the cottonwoods peaceful and remote. The chirping of crickets mingled with the sloughing sound of the buckboard's wheels, and the river's lazy flow was almost hypnotic. While she listened, she covertly watched Brady, studying him with a close and critical appraisal. The origin of the black eye teased her curiosity. Even so, she found him handsome in a way that was both exciting and disturbing.

She wondered at the tight set of his jaw and the grim frown that marred his rugged good looks. She knew of his life, of his bitter quarrels with his stepfather, and she knew of Hogue Wilkes' relentless tormenting of Brady.

Intuitively she knew that people who had once appreciated his wild, reckless, and fun-loving ways now mistrusted Brady because of his sudden position of wealth and the mystery of who killed Hogue Wilkes.

Remembering her purpose for the ride, she stirred herself and in a subdued voice said, "I suppose you're wondering why I was really at the Bjorns today. . . ."

"Isn't my business, Hannah."

He caught and held her gaze. "Have to admit, though, I did sense I'd intruded where I didn't belong." He flicked the reins for the horses to pick up their pace.

She was suddenly worn to the bone, not just physically,

but emotionally as well. She placed a hand on his arm. "Stop the horses, Brady. We need to talk."

There in the moonlight among the cottonwoods, she told him of Spearman's scheme to ruin Sven and Gunnar and that he had sent her to deliver the message. She explained in detail the plan she'd devised to help the brothers and how she prayed it wouldn't backfire, and she found herself wanting desperately to convince Brady of the rightness of her decision.

The corners of his lips turned down into a dour smile when she finished by telling him of the Bjorns' decision to take her advice about moving their stock and boarding up their building.

She watched him, waiting.

He took a match from his pocket, struck it against the side of the buckboard, and lit a cigarette. Waiting for him to answer, doubt crowded in, causing her to wonder if she were making a grand mistake in confessing Spearman's scheme to ruin the brothers and of her part in helping Sven and Gunnar. No, she would lay a bet that she could trust Brady.

He pulled a few draws, then stubbed out the cigarette, tossing it aside. "What's worrying you Hannah . . . me?

"Yes, I think so."

"Don't fret over it. You've given the Bjorns good advice."

"It's just that Mr. Spearman has been good to me. . . ." She dared a hesitant smile.

"And you're feeling disloyal to him. Am I right?

"I guess so—a little."

He reached for both her hands and held them tightly.

"You're a good person, Hannah. Would you rather live with feeling disloyal, or with the memory of standing by and doing nothing while Spearman strangled Sven and Gunnar out of their livelihood?"

Her answer was quick and certain. "If I had to choose, I'd rather feel disloyal."

"Spearman has that ability, doesn't he?" Brady's voice was laced with acid. "You shouldn't have to live with either." He looked at her. "Why are you working for him?"

The transitions between the two questions were too abrupt for her, and she remained silent. She wanted to ask Brady if he, too, saw Spearman as she did. The chance passed, and she answered his other question.

"Again . . . loyalty. After my father died, Mr. Spearman gave me work so I wouldn't have to live on Judge Parker's charity."

A look of astonishment crossed his face. "Judge Parker? Explain."

"Papa was one of Mr. Spearman's teamsters until he got too old to make the freight runs; then he worked as a hostler. One day a horse kicked Papa in the head. When Papa died, the judge asked Mr. Spearman to find a place for me in his employment. That's when he created the freighting business and hired me to manage it and old Mr. Copeland to keep the books."

"Where was I when all this happened?"

"Away."

"*Drifting* is what you really meant to say, isn't it?"

"It isn't a word I would have used, but, yes, I guess."

Brady stared out over the horses' rumps, and Hannah had

a feeling she had trespassed on a part of him she didn't understand. She was speculating on that when he asked, "Did
Kate like you?"

"I don't think so," she said. "I'm sure if you ask her, she'll
tell you she didn't like it when I refused to accept a room
she'd arranged for me with the Hudson family."

"You mean Mr. Hudson, the banker? Why didn't you want
to stay there?"

"I was seventeen, and I wanted to live at the boardinghouse."

"Surely Kate was looking out for you." Then his voice filled
with curiosity. "Why did you want to take a room at Ma
Smalley's rather than live in luxury with the Hudsons?"

Hannah shrugged, amused by his curiosity. "Mr. and Mrs.
Hudson are society people. If I stayed with them, I'd be in
the right house, the right men would call on me, and after the
right amount of courting, I would have the right husband."

"And you didn't want a husband?"

Without hesitation Hannah said, "Eventually, but one of
my own choosing."

"I see. Do you like living at the boardinghouse?"

At this, she laughed a little. "I'm not like most women,
Brady. You see, I enjoy sitting in the parlor, talking with the
catalogue drummers, and listening to stories about what's
going on beyond the mountains and the plains. I like to play
poker with Doc Bell, Mr. Rikker, and Mr. Proctor. And unlike most young ladies, I like to drink a beer with old Jake
Newton when he isn't driving the stagecoach. I like to go un-
escorted to the dances at the Willow Creek schoolhouse, and

if some homely cowpuncher wants to walk me home, I don't mind." She sighed. "I'm not exactly what Kate Parker would call a lady."

"Uh-huh. I guess you're right."

They smiled at each other in a strange communion. "It's late. Maybe you'd better head the team back to town, Brady."

They were both silent, and Hannah felt a pleasant contentment. She had needed his offhand reassurance, and without knowing, he'd given it.

He halted the team in front of Ma Smalley's Boardinghouse and set the brake before jumping to the ground. He reached up to help Hannah down. His hands fit easily around her tiny waist.

She glanced down at him. In the dim light she could see the outline of his broad shoulders and narrow hips. His hair looked as if it had been kissed by the sun, curling from beneath his Stetson. Her skin prickled with excitement, a heat grew under her starched white collar, and she knew she needed to get away from him.

Setting her feet on the ground, Brady held her for a moment. In a husky voice, he said, "Mind if this homely cowpoke walks you to your door?"

Her smooth brow furrowed as she pondered her feelings for Brady. She'd kept those emotions tucked away. For the first time in her life she felt emotionally fragile. This was not how she envisioned love, for that seemed to render its victim giddy and senseless, and she did not feel that. Instead she found herself on some erratic pendulum, swinging precariously from contentment to worry, all of which was unlike her.

If this was love, she decided disdainfully, it was worse than she had ever imagined.

Suddenly she reminded herself that he was betrothed, and she pulled away from him, eager to be away from her troubling musings.

"I don't think Miss Kate Parker would take kindly to knowing we shared an evening buggy ride, much less your walking me to my door."

Brady brushed a wayward strand of burnished copper hair from her cheek. "Considering all you've told me tonight, it isn't Kate you need worry about."

He held both her hands in his. "How old are you, Hannah?"

Her eyes widened in surprise. "Brady Wilkes, why would you ask such a question?"

"Curious, I guess. In many ways you seem a bit older and a lot wiser than Kate."

"Are you paying me a compliment or insulting me?"

He winced at the frown on her face and placed her hands against his heart. "I'd never deliberately insult you, Hannah. In fact, I wish Kate were more like you."

She heard regret in his tone and realized he was apologizing and didn't try to pull her hands free.

Her voice was soft and whimsical. "I'll celebrate my nineteenth birthday next Sunday."

"Allow me to take you on a picnic, then. I'll bring a storebought cake, and I'll pick you a bouquet of wildflowers." A grin flashed across his face, and then he grew serious.

Crickets playing their night songs blended with the piano music spilling from the Four Corners Saloon on the warm breeze.

Brady bent toward her, and she stood on tiptoe, lifting her face and parting her lips.

Tears formed behind her closed eyes. He still held her hands to his chest, and the fierce beating of his heart matched her own. She realized that her distant affection was growing into a deep and passionate love—a love she must deny.

She pulled back, giving him a weary smile. "No, Brady. This is wrong."

"I don't understand, Hannah."

"It's simple. You are betrothed to Kate." Hannah removed her hands from his. "I decline your offer to help celebrate my birthday. From now on our meetings shall remain strictly"— she searched for the correct word—"impersonal."

They were beginning to attract an audience. The baker walked out of his shop, two ladies nodded in their direction, and a cowpuncher yelled a greeting to Brady.

Brady took a step toward her and stopped when she backed away. "I can always count on your honesty, can't I, Hannah?"

She colored. "Night, Brady. Thanks for the ride."

In the dimly lit street, she watched him remount the buggy and turn it toward the Bjorns' freight yard. In the lobby, she collected her key and hurried up the stairs to her room. She inserted the key in the door and, not bothering to light the lantern, made her way to the window to look out over the quiet street.

She stayed there, knowing it necessary for Brady to pass the boardinghouse to follow the road leading to Anchor. It took longer than she imagined before she spotted the buckboard rattling down the street. Brady sat tall on the bench seat. He'd tied his horse to buckboard's end gate.

Remembering his parting words and the look of pain in his eyes, she felt oddly disturbed, and she decided she needed a padlock on her heart.

Chapter Eleven

Rounding up Brady's horses in the August sun had given Wally Sims a long, hard day in the saddle. After a restless night, he was almost thankful when his usual hour of rolling out of his bunk came around. An hour before daylight, he pulled on his trousers, picked up his boots, went over to the cook's bunk and shook him awake, then passed softly on stocking feet down the bunkhouse aisle between the rows of snoring men. Outside, he tugged on his boots and stared into the night. He stretched and yawned and scratched.

After pouring a basin of water, he bent over and splashed it over his face and head. He lathered his rough, gnarled, and calloused hands, to scrub behind his ears and over his weather-seamed face. He washed his mustache until it was soft and silky and soaped his thinning gray hair, then poured the basin of cold water over his head to wash out the suds. He

111

dried himself and slipped on a shirt, then automatically rolled a cigarette.

When he lifted the match, he noticed a lamp lit in the main house. It had been a long time since he'd seen a light in that end of the big place. He puzzled over it for a moment before remembering Brady. He wondered if the younger man was just going to bed or getting up.

Wally lit his cigarette and savored the raw shock of tobacco smoke as it filled his lungs. During that time he observed Brady pass back and forth in front of the window several times. Curiosity pulled him toward the house. He strolled to the yard fence and watched, but even this close, the movements made no sense.

He considered. A few days ago his antagonism toward this young cur wouldn't have brought him as far as the fence. Not knowing Brady firsthand, he'd believed the bunkhouse gossip. After witnessing the beating, and then sitting at the boy's campfire, he'd formed a different opinion. A good judge of horseflesh, he also fancied himself a good judge of men and had made his offer to help. An offer Brady had accepted.

Wally shoved open the gate, eased over to Brady's window, and halted just short of the sill, silently regarding the lamplit scene before him.

Brady had lain out a coil of rope on the hardwood floor. At every eight feet of its length he was fastening to it a three-inch ring, then wrapping the ring with wet rawhide. As soon as he finished with one ring, he'd coiled up the completed section of rope and then measured out another eight feet. He worked so intently that he didn't notice Wally, who watched a five full minutes before he spoke.

"Ain't seen that type of rigging used since the war," Wally observed.

Uttering a startled oath, Brady wheeled around. When he saw who it was, he grinned. "How 'bout helping me splice the big ring into the end?"

The ranch hand walked around to the porch, through the front door, and down the hall to Brady's room. He picked up the lone ring, bigger than the others, and began to unravel the rope. "Didn't know a youngster like yourself knew about such as this."

They worked in silence, during which time Wally covertly regarded the younger man. There was a certain grim temper in Brady's normally cheerful face, and Wally wondered what had gone on with the sheriff yesterday. Presently he said, "How big a string you goin' to drive, Brady?"

"How many horses did you and Clem round up?"

"Fifty."

"Between your bunch and mine, I'll cut out forty."

"Where you drivin' 'em?"

"Fort McClaren."

Wally eyed him blandly. "You been there?"

"This summer."

"Then why don't you loose-herd 'em? It's wide-open country, only a hundred thirty miles, give or take a few."

Brady sat cross-legged on the floor. He let his hands fall to his lap and looked up at the tall, work-worn man. "I may be traveling at night. Besides, the purchasing quartermaster leans toward cranky, and I want my horses in good shape." He hesitated. "Another reason too—this might end up being a race."

Wally reached under his hat to scratch an itch. "Yeah, with who?"

"Spearman." Brady's voice was dour. He went to work again and, without looking up, said, "Want to ride along, Wally?" He glanced up with questioning eyes.

"Dang sure would. You'll need more than me, though."

"I'd like Clem to go, but with his being foreman, he can't leave the ranch. Got any suggestions?" Brady figured none of the hands would want to work with him.

"Acosta and Meade are both top hands. They never put much truck into anything Rube mouths off about, and as for the thing between you and Hogue, that's your business."

By the time Brady and Wally finished with the ropes, it was full daylight. They lugged the gear down to the black-smith shop on the other side of the main barn.

The buckboard he'd traded with the Bjorns for stood in front of the shop's open door where Brady had left it the night before. He explained to Wally what he wanted. "Let's get busy."

Down-hoops and double rings, which he had bought in town after leaving Hannah, were to be installed on the buck-board. A hand brake was rigged up, the free end of the rope was to be spliced into the buckboard's tongue, and the buck-board was loaded with sacked oats, bedrolls, and grub to last a month.

The triangle clanged for breakfast.

"Go ahead and finish up. I'll make sure the cook saves a plate for you, Wally."

Wally answered with a smile. "You're the boss, Brady."

True to his word, Brady stopped in at the cookshack and

asked that Wally's breakfast be saved. It was a measure of Wally's acceptance here that the cook acknowledged the request without protest.

Stopping by the wash bench, Brady doused himself with cold water. The shock of it wakened him. His sleepless night was forgotten, and he went in for breakfast.

This was his first appearance since the fight, and he spoke only to those who greeted him. He kept silent and aloof, but the tightening in the pit of his belly told him something wasn't right, and the crew knew it. Concentrating on his food, Brady surprised an occasional speculative look in his direction. Breakfast finished, he tramped over to the office where Clem Garrett parceled out work to the crew.

Clem, seated in his wooden swivel chair, listened carefully while Brady made his request.

"I need three men. Wally Sims volunteered, and I hear Acosta and Meade might be willing to work for me."

Clem leaned back in his chair. "Mind telling me what for?"

"I'm taking my herd to Fort McClaren, and I need the help."

While the foreman seemed to ponder this, Brady added, "The men are a loan from you to me, Clem. They're on Anchor's payroll. If you can spare them, ask Meade and Acosta—don't order them."

Clem nodded. "They'll go, and I can spare them."

"Thanks, I appreciate it."

A dozen or more men idled around the office door enjoying their morning smoke when Brady stepped out into the sunshine. He made his way down to the corral and caught up and saddled his blue roan, then rode out to the pasture and, with the help of Wally, rounded up his fifty-odd horses and drove them into the big corral.

The morning sun was warm and pleasant, and Brady enjoyed this particular job. At the big corral he found a curious trio of men perched atop the rail to watch what he was doing.

By the time he and Wally had cut out all the horses that were not solid-colored or were over seven years old and had turned them back into the pasture, six more men were perched atop the corral railing. Clem Garret sat among them.

Brady knew that in their silent way the men were measuring him, this time for his horse knowledge, which would go a long way in letting them know he was also capable of handling the business end of running a ranch.

Acosta and Meade climbed down from the rail and approached Brady. Acosta said, "Heard you're lookin' for two good wranglers."

Brady eyed the man. "That's right."

Meade stood next to Acosta. "I don't hold truck with what happened the other morning at the cookshack, and I ain't got no hard thoughts against you, Mr. Wilkes."

Brady shook hands with each man. "Call me Brady."

Both men nodded.

Feeling a little uncertain about his new station in life, Brady told Acosta and Meade what he needed them to do.

"I want you to go inside the holding pen, pick out a horse, and put a rope hackamore on him. When I give the signal, lead 'em out, one at a time." He inclined his head toward Wally. "Wally will work the gate."

Without questions the two men gathered their lariats, jogged over to the holding pen, and eased through the gate. Each man shook out a loop in his rope and with expert precision swung it over his head and let it fly in the direction of the horse he had singled out.

Brady took up his position in the center of the main corral, and Acosta led the first horse out. The animal was a chestnut gelding with a coat that glistened like burnished gold in the sun. Brady walked around the horse, running his hands down the withers. He lifted the lips and checked the teeth. "Turn him out."

One of the men perched on top of the rail objected, "Brady, I been usin' that horse, and he's sound as a dollar."

Other's added a few loud *amens*.

This was it—the first challenge. Keeping his expression businesslike, Brady said in a straightforward voice, "He's nine years old. The Army says no more than seven, Reno."

Now the men knew what Brady was up to, and while there were some good-natured rumblings of doubt, nobody openly questioned him, and the chestnut was turned out to pasture.

The next four horses proved acceptable and were led to a smaller corral. Brady watched more men climb up and roost on the top rail and knew they would be quietly but mercilessly critical. All of them were horse experts, and he needed to prove that his knowledge matched theirs.

Acosta led the fifth horse past him. The horse was as compact as a boxcar, with flat shoulders and a rounded breadbasket, the kind of animal the Army coveted. Brady glanced once at him as he walked by and said, "Take him out, Acosta."

From his perch, Clem Garret called out, "I'll fight you on this one, Brady."

Brady said, "Sweenied shoulder, Clem." He walked up to the horse and pointed to a faint, flat depression in the smoothly bunched muscles of the right shoulder, which indicated an atrophied muscle. "That might get by the line officer but not the Army vet."

Clem rubbed his chin and said nothing. The men grinned. And Clem, too shrewd to argue, allowed a faint smile to enter his eyes.

By the time Brady had turned out the twentieth horse, a cow-hocked animal, as all could see, only Rube Winters, the blacksmith, objected.

The thirty-fifth horse brought a round of good-hearted guffaws and arm-punching when Brady loudly declared, "Solid color, fifteen hands, three inches, close-crop chest, just like the Army wants—except they don't take mares."

Acosta quickly led the horse from the corral. "Sorry 'bout that, boss. Reckon I need to pay a little closer attention."

The man had called him *boss.* Brady felt as if he'd won round one and wondered how many more he'd need to win.

The fortieth and last horse was a bright-eyed chestnut, alert, fat, and sleek. The crew looked at the gelding and rippled their approval.

Brady watched Meade lead the horse past him and made no comment. He made a circle with his finger, and Meade brought the horse around for a second pass.

Brady stroked his chin. "Turn him out."

A wave of protest rose from the men, and a sudden grin

came over Brady's face. He invited the men to come down and take a closer look at the animal.

Every last man climbed down off his perch and formed a circle around the chestnut. Each man regarded the horse in silence. Clem Garrett spoke up. "Fifteen-three."

"No, sir, fifteen hands and two," Brady said.

One of the men spoke up and said, "He's joshing you, Clem. The quartermaster'll buy this hoss for sure."

Brady said, "Nope. Look closer—capped hip." He touched the chestnut's left hipbone, which held a faint depression in its curve. "If this horse has to do much long-distance running, he'll stumble."

Clem walked behind the chestnut, bent his knees a little, and sighted over its back. When he straightened, he shoved his battered, sweat-stained hat off his forehead. "Danged if Brady didn't call it right. This horse is hip down, all right."

He slapped Brady on the shoulder, "Son, with an eye like yours, you could slicker the best of us if you had such a notion."

The crew laughed at that, and Brady joined them. He knew a truce had been called and that the men had accepted him, not as Hogue Wilkes' heir but as a man. He'd paid for part of his readmission to Anchor.

From the animals he rejected for Army mounts, he chose four to make up two teams for the buckboard.

The sun was high by the time Brady and his three men had tied the horses two by two with their new rope halters, a pair to each ring, a horse on either side of the big rope.

He pulled a bandana from his back pocket, removed his

hat, and wiped sweat from his forehead and from around the hatband.

"Meade, while we're finishing up here, mosey on up to the cookshack and tell Amos to put together enough sand-wiches for the four of us to eat in the saddle. Tell him that Acosta and Wally will be over later to load the buckboard with beans, bacon, dried beef, and flour to last a couple of months.

"Acosta, you and Wally load the buckboard with grain and salt blocks and then drive on to the cookhouse. I'll stay and cut out eight horses, six to go in our remuda as remounts. The other two, I've promised to the Bjorns."

A few minutes short of noon Brady told the men that each would take a turn at driving the buckboard. He looped up the tugs and tied them to the end gate.

Mounting his blue roan, he glanced at the Anchor ranch hands.

Clem Garret reached up and shook Brady's hand. "That's five thousand dollars on the rope, Brady. I'm wishing you luck, son."

Brady tipped his hat to the man. This time he wasn't run-ning away from trouble, but racing toward his future. He held up his right arm and motioned forward. "Get 'em mov-ing."

By the time the long string was out of the meadows and headed toward Willow Creek, Acosta and Meade had learned to keep the tugs tight, and Brady relaxed a little. He hoped his gamble worked out in a big way. To succeed, he'd need to beat Spearman's men to Fort McClaren, and they were a day ahead of him.

But the advantage lay with Brady, for Spearman's crew didn't know they were in a race and would plod along, allowing their horses to graze at every opportunity.

Shortly before reaching the grade above Willow Creek, Brady gave orders to skirt the town. "We don't want to arouse Spearman's curiosity."

"Whatever you say. You're the boss." Wally nodded from the buckboard.

"I'll haze the two loose horses over to the Bjorns. I owe them for the buckboard." Before he turned back, he said, "Drive the bunch until dark. Follow the river."

He checked on Acosta and Meade to make sure they were keeping the ropes tight and watching for tangles.

Brady hazed the two horses down the road until he was above the town. He released a long, deep sigh. He thought of Hannah. It had been wrong of him to try to kiss her. Still, he liked the way her mouth curved into a smile, the feathery touch of her hand on his arm. But most of all he recalled the worry he'd seen in her eyes when she warned him about the sheriff's inquiries as to his whereabouts when Hogue was murdered.

Brady cleared his throat, discomfited. He pushed Hannah from his mind and focused on Kate and the way she had flounced out of her father's office. He decided to ride over to make peace with her and to explain his plan not to take immediate ownership of Anchor. He had no intention of telling her where he was going. She would only accuse him of shirking his responsibility to her. Nevertheless, he knew he had to see her before he left.

He turned the two horses into the side street and approached Judge Parker's house with its neatly groomed lawn, whitewashed and cool under the shade of cottonwood trees.

Seeing the lush green yard, the two loose horses trotted to it and lowered their heads to graze.

Brady, some distance behind them, saw Kate kneeling next to a flower bed in front of the house. When she spotted the horses, she rose and brushed grass from her apron.

"Shoo!" she scolded. "Get away!"

Brady reined in and grinned. When Kate caught sight of him, she cried in exasperation, "Brady Wilkes, your horses are ruining my lawn!"

A teasing grin on his face, Brady spoke to the horses. "Boys, stop eating. You're upsetting the lady." The geldings went on grazing, and Kate had to laugh. Brady stepped out of the saddle and moved across the walk. Her face was alive and lovely from her laughter.

"Shall I invite the three of you in?" she asked.

"No, they're a bit shy." Brady was solemn when he spoke.

Kate stood on tiptoe to kiss him. "Stay for supper?"

"I'll be gone a while, Kate," he said. "I'm horse-trading."

Kate pouted. "I guess that means you won't be here Saturday."

Brady thought for a moment. "What's Saturday?"

"There's a barn dance." She protested, "Oh, Brady, I'll just die if you're not here to take me."

"Sorry to disappoint you, Kate. There'll be other dances."

"How long this time—a week? A month? Three?"

Brady laughed, unintimidated by her wrath. "If all goes

well, two months—three at the most." He took a step forward. "I'll promise you this, when I do return, you'll never miss another dance." He grinned and crossed his heart.

She raised an eyebrow in mock suspicion. "Who're you trading for? Lou Spearman?"

"Uh-uh. Wilkes and Company, Horse Traders."

Her eyes widened. "Who's the company?

"Me and riders from Anchor, and the five thousand dollars I hope to clean up on the deal."

She didn't smile. "So you've decided to give up ranching for horse-trading?"

"If you've got horses to trade, then you're a horse trader, right?

She tapped one foot. "If that's all you've got to trade. What about the ranch, Brady?"

He sighed. "We're arguing, aren't we? And it's not getting us anywhere."

Kate nodded while she gazed at the horses on her lawn lazily cropping grass. "No, it's not." She looked up at him. "You can't stay put, can you, Brady? It's in you to drift."

"That's not it." He needed to make her understand. "I've got to make this trip, Kate."

"Why?" She scowled at him. "So you can stop the itch in your feet?"

He tried to draw her into his arms, against his chest. "This is for us, Kate. Try to understand—"

She pushed away from him and made a shooing gesture with her hands. She pursed her mouth in reprimand. "Go, Brady. Go on. I've got flowers to water."

"Kate—"

She stooped to pick up her watering can and, with her back straight and head held high, she walked toward the rear of the house.

Brady stepped into the stirrup and swung into the saddle. Guilt tugged at him for disappointing Kate—again. He had been home so little and had spent even less time with her. In a remorseful whisper, he said, "I'm sorry, Kate."

He pushed the two bay horses down the dusty street and, with neither Sven or Gunnar about, left the horses in the hostler's care.

He kept to the river, following the main wagon road, and though the horse string was somewhere ahead of him, he was in no hurry to catch them. The heat was oppressive and crowded in on him. And the memory of his parting with Kate was a nagging worry in his mind, taking the pleasure out of the day. There had been an edge to her words. It rankled him that she'd managed to turn his horse-trading trip against him, making it sound as if he were exercising a whim.

Perhaps her skepticism was justified. It was true that he was glad to be away from the ranch and town. Doubts rose up inside him. Maybe he was avoiding Bass Young and more of the sheriff's questions, and maybe he was running away from Spearman's ultimatum, and maybe he was postponing the inevitable.

A realization came to him that he had reacted to Spearman's ultimatum the way he reacted to most things in his life, and that was without thinking things through in a rational and logical manner and by running away rather than meeting his problems head-on.

He tried to remember what had prompted him to become a runaway. Had it been the merciless lash of Hogue's leather strop against his bare flesh? Perhaps it had been the sting of cruel words against a boy too young to defend himself. Maybe it was the hordes of women Hogue had paraded in and out of the house, comparing each of their tainted reputations to that of his mother until he could no longer stand the taunting?

Thinking on it, Brady rationalized that Spearman's ultimatum had affected him much as Hogue's accusations had. Brady thought about Spearman's threat and what would happen if he didn't acquiesce to the partnership. "*I can do anything I want with you, Brady, as long as I've got the soldier uniform.*"

It was true—Spearman could do anything. Any rancher whose name was on a bill of sale with Brady's signature could identify him as the man impersonating a lieutenant in the United States cavalry, notwithstanding Spearman's men who, for a price, would back Spearman's innocence in the scam.

A bleak awareness washed over Brady, so strong it almost shook him out of the saddle. By his own admission, Spearman had murdered Hogue and then, for the price of clearing Brady's name, demanded a partnership in Anchor. His thoughts were morose. *Spearman wants more than a partnership. He wants it all.*

Chapter Twelve

One-Eyed Lester followed the same routine every morning after the horse yard opened for business. After an early breakfast at the boardinghouse, he enjoyed a fresh cigar while he sauntered down the boardwalk past the Bjorn Brothers' Freight Company, and then he'd follow the creek up to Spearman's.

He'd left strict orders with the hostlers to take every horse on the lot down each morning to drink. It was his theory that horses fared better drinking fresh water from the creek rather than water that stood stagnant in long troughs. But driving the horses to water was a laborious task and one the hostlers disliked and often shirked.

From long practice, Lester had learned to read tracks, and could tell fresh ones from those a week old. From the number of hoofprints leading from the yard to the creek and

126

back, he could tell if his orders had been carried out or ignored altogether.

With the fifty head he'd sent to Fort McClaren and no new stock brought in, today's signs were easy to read. All the horses had been driven to water. He strolled through the back gate and headed for a smaller enclosed area attached to the main barn, where ailing horses were stabled. He always looked over them to see which ones were salvageable enough to pass off as healthy and which ones to dispose of. To keep from having to check if every stall had been cleaned, he'd learned to gauge the height of the manure pile.

By the time he'd finished his rounds, the crew had gathered in the main barn, ready for their work assignments. He'd always send a man to the office to collect Hannah's freight schedules for the day, and then he would pick the teams, choose the teamsters, and oversee the loading of the wagons before meeting with Spearman.

After assigning the last wagon, he walked into the cool darkness of the office, taking a moment for his eyes to adjust to the dim interior. Standing on the other side of the rail that separated Hannah's work space from customers and teamsters, he paused. "The Bjorns look as if they're boarding up their freight office," he observed.

"Really? I hadn't noticed." Hannah kept her voice pleasant. He adjusted his eye patch. "Hannah?"

She looked up from her journal, careful not to offer a smile that he might read more into than she intended. "Yes?"

"You got somebody escorting you to the dance Saturday night?"

"I do."

He gave her a friendly grin and moved on down the hallway to Spearman's office. Spearman sat in his swivel chair with his feet propped on the windowsill next to his desk.

Lester went to stand where he could look out the window. "Bjorns are beginning to board up."

Spearman answered with an unconcerned grunt. "Fiske Cooper rode in last night."

"Yeah. Where is he?" Spearman glanced up.

"Sent him out to the shack at Rimrock Canyon to cool his heels for a few days."

Spearman smiled. After a moment he said, "Any scuttle-butt around town about our little ruckus with Brady over at the barbershop?"

"Haven't heard none, and apparently Bass Young is keeping his lips tight."

"How so?"

"Passed Judge Parker this morning, and he didn't inquire."

Spearman hoisted himself to his feet and stretched and yawned and scratched his belly. A mischievous twinkle in his otherwise bleak eyes glinted. He picked up his dusty bowler, situated it aslant on his head, and tapped the crown. "Think I'll pay my friend the judge a little social call."

In his normally ponderous step, he whistled while walking toward the courthouse. He tipped his hat at a storekeeper's wife and stopped to chat with the barber before crossing the street and mounting the courthouse steps.

Judge Parker glanced up from a paper he was reading at Spearman's tap on the frame of the open door.

"Got a minute, Judge?"

Parker offered a spare smile of welcome. "I don't often see you here, Spearman. What brings you by?"

"You know how it is, Judge. A horse trader usually tries to stay clear of the courthouse and a judge." He guffawed at his own joke.

Judge Parker managed a weak smile. Spearman knew he could afford to make the joke, and he also knew that Judge Parker knew it too, which put them on an amiable footing.

"Mind if I seat myself, Judge?" Not waiting for a response, Spearman seated himself. He removed the bowler and perched it on a crossed knee, making a pretense of brushing off some of the dust.

"I see your daughter out and about more than I do you, Judge."

"Kate has the same chores most women have."

Spearman chuckled. "Now that Brady's back for good, I suppose she hasn't much time for her father."

The judge offered Spearman another of his noncommittal smiles.

Spearman managed to sound suitably downcast, "It saddens me that the boy had to come home to Hogue's death." He clucked his tongue. "Even missed the funeral."

"That was unfortunate," the judge agreed.

Spearman frowned and then asked in a polite but confidential manner, "Does Brady seem moody to you, Judge?"

Judge Parker shuffled a few papers into a stack, his answer dry. "Considering the tack Bass Young's taking, can't quite blame the boy."

"Damned shame," Spearman growled. "If you ask me, Bass is going about this all wrong. I don't like the way he's been pestering me. Why, I practically took that boy in—even gave him a job."

"What do you think Bass is after?"

Spearman twisted the bowler around on his knee. He pursed his lips as if in deep concentration. "Brady can't account for his whereabouts for some days in May. Bass seems to think that's when Hogue was killed." Spearman snorted in disgust. "This is costing me a pretty penny. Why, I've had to send all the way to Utah for a man Brady claims can prove his whereabouts."

"Let's hope your man has a better memory than Brady," Judge Parker remarked.

After a solemn second Spearman decided it was time to get down to the real business of his visit. "Judge, are you handling Brady's legal affairs?"

"I'm Hogue's executor, if that's what you mean."

Spearman nodded. "I heard Brady is looking for a partner, and I want to know how serious he is."

With a somber expression, Judge Parker regarded the big man before answering. "I didn't know he was looking for a partner."

Spearman's bushy eyebrows rose slowly, then settled. "Then maybe I'm speaking out of turn."

"Out of turn or not, I wish you'd speak plainer." The judge's voice was dry. "As Brady's lawyer, I'd say I have the right to know."

Spearman ran a finger around his collar and cleared his throat while suppressing the laughter building inside his chest.

"I suppose it's no secret. Brady came down to the lot the other night. He talked with the boys for a while before drifting into my office. I could tell he had something on his mind, the way he fidgeted about, and he finally he asked me how I'd like to go into partnership with him." Spearman snapped his fingers. "Just like that."

"What was your answer?"

In an air of innocence, Spearman spread his beefy hands apart. "I have to dry feed every horse on my lot, and if I hold one horse for two weeks, he's eaten up my profit. Naturally, if I had grazing land, I could run more horses and make more money, and that's what Brady offered."

"Meaning Anchor?"

"Exactly. I'm a horse trader, and I know a good deal when I hear one. I'd supply the money to back the deal, and Brady would buy the horses and supply the graze."

Judge Parker lifted the stack of papers from his desk and walked over to set them in a basket on top of a wooden file cabinet. "Sounds like a horse dealer's boon."

"Most certainly. That's my thought."

"Why are you here, Lou? Something about the deal bothering you?"

"You know Brady's reputation. Before I jump into this venture, I need to know if he's serious."

The judge clasped his hands behind his back. "If he is, it'll be the first time in his life."

"Why, Judge, you sound peevish. Has Brady done something to distress you?" Spearman hadn't missed the critical tone in the judge's voice.

The judge closed his eyes and rubbed them with his

forefingers. "He keeps my Kate upset. She wants to wed, have a family, and Brady's broken every promise to settle down.

"He came to see me the other day and said he doesn't want Anchor—at least until he can clear his name." After a short silence Judge Parker continued. "Strange, how Hogue antagonized the boy all his life yet willed the ranch to him. Kate was here." He released a heavy sigh. "To my daughter, this means more waiting on a man who may never settle down."

"I'm sorry your daughter was upset, Judge. Kate is a fine young woman who deserves better." Spearman tried to keep the amusement from his voice. "But you do have to admit that if he does take immediate possession of Anchor, it makes him look guilty as sin."

With a wry grimace, the judge looked at Spearman. "Brady isn't dependable."

Spearman puffed out his chest and blustered, "He's the sharpest horse buyer I know. He's always worked well for me."

"Then maybe you've got a knack for handling him."

"Boy doesn't need handling, Judge."

"I didn't mean *that* type of handling, Lou." The judge shrugged. "I meant, maybe you're the right person to partner with him."

Without knowing it, Judge Parker had given Spearman the answer he wanted to hear. Still, he managed to look baffled and remained silent.

Judge Parker said, "You've got a good business in that horse lot, haven't you, Lou?"

This was no time for mock modesty, and Spearman knew

it. He nodded and said, "Going on twenty years with no complaints."

When the judge stood up, Spearman rose too. "I'll talk with Brady," the judge offered.

The two men shook hands. "That's all I ask, Judge. I want everything legal and aboveboard. Last thing I want is for folks thinking I took advantage of Brady during this grim period in his life."

He set the bowler at the same jaunty angle atop his head. "Please pass on my regards to your daughter, Judge." He paused at the door and offered a small smile. "You're charging your usual fee, of course?"

"No different than from our other arrangements, Lou. Don't forget the little something extra for my personal fund."

Outside in the bright sunlight, Spearman smiled as he paused to light up a cigar. Generosity wasn't in his nature. Today was different, and when he walked passed a raggedly dressed little girl sitting on the boardwalk outside the general store, he handed her a coin. "Go inside and buy yourself some penny candy."

When news got around that Brady was taking a partner, folks around town wouldn't be surprised. He slapped his hip and laughed outright at the irony of the judge's thinking that he, Lou Spearman, would be a good influence on Brady.

Chapter Thirteen

Brady crouched in the high grass above the canyon and watched the spiraling smoke from the smoldering embers of the campfire below. He didn't like what he saw. Spearman's crew had selected their last camp before Fort McClaren well.

He noted that Long Tom had made camp at the lower end of the meadow, where the canyon walls crowded close together. That bothered Brady. The Kiowa reservation lay twenty-odd miles from the fort, and Long Tom had enough Indian in him to recognize that a loose band of horses was a tempting prize, no matter how many guards were posted. He'd roped off one end of the passage, blocking it so that no one could get through.

Of the two other men with Long Tom, Brady recognized only Poco Crawford, a wiry man whose penchant for savagery caused Spearman to keep him away from town as much as possible.

In the lowering dusk, Brady watched a few minutes longer. He scooted back from the bluff until it was safe enough for him to stand without being spotted. Then, in a low crouch, he sprinted toward a thicket a few hundred yards away, where he'd ground-tied his horse.

Climbing into the saddle, he turned the blue roan along the sun-baked road to where his men waited with the herd. Sweating by the time he arrived, he stepped down and loosened the girth on his roan and led the horse to the streambed to drink. Brady bellied down to slake his own thirst and to scoop handfuls of cool water over his face and head.

He led his horse back to camp and relayed what he'd observed to his crew. "Long Tom has the wagon road blocked off and has bedded his herd inside the canyon, a good defense against any Kiowa scouting party. Not good for us."

"Why's that?" Meade asked. His question made it obvious he'd never trailed to Dodge City or Fort McClaren.

"Because it's the only way to the fort," Brady answered patiently.

"Don't sound good. What's the plan, boss?" Acosta bit off a large chew of jerky.

"We ain't turning back, are we?" Meade wanted to know.

An almost pleasant anger stirred in Brady. For nearly a month he and his men had trailed behind Spearman's crew, eating their dust, staying far enough behind not to be spotted, ever cautious.

It was full dark now. Following his orders, the men had

made no campfire but lay sprawled out on the riverbank. Only the coals of their cigarettes lit the night.

"If we decide to walk 'em past, Long Tom might think another dealer is trying to push ahead of him, and that could spell trouble," Wally said.

"It's a possibility, for sure." Brady wished for a fire to see the expressions on the men's faces. He needed to know their thoughts. "What if we ran them through?"

"Sounds like a plan, Brady." Wally tramped back to the buckboard and brought out a lantern and lit it. Afterward the men squatted around the lantern and planned their moves, Brady drawing a rough map in the dirt to guide them.

Brady hoped his plan would work without any danger to his men or the horses. "Long Tom will have a nighthawk with his herd. My guess is, the bunch is green-broke and skittish. Acosta, you hook a lantern to the buckboard's tally pole while you're passing their camp. Sing as loud as you can. Hell, sound a little drunk if you can manage it. Oh, and tie a saddled horse to the buckboard's end gate."

This brought a round of low chuckles, for they'd all heard the cowpuncher's off-key caterwauling.

"You got it, boss. But, boss, why you want me to sing?" The curiosity in his voice was evident.

"Simple, Acosta. Long Tom and his crew will think you're a drunken farmer on the way to the fort."

"Aiee, smart thinking, boss." Acosta slapped his hands together. "This gonna be more fun than I had in a long time."

Brady laid out each man's position. "I'll take the lead gelding with me. Wally, you ride flank, and, Meade, you keep 'em moving from the rear.

"Acosta, once you get a hundred yards past the camp, pull over and get astride your horse, *muy pronto*. All hell is going to break loose."

"Ho-kay, boss. Then what?" Acosta wore a bright, malicious expression on his face.

Brady offered a mischievous smile. "I'll fire one shot into the air, and when I do, I want all of you to yell like a Kiowa war party and keep yelling until we're at least two miles beyond the canyon."

"Gotcha, Brady." An experienced horse wrangler, Wally said, "Spearman's green-broke herd will spook, and hearing our bunch will likely break the strongest barrier to join them."

"If the stampede is effective, Long Tom and his crew will spend the next two days rounding up their string." The glee in Meade's voice was unmistakable.

"Bass Young confiscated my pistol. Mind if I borrow yours, Wally?" Brady exchanged a brief glance with the wrangler.

Wally Sims unholstered the Colt .45 and handed it over.

Brady spun the cylinder, making certain a cartridge was in the round.

There was, Brady knew, a chance his plan might fail, and if things went wrong, he was risking injury to his horses and, afterward, a gut-busting fight with an angry Spearman and his crew. Recognizing this, he said, "This thing could go wrong, men. If any of you wants to pull out, I'm beholden to you for coming this far with me."

"You can count on me, Brady."

"Me too."

"And me, boss."

At that moment, the boy Hogue Wilkes had larruped into a shiftless drifter ceased to exist. Brady felt the men's smiles in the darkness, and he knocked back the emotion welling in his chest. He put out his hand to each man and shook it.

"Luck to all of you." Brady nodded at his companions. "After we bust through their lines, we'll run the herd hard for ten miles, then walk 'em the last ten to the fort."

No other words passed among them. The men fell silent as they went about the tasks of saddling their horses and bunching the herd. Acosta tied his mount to the end gate and then climbed up on the buckboard's bench seat. After he struck a match and lit the lantern, he clucked the team into motion.

In the faint starshine that illuminated the buckboard, tension mounted in Brady. He waited until the lantern was out of sight before signaling with a low whistle for Wally and Meade to move out.

At a shuffling pace, Brady kept the rope taut on the lead gelding. Slowly the group moved out of the meadow and toward the road, keeping to the canyon walls until Brady spotted the flickering campfire at the far end of the canyon. His eyes had grown accustomed to the darkness, and he made out Spearman's horses gathered at the rope barrier, probably watching the distant lantern.

Then the silhouette of the nighthawk, his horse pointed toward the swaying lantern, as if he were listening to the raucous and discordant caterwauling from Acosta, came into view. Brady watched the rider trot his horse toward the wagon.

When the lantern ceased movement, Brady knew it was

time. He glanced to his left and saw that Wally was flanking the herd as planned. The clip-clop of the ponies' hooves echoed sharply in the stillness.

Brady prodded his roan into a lope, the lead gelding following closely behind. As he approached the night rider's horse, Brady removed his hat and slapped it across the horse's face, startling the animal into rearing up.

He pressed his horse into a run, pulled the Colt .45 from his waistband, and mouthed a bloodcurdling Kiowa howl. His shot and loud whistles cut the night like a knife.

Confused yells and shots from Long Tom and his men rent the air, causing Spearman's horses to panic. Their fright was contagious, and they pushed against the rope barrier. Brady heard the mounting rumble of his herd's hooves hammering the rocky ground.

Spearman's horses' screams communicated to Brady's own herd. The nighthawk had waited too long to calm the panicked animals. Brady, riding at the head of the herd, saw the men waving blankets, trying to turn the terror-filled horses before they broke through the rope barrier.

He dropped the lead gelding's rope, giving the horse his head, knowing the herd would follow. He angled off to the right to help Wally flank. He saw an explosion of sparks as the horses raced through the campfire.

He turned in time to see the nighthawk's horse racing toward him, then felt something slam into his roan with the force of an avalanche. He felt his horse falling, and he kicked free of the stirrups before he was trapped under a thousand pounds of horseflesh. He heard his horse squeal in pain.

Brady landed heavily on his back, and the breath was driven from him. The nighthawk's horse somersaulted over Brady. A cold urgency filled him, and he pushed himself away from the tangle, rolling wildly to avoid thrashing hooves.

He lay there only seconds, his shoulder numb, his breath coming in great, gasping heaves. The sound of it was drowned out by the thundering of a hundred frightened horses.

He scrambled to his feet, stumbled, and fell, and then yards behind him heard Wally calling, "Brady. Brady? By god, where are you?"

He rose toward the voice and, lifting an arm, shouted, "Over here!"

He made out the shadow of the tall, lanky man astride a sturdy horse galloping toward him. A strong arm reached out. Brady reached up and clasped hold, swinging up behind the rider.

He hung on as Wally spurred the animal and at a dead run continued pushing the herd through the canyon passage.

Behind him were the loud curses of Long Tom and his men as they struggled in the melee to rope and saddle horses and to catch the renegades who'd scattered their herd four ways to Sunday. And he knew there would be double hell to pay when it was discovered that he was responsible.

His thoughts were interrupted when Wally shouted, "Where to, Brady?"

"Keep 'em moving. The herd will follow the lead gelding. He knows the way. Once we break the clearing, get me close to the gelding. I'll transfer to his back."

"How the devil you gonna keep from falling off?"

Breathing hard, Brady said, "I'll ride Indian style. Hopefully I can latch on to the lead rope and pull it up. If I'm lucky enough to not fall off and get trampled, I can use the rope as a single rein."

"Good luck to you, son. You've got enough sand for ten men."

Wally removed his hat and fanned it. His yells and the loud *hi-ya*s from Acosta and Meade kept the horses running almost single file through the long canyon pass. Wally guided his horse in line to keep from being crushed against the stone walls.

Chapter Fourteen

In the early morning's already blistering heat, Brady slowed the gelding to a walk. His entire body quaked with exhaustion, and blood caked the side of his head where he'd hit a rock when his roan was blindsided by the night rider's horse.

Acosta rode up to him and swore softly, "I never even saw you after we started, boss. What happened? Where's your roan?"

Brady told him and afterward asked, "Is Meade okay?"

"Yeah, boss. Sorry 'bout your horse. He was your favorite, huh?"

Brady nodded. His brow puckered into a frown. "What about the herd?"

Acosta laughed. "Take a gander for yourself. It's true that Spearman fellers' bunch is strung out all the way to Kiowa territory." He touched his temple and laughed again. "But the smart ones, they joined our herd."

It's all coming together, Spearman. With a little luck, I'll have you all wrapped up in a tidy package. Brady smiled and, keeping his voice soft, said, "That's fine, Acosta. Just fine."

Gradually the prairie resumed it natural rhythms. Birds chirped, and an eagle swooped down to capture a hare in its talons. The sun was hot and dry, and the stubbly ground gave off waves of shimmering heat.

Shifting on the horse's bare back, Brady placed a hand on the animal's broad rump and viewed the scene behind him. Through thick clouds of dust kicked up from beneath the herd's hooves, he spotted Meade riding drag and watched Wally approaching at a casual lope.

Brady's shoulders slumped. He was bathed in dust and relief. The danger had passed, and he was eager to reach the fort.

His sweat-soaked shirt clinging to his body, Wally slowed his horse alongside Brady's mount.

"After the herd settled into formation, I skedaddled on back to where you went down. Brought your saddle."

"'Preciate it. The roan?" Asking the question didn't ease the answer Brady already knew.

Wally shook his head. "Didn't suffer—broke neck."

Brady called out to Acosta, "Keep 'em moving due east! We'll catch up."

The wrangler waved his acknowledgment. Cutting to the right, Brady kneed his horse toward a lone buckthorn tree and motioned for Wally to follow. His mouth was dry, and he was queasy with pain and fatigue.

Reining the horse next to the tree, Brady willed his knees

not to buckle when he slid to the ground. He looped the rope around a branch and knelt, then lay down, using a hand to shade his eyes from the morning sun.

Wally dropped the extra saddle to the ground and dismounted. Trusting his horse to stand ground-tied, he remained silent while rigging Brady's gelding.

Expelling a weary sigh, Brady rolled to a sitting position. "Any activity from Long Tom and his riders?"

The horse grunted when Wally tightened the girth. "Don't reckon you've got much to fret about, Brady. It'll take a while before those ol' boys can rope themselves a half-wild mustang to throw a saddle onto."

"They'll hunt me down, and there'll be hell to pay. Spearman stands to lose a lot of money. He's not a man to easily reckon with." Brady's voice was hard.

"Yep." Giving the gelding a good-natured slap on the rump, Wally removed his hat and ran an arm across his sweaty brow as he sat next to Brady, trying to soak up some of the tree's sparse shade. "Shorely wouldn't mind a swig of Kansas sheep dip to wet my whistle."

Brady moved cautiously as he stood. His right shoulder pained him, and his right hand was swollen and purple. He loosened the bandana from around his neck and tried to fashion a sling.

Seeing the boy's struggles and without making a to-do, Wally finished tying the knot. "Looks like you might've broken your wrist. Lucky you didn't break your dang fool neck when that night rider rammed into you." He felt along Brady's shoulder. "Don't feel no broken collarbone, though."

Brady bit down on his lip to suppress a groan. "I could use

a shot of whiskey myself. In fact, after we settle with the quartermaster at the fort, I'll buy the first round."

"Won't have to ask me twice—Meade or Acosta, either."

Feeling an urgency to get moving, Brady found it awkward trying to mount without the use of both hands. "Hold this bangtail's head, Wally. Mind giving me a leg up?"

Brady set his foot into the stirrup and grabbed the saddle horn with his good hand. He lifted his right boot, and Wally gave him a boost.

"How much farther?" Wally handed the reins up to Brady.

"There's a watering hole about four miles from here. After that it's another ten miles to the fort."

"Want to let the horses rest?"

Brady gritted his teeth against the pain as he settled into the saddle and urged the gelding forward. "Only long enough to drink. We'll walk 'em another five miles before we bed down for the night. I don't want to chance running into a Kiowa scouting party."

Morning gave way to afternoon. Sun beat down, creating heat swells. Brady's head bobbled against his chest, and he jerked his eyes open, not knowing how long he'd dozed in the saddle.

The plodding pace of his horse picked up. The animal stretched its neck against the bit and squealed. Acosta's voice called out, "Water, boss!"

Brady yelled back, "Let 'em run!"

The sun reminded Brady of a blazing ball of fire. He cradled his aching arm against his chest. Relief washed over him when he spotted spirals of smoke. A few Kiowa lodges were scattered outside the fort. Little had changed since his last delivery of remounts to the post.

A lookout yelled, and moments later the large log gates opened. A handful of troopers strolled out to watch the herd follow the lead gelding to the quartermaster corrals.

Brady glanced at his crew of three. They were dusty, their shirts ringed with the white salt stains of sweat. Knowing they were exhausted, he noticed that each man sat a little taller in the saddle as they neared the fort. He urged his horse into a lope and rode on ahead, turning past the stable and on to the corral.

"Open the gate!" he yelled.

Sergeant Pendergrast crossed the yard buttoning his shirt collar. The lieutenant was expecting horses from Spearman, and although Brady had developed a good rapport with the man, he wasn't certain if the officer would turn down a deal with Brady acting as an independent agent. He knew the trouble would come when the sergeant requested the check be made out. Spearman, wise in the ways of horse dealing, had long since cemented his friendship with the quartermaster by gifts of blended whiskey, hand-rolled cigars, and money paid under the table. And if the quartermaster had occasion to visit Dodge City, Spearman paid for a night upstairs at the Golden Slipper.

Brady also knew that Spearman wasn't above sending men to pay calls on ranchers who tried to interfere or complained when the line officer gave contracts to Spearman over buying their stock, and the results were usually bloody.

Brady didn't care. These were sound horses, broken to saddle and better than any animal Spearman had ever offered the Army. He knew that an honest line officer or veterinarian could not turn up faults with any of them.

He dismounted by the big corral where a blue-clad trooper held open the gate. Brady removed his hat and waved the horses into the vast pen.

As soon as his men rode up, he instructed, "Acosta and Meade, I want only Anchor horses in the big corral. Cut out those wearing the Trident brand and put them into the smaller pen."

Brady thought back to another horse dealer who had dared to file a written complaint and remembered the grisly results. He called Wally aside. "Follow me."

Although out of earshot of the trooper, Brady chose to keep his voice low. "I know you and the men are tired, but no matter what, don't leave the herd unguarded."

"You expectin' trouble, Brady?"

"Let's just say I've seen sound horses turn up lame and suddenly develop leaking lungs without any reasonable explanation."

Wally propped a dusty boot on a bottom rail. "You saying some dagnabit guttersnipe would deliberately cripple a good horse?"

"With Spearman, money is the reason."

"Reckon you'd know firsthand."

Had that remark come from any of Anchor's other ranch hands, Brady might have taken offense. Sharing a campfire was a good way to learn about men, and he'd come to know Wally, Acosta, and Meade as men he could rely on, men who would back him in a fight.

"I've come to know a lot about Spearman and most of his

dirty tricks, and I'm not proud of it." Brady looked up at the sky, trying to judge the time. Weariness throbbed in him, and he supported his elbow, trying to take pressure off his wrist.

"Go on over to the mess and grab yourself some chow and then find a place to bed down for a little shut-eye." Brady gazed out over the milling horses. "I'll stick here with Acosta and Meade. I want two men watching the horses at all times until I strike a bargain, get a signed check, and hightail it of here."

"Your wrist looks bad, Brady. I'll stick here whilst you go see the sawbones. Don't you worry, me and the boys will watch after the horses."

Without another word, Brady crossed the yard in long strides toward the infirmary. An hour later, his wrist secured in a splint, wrapped tight, and resting in a sling, he returned to the corral where one man slept and two remained vigilant.

"Everything okay here?"

Silent nods answered him.

"The mess tent is closed," Brady told them. "Since Meade is asleep, Acosta, you and Wally head over to the general store. Mrs. McCutcheon makes a fine sandwich and always has hot coffee."

"What say we stop by the canteen and have us a beer? Shorely would like to wet my whistle." Wally rubbed his mouth with the back of his hand.

Brady held an appreciation for the men's long dry spell. Still, he didn't want to risk trouble. "I don't have to tell you not to take part in any discussions with the troopers."

"Reckon they'll be curious about the Anchor brand?" Acosta asked.

"Probably, since we had a few horses wearing the Trident brand mixed in with ours."

"That gonna be a problem, boss?"

"Can't say . . . maybe."

"What then, Brady?" Wally wanted to know.

"Nothing we can do until morning. We'll sleep in shifts. Wally and I will take the first watch. Acosta, you and Meade will spell us at midnight."

"You got it, boss."

Brady walked over to the trough, where fresh water ran from a pipe. He cupped his good hand to catch some and drank until he'd slaked his thirst and eased his parched throat. He soaked his bandana and used it to cool his face and the back of his neck. He longed for a bath and for a plate of Kate's fried chicken.

Propping his good arm on the corral's top rail, he listened to the soft shuffle of hooves on packed dirt while he thought about his future with Kate. He didn't blame her for getting all riled up when he'd announced his decision to delay taking legal possession of Anchor, and he couldn't fault her for still believing he was shiftless. He hoped when he returned to Willow Creek, proved to her that he was capable of making sound horse-trading decisions, and showed her the money he'd earned, she would agree to set a date for the wedding.

Then his thoughts took a different and troublesome direction, and he wondered why he should suddenly think of Hannah Osterhaus. For years he had loved Kate, had proposed marriage to her, and she still hadn't set a date.

Every instinct told him to push Hannah from his thoughts, yet he found himself comparing the redheaded, outspoken girl who didn't mind playing a game of poker or who, by her own admission, enjoyed a mug of beer, craved adventure, and bossed a crew of teamsters to the prim and proper Miss Kate Parker.

The two women were as different as night and day. Kate believed in fairy tales and yearned for the role of a princess who became queen of a large empire. That last thought struck a chord with Brady—a troublesome chord. Did she love him, or did she desire Anchor?

That avenue of thought cut too close to the bone and left him nowhere except in a quandary. He knew what Kate thought of his decision and knew he had to convince her that his plan wasn't rash, no matter the consequences to himself.

Stifling a yawn, he turned his eyes from the horses to a small red glow on the far side of the corral. Cigarette smoke drifted across the stillness. Hoping to draw the man out, Brady said, "Howdy, friend. You mind rollin' me a smoke?"

The voice answered, "Who's there?"

"Brady Wilkes."

The voice moved closer, and, not having a weapon, Brady edged nearer to where Meade slept.

"Yeah, saw you comin' out of Doc's. You got a busted wing?"

"Nope, a bad sprain." Brady spoke louder than necessary. "Doc said it'll be right as rain in a few weeks. About that cigarette?"

A voice off to his left whispered, "Got 'im covered, Brady."

"Thanks, Meade." Relief pooled in the bottom of Brady's gut.

"Say, didn't catch your name, trooper." Brady's eyes sought the man.

"Didn't give it. 'Fraid I'm fresh out of tobacco."

To make his presence known, Meade spoke up, "I've got plenty, Brady."

Wally and Acosta's voices carried across the yard as they approached the corral, and the soldier slipped away without a word.

Brady and his crew were up before the bugler sounded reveille. Taking no chances, not even in the broad daylight, his order for eating in shifts remained.

He and Wally stood looking over the horses. "I had my doubts about bringing them in last night." Brady spoke more to himself than the man beside him.

"Yep, they've had a chance to shake off some of that trail dust."

"Grain, fresh water, and a night's rest, and they're frisky as colts." Brady felt a swell of pride in the horses he'd hand-picked for sale.

An hour later, Sergeant Penn approached the corral, followed by six blue-uniformed men. His handlebar mustache drooped in the heat, and in an attempt to right the ends, the sergeant twisted the tips. He was a rotund man gone to flab from too many years behind a desk. Military protocol didn't allow him to remove his black campaign hat to wipe the sweat beading on his forehead.

Brady was glad his right arm was in a sling, knowing from experience that the palms of the sergeant's hands were soft and moist.

Sergeant Penn stopped in front of Brady and acknowledged him with a nod. "How's the arm?"

Brady wiggled his fingers. "Fair."

"How's my old friend Spearman?"

It was a courtesy question. Brady knew the sergeant was more interested in the gratuities than in Spearman himself, and he shrugged off the question with a brief answer. Penn was already looking at the horses.

At the sound of his name, Brady turned and smiled at the post's veterinarian, an amiable man with a mop of mussed white hair who looked as if he should have retired years ago.

"Howdy, Doc."

"Brady Wilkes, meet Lieutenant Cabot, fresh from West Point. Been here all of ten days."

"Where's Captain Dillard?"

"He and his company are on patrol—due back anytime." The lieutenant stood ramrod straight, and there was a kind of cheerful impudence in his face when he nodded at Brady. "Fine lot of mounts you've brought in, Wilkes."

Lieutenant Cabot regarded the horses a moment. "How many are you buying, Penn?"

The sergeant stepped forward. "I asked for fifty, sir."

"I count forty-seven." Cabot looked at Brady.

"We had a little trouble on the way in, Lieutenant."

"What about those in the far corral?"

"Not wearing my brand. Can't sell what I don't own."

"Yes, of course."

Brady read the curiosity in the officer's eyes and figured an explanation would be asked for later.

"I'm afraid if the contract specified fifty, we'll have to forfeit our deal, Mr. Wilkes."

Here it comes. It's now or never. "The contract is with Lou Spearman. These are my horses. I run the Anchor brand."

"Then I'm afraid we can't—"

"Spearman's men ran into the same trouble, Lieutenant. It might be days before his men show up, and when they do, it won't be with fifty horses." Brady's stomach knotted. He inhaled and exhaled the tension, hoping the officer would assume the trouble had been with Kiowa raiders.

"Still, you're three shy of fifty." Cabot grinned. "And what about the ones we reject?"

"Not in my bunch." Brady grinned back.

Sergeant Penn stepped forward. "Sir, we have a written contract with Lou Spearman. He has supplied us with horses for several years, and I am duty-bound to honor—"

The humor left Cabot's face, and he held up a hand. "The Army is not, Sergeant Penn, required to conduct business with one contractor. Mr. Wilkes is here, his horses are here, and as such we will consider his string. Is that clear?"

"Yes, sir, Lieutenant." Sergeant Penn sought the shade of the stable wall and sat down on an upturned keg.

"Have your men ready to bring out each horse on my signal, Mr. Wilkes."

Wally walked out a red dun and held the horse while the lieutenant looked for faults of conformation, and the veterinarian examined its mouth and feet. When they were finished, one of the troopers was signaled to saddle the horse. After Lieutenant Cabot tested the gelding for gentleness, he stepped into the stirrup and swung into the saddle. Brady supposed Cabot was substituting for Sergeant Penn as inspecting line officer.

Cabot galloped the horse to the far end of the fort and back to the corral, stopping in front of the vet. Brady knew this was a test for wind.

The vet put a stethoscope to the horse's chest and listened. "Sound as a dollar. Bring out another."

Brady drifted over and squatted next to the sergeant in the shade. "Spearman won't like this, Brady." Penn's voice sounded nervous.

"You write out the check, and I'll deal with Spearman."

Not liking the company, Brady returned to the corral. Penn followed. When the last horse was brought out, Penn objected.

Cabot said, "What's wrong with him, Sergeant?"

"He's cow-hocked."

An argument ensued between the veterinarian and the sergeant until Lieutenant Cabot backed up the old veterinarian's observations.

Cabot offered his hand to Brady. "An excellent lot of horse-flesh, Mr. Wilkes. Sergeant Penn will issue you a check for a hundred fifty dollars per head."

"Nice doing business with you, Lieutenant."

Brady fell in beside the sergeant, and to all on the parade ground the two men would have looked as if they were the best of friends. Once inside the officer's building, Penn said to a young private, "Write out a check for five thousand dollars payable to Lou Spearman, and bring it in for my signature."

Brady rocked back on his heels and in a mild voice said, "Better write it for seven thousand and fifty dollars, Private, and payable to me, Brady Wilkes." He leveled a look at Penn.

The sergeant looked startled. "Hold on, Private." He opened the door to his office and stepped inside. "Brady, we need to talk."

He closed the door and in a stance of defiance blocked Brady from leaving. "Those are Spearman's horses, aren't they?"

"Spearman's wear the Trident brand, and you know it."

"Be a good lad and say that Spearman bought the horses from you and you are acting as his agent."

"That would be lying."

"Come now, don't be difficult. I know things about you, Brady. Things that could make the lieutenant change his mind and back out of the deal."

Brady stood in the middle of the room, his legs apart, left thumb hooked in the front of his belt. A smile played on his lips. "And I know 'things,' too, Sergeant, if you catch my drift."

Penn looked confused and walked to his desk. He sat heavily in his chair. "I don't understand. What's going on?"

"It's easy. You sent a wire to Spearman requesting fifty horses. Spearman told me, except he and I have had a parting of the ways. You've got forty-seven of my horses, and they've all passed inspection. There's ten wearing Spearman's brand in the smaller corral. See if the lieutenant approves of them."

Penn leaned back in his chair. "Long Tom was bringing the horses. You said he ran into some trouble." He stood again and paced about the office, his hands clasped behind his back. Without waiting for Brady's answer, he said, "Yes, of course, I see."

His lips folded into a sneer under his mustache as he jabbed a pudgy finger against Brady's chest. "You were the trouble. What did you do, Brady?"

"Nothing that Long Tom wouldn't have done to me first if he'd had the chance." Brady's patience teetered. "Tell the private to write the check."

"I think not. I'll wait for Long Tom to bring his string."

Color crept into Brady's face. "Spearman's ten horses haven't been inspected or vetted. I think it's about time Lieutenant Cabot and the horse-doc take a look at them."

Sergeant Penn's piggy eyes darkened with dislike. "You young upstart, you wouldn't dare."

"You afraid the new lieutenant will figure out you've been paying top dollar for horses with sickle hocks and herring gutted and paying off the post farrier to keep his mouth shut?" Brady turned on his heel and started for the door.

"Wait!" Penn shrilled.

Brady halted and faced the sergeant, who was sweating profusely.

Penn chewed on a tip of his mustache. "I'm acting within my authority as line officer and quartermaster to deal with contracted horse dealers. You are not on the list." His voice was flat.

Brady swung open the door and said, "Private, I'd like an audience with Major Erlich."

For a man gone to flab, Penn crossed the room amazingly quickly to stand next to Brady. "Belay that request, Private, and write out a draft to Brady Wilkes in the amount of seven thousand and fifty dollars."

Penn signed his name to the check and without a word or look at Brady tramped past him and into his office, slamming the door.

Brady pocketed the check and stepped into the bright sunlight. He felt no elation, no victory. He had used all his rope and had stuck his head into the noose.

He strode across the yard to where his crew lazed in the shade. "Saddle up, boys. We're heading home."

"I figgered it up in my head, boss. You got a right smart amount for those cayuses." Acosta grinned over the back of his gelding.

Brady patted his pocket where the folded check lay. "You men have earned more than the pay I promised. There's a bonus for each of you, soon as I can get to the bank."

"What about you, Brady? You plan to kick up your heels when we return to Willow Creek?" Wally tightened the saddle's girth on Brady's horse and handed over the reins.

"I've got business to settle with the sheriff." Whatever the outcome, he intended to face Lou Spearman and take whatever the fates handed him.

Chapter Fifteen

Fiddle music and laughter filled the streets of Willow Creek. As was the custom, Leon Tisdale had flung open the doors of his hay barn situated at the rear of his feed store, and the ladies' auxiliary had swept and cleaned and decorated for the Saturday night dance. The end of the summer had arrived, and this was the main festivity before fall roundup and winter.

Wagons, buckboards, saddle horses, and buggies overflowed the hitch rails on the main street and filled the side streets and alleys.

Teams were unhooked and tied to end gates, where they could munch on the hay in the wagon beds.

From all points up and down the river, families would come with box suppers. Cowboys looking to kick up their heels, and widows both young and old dressed in their best finery hoping to catch a husband would put on their finest smiles.

Except for the saloons, the town was closed up tight, for this would be an all-night dance.

Through the open window of her room, Kate hummed along with the fiddles and accordions as she stood in front of the long mirror, giving her blond curls a final caress. She had no misgivings about her appearance. She had ordered her dress from a catalogue, an off-the-shoulder gown of palest pink satin with a neckline cut low enough to reveal the swells of her décolleté. She had picked pink rosebuds from her garden and woven them into her hair.

Around her neck she wore a pink velvet ribbon upon which she had pinned a cameo. She gave her cheeks two hard pinches to color them.

She blew out the lamp and walked downstairs, delighting in the silk's swishing sound, and smiled at the two men staring up at her.

Woodrow Stern stepped forward and offered his hand. "You look lovely, my dear."

She rewarded him with a dimpled smile.

"We're late, Daughter."

Kate patted her father's cheek. "Don't scold, Daddy. Being late and making an entrance is fashionable."

She looped arms with her father and her new husband, allowing them to escort her to the carriage at the end of the walkway.

By the time they arrived, the building was crowded with men in dark suits waiting impatiently for more women to arrive.

Gunnar Bjorn broke away from a couple of scrubbed-clean wranglers and met Hannah Osterhaus at the door.

By the flush on his usually morose face and the brightness of his eyes, Hannah guessed he'd made several trips to the punch bowl reserved for men only. His blond hair was slicked back with pomade. He wore a stiff black suit, and a black string tie adorned his starched white shirt.

His inebriation was apparent when he said with unaccustomed gallantry, "My brother and I are no longer owners of a freighting company, Miss Hannah, but you honor me by being der prettiest lady at der party."

When he bowed low, Hannah was certain he might topple over.

"You flatter me, Gunnar." All the same, she was pleased.

"May I fill up your dance card, Miss Hannah?"

She extended her hand. "Escort me in, and I shall reserve as many dances as possible." With a playful smile, she waggled her fingers at him. "But no promises for *all* of them."

Hannah and Gunnar crossed the jam-packed room and joined a quadrille. She looked around when someone called her name, and she waved to the foreman of the Slash T.

Gunnar clasped her hand and bowed over it as the music sounded and couples faced the center of the square. She smiled and flirted with each man who whirled around the floor. When the set ended, sun-darkened cowboys gathered around Hannah.

She fanned herself. "My goodness, it's hot."

"Vait here, Hannah. I'll get you some punch."

She found she had to tilt her chin up rather far to get a good look at Gunnar, and she offered him a smile.

Before he could make his way back across the room to

her, the next dance had started, and she was swept away in a swirl of skirts and cowboy boots.

After that dance ended, she retreated into a room set aside for ladies to refresh themselves. She leaned against a wall to catch her breath and watched as Kate Parker primped in front of a mirror.

The wife of the banker, Hudson, announced to the room in general, "You are the belle of the ball, Kate, and your gown is lovely. Pink suits your complexion," Mrs. Hudson added as she adjusted the pins in her crown of gray braids.

Kate fanned herself. "I wish it were a real ball instead of a barn dance."

The older woman patted Kate's hand. "You and Woodrow will attend many balls once you move to Topeka. When are you leaving?"

Hannah worried about how the news of Kate's sudden and unexpected marriage to Woodrow Stern would affect Brady Wilkes.

"Next week." Kate released an exaggerated sigh. She held out her hand for all to admire the gold wedding band. "I still can't believe it—Mrs. Woodrow Stern, Esquire, wife to the governor's new aide."

Hannah glared at Kate. "You should have at least waited until Brady returned. Don't you care about his feelings?"

Kate tucked an errant rose back into place, patting her curls. "Not that it's any of your business Hannah, but Brady and I were never formally engaged. Besides, he's always going off trading horses and is gone for weeks at a time, with never so much as a telegram or a letter."

The woman's smug tone irritated Hannah. "I think it's a

little odd that Woody's practiced law in Willow Creek for over a year, and until a month ago the two of you weren't an item."

"*Woodrow.*" Kate emphasized the name. "He and Father often worked closely on criminal cases." She cut another smug glance toward Hannah. "So it isn't as if we didn't know each other."

"You always were enterprising, Kate. One can only wonder if you married Woody for love"—Hannah tilted her head to one side—"or money, position, and power."

Kate arched a perfectly shaped eyebrow, her voice punctuated with insolence. "Why, Hannah, my dear girl, if I didn't know better, I might think that you were jealous."

Hannah's chin tilted upward, and her tone was one of strength in her convictions. "Jealous? Of you?" She placed her hands on her hips and harrumphed. "I don't know which to feel sorrier for—Brady, when he finds out you've jilted him, or *Woody,* when he figures out his lovely wife married him for—"

Hudson's wife intervened. "Hannah Osterhaus, you would do well to hold your tongue. Look at you, working around ruffians every day down at the horse yard. You should take some direction from Kate before you end up an old maid, or worse."

The woman reminded Hannah of a barnyard hen with ruffled feathers. She let out a gentle laugh to show that she took no offense at the older woman's remark, though it had stunned her. She proceeded with another query of Kate. "Is it true that Mr. Spearman bought your father's house?"

"It's really none of your business, but yes," Kate replied.

And though her eyes glinted fire, Hannah's smile broadened. "Gossips say Mr. Spearman also bought your father a position in Topeka."

Kate sucked in an indignant breath. "Why, if I weren't a lady, I'd slap your face." An angry blush shone on Kate's cheeks. She gathered her skirts and with a disbelieving sniff insisted, "Father is retiring and moving to Topeka to remain close to me. I *am* his only child, after all."

Hannah answered with a nod. If only Kate knew how conniving Lou Spearman really was. She knew her accusation was true, for she'd overheard a conversation between Spearman and the judge—a conversation not meant for her ears.

Hudson's wife and another woman followed Kate from the dressing room while a third winked at Hannah and whispered, "Takes spunk to speak the truth." She gave Hannah's shoulder a little squeeze.

Hannah noted Kate's rich-looking pink gown and compared it to her own high-necked blue gingham, with its velvet collar worn shiny from too many washings. It was her only good dress, reserved for Sundays and special occasions, though special occasions were few and far between.

Her eyes had detected a pinched look of discontent in Kate, and Hannah wondered if Brady had ever taken notice of it. She wondered if he was troubled by it.

As for herself, she had made her peace with Kate Parker years ago when Kate had angrily accused her of being ungrateful for not agreeing to the live with the banker Hudson and his wife, opting for independence instead.

Gunnar waited outside the door to claim a dance with Kate. He handed her a cup of punch. "For you, Mrs. Stern."

"My goodness, aren't you sweet, Gunnar?" Before she took a sip, the music started, and her new husband claimed her.

Noting the disappointed look on the big Swede's face, Hannah said, "Kate's beautiful, isn't she?"

"Ja, on der outside." He pointed a finger at his heart. "Not so beautiful in here." A grin lit his rosy face. "Dance vit me, Hannah." He set the two cups aside.

When he'd stepped on her toes more than once, Hannah said, "You're going to have a whale of a headache in the morning if you keep dipping into the punch bowl."

She accepted his inebration with an easy tolerance because he usually didn't let loose and have a good time. When the dance ended, Gunnar stumbled. Hannah clutched his arm to steady him.

"Are you celebrating something special, Gunnar?"

His grin reflected little humor. "I'm celebrating, ja."

"Is it your birthday?"

"No." He drew himself up and declared, "I'm celebrating going back to punching Slash T cows for fifteen a month mit board and beans."

Hannah pressed her hands against his broad chest to steady him as he leaned forward. "It's only temporary, Gunnar. You'll see."

The gloom in his voice tugged at her heart.

"Maybe," he said. "Maybe it's permanent too. Me and brother Sven, ve not know how fat Spearman's bank account is."

Before she could give comfort to her friend, she was claimed by Mr. Hudson, the banker, after which she danced with old Jake Newton, the stagecoach driver, and chatted with Doc Bell. She was claimed for dances again and again.

Standing in the doorway to catch a breath of fresh air, she watched Judge Parker waltzing sedately with the widow Jackson and the new Mrs. Woodrow Stern flirting and teasing with drovers from outside Willow Creek, men Hannah didn't recognize.

"Evening, Hannah." One-Eyed Lester spoke from the shadows.

Startled, she said, "I didn't see you, Lester."

"There's a waltz playing. May I have this dance?" He offered his hand and led her inside.

His massive chest filled out his clean shirt, and there was a kind of mocking courtliness about him that amused Hannah. He danced with precision, the way he did everything, and he regarded her with the same bland good humor he showed every day at the freight office. But there was an unruffled arrogance about him, and she found it faintly disconcerting.

The waltz ended, and he still held her around the waist, when a voice spoke over her shoulder. "Evenin', Hannah. Lester."

She recognized the sheriff's voice and unwrapped herself from Lester's hands. "Good evening, Sheriff Young."

The sheriff regarded the one-eyed man with distaste. "You heard from Fiske Cooper?"

"He ought to ride in tonight, Bass," Lester said. "I left word at the horse lot where he could find me."

Bass Young nodded and then tipped his hat to Hannah. "Enjoy yourself, Hannah. Nice to see you havin' a good time."

Hannah waited until the sheriff was out of earshot. She kept her eyes level and the corners of her lips down.

Almost as tall as Spearman's right-hand man, Hannah said, "Fiske Cooper rode in from Colorado two days ago, Lester."

He gave her a bland smile. "What Bass Young doesn't know won't hurt him. Nothing for you to worry your head about."

Hannah figured that this was his way of telling her to mind her own business.

He delivered her back to a scowling Gunnar. Lester offered a slight bow and said, "Thank you for the dance, Hannah."

The fiddle player called, "Grab your partners, ladies and gents! It's polka time!"

Gunnar moved Hannah to the center of the floor. From the corner of her eye she spotted Brady Wilkes standing in the doorway looking over the crowd. He wore dusty trail clothes, and the dark stubble gracing his face made him look more handsome than she'd ever observed. He held his hat in one hand, his blond hair curly and tousled. Her heart quickened, then settled when she saw the smile he gave Kate and how Kate hurried across the room, flinging her arms around him, not caring who noticed.

Gunnar had spotted him too. "Dere's Brady." He grabbed Hannah's hand and dragged her toward the door. "Brady, my friend, you haf come to der dance." He thrust Brady's hand up and down as if it were a pump handle.

Hannah grinned up at Brady. "I guess you can tell by his speech that Gunnar has visited the punch bowl a few times tonight." She had to crane her neck to look at Brady's face.

His glance shifted from the Swede to her, and she saw instant approval in his eyes. "How are you, Hannah?" He greeted her in a warm and friendly voice.

Kate clung to Brady as if afraid he might try to escape. Gunnar said, "Come, Brady, haf a drink mit me. Dese girls are dancin' mine legs off."

Brady looked down at his clothes. "Another time, my friend."

"Tell him, Hannah. He cannot miss der fun."

Kate touched Brady's face, rubbing his beard stubble with one small hand. "With months' of fur on his face"—she wrinkled her nose—"and reeking with horse stink, he won't claim many dances tonight."

Hannah watched Woodrow Stern thread his way through the crowd and noted the uneasy smile on his face as he observed his wife clinging to Brady's arm.

He spoke as if he were addressing a jury. "Good evening, folks." He wrapped his arm around Kate's waist and hugged her close. "I don't suppose Kate's had time to tell you she's now Mrs. Woodrow Stern—my wife." His eyes offered Brady a challenge.

Hannah felt every muscle in her body tense with anticipation as she observed the bewildered look in Brady's eyes. She watched him stiffen and give Kate an inquiring glance.

Kate jutted her chin forward and sniffed. "Oh, don't look so surprised, Brady. I never officially agreed to marry you."

Brady looked profoundly perplexed. He gazed at her as if that might produce the answers he sought.

The moment Hannah saw Brady bunch his fist, she gave Gunnar's ankle a swift kick to arouse him from his stupor.

She kept her voice quiet. "I'd like it very much if you would dance with me, Brady."

In a determined voice Gunnar said, "Brady, you come over to my room. Vash up, use my razor, and get on a clean shirt. Der ladies vill put out the food soon. Ve hurry, okay?"

Hannah watched the way Brady's jaw clenched as he looked at Kate and then at the lawyer. "Woodrow . . . Kate, I'm certain the two of you . . . deserve each other." Then Brady growled, "Lead the way, Gunnar."

The big Swede grinned at Hannah and led Brady by the arm down the street to the back stairs of his room over Miss Emma's Dress Shop. He stumbled once on the stairs and caught himself. Inside, he lit the lantern, and Brady noticed the alcoholic glumness on Gunnar's face.

The room was small, holding two single beds, a chair, a small potbellied stove, an armoire, and a washstand with a mirror above it. Like the two brothers who lived there, the room was tidy and clean. Though it was a poor man's room, Gunnar made no apologies for it.

"You vant hot water or cold, Brady?" Gunnar lifted the razor from the washstand and sharpened it on the leather strop.

Brady stripped out of his shirt and bathed in cold water, and while he lathered his face, he noticed Gunnar slouched on the end of a bed. His large, callused hands propping up his chin, brooding anger on his face. It wasn't like the Swede to be bitter.

"Where's Sven?" Brady asked.

Straightening his shoulders, Gunnar said, "Sven take our horses to der mountain. Starting Monday, ve go back to vorkin' cows again, Brady."

Hannah had told Brady about Spearman's scheme to put the Bjorn brothers out of business. "Be patient, my friend. Spearman's time will come soon enough."

Gunnar listed sideways when he stood. "You tink Hannah has dis figured right, dat Spearman vill quit when it begins to hurt his pocketbook?"

"Hannah's smart, Gunnar, and I agree that mountain freighting in the winter will break Spearman's bankroll."

Brady used the scissors on the table to snip the ends of his unruly hair. He watched the Swede move restlessly to the window.

As Brady brushed hair from his bare shoulders, his own thoughts were sober. *But my troubles with Spearman and the sheriff are just starting.*

The memory of Kate's disappointment and his need to keep his promise to escort her to a Saturday night dance had justified his riding straight to town while his weary crew rode on to Anchor. He'd been away nigh on three months, and the jolting news of her marriage had hit him in the stomach like a sledgehammer. He clamped his jaw and drew air into his lungs. Laying the scissors aside, he splashed cold water over his face.

Thoughts of Kate rankled him. In truth, the emotion that struck him the hardest was disappointment. Her sudden marriage confirmed what he had suspected but refused to admit. She was after money and prestige, and she'd latched on to Woodrow Stern to get it.

He felt a sudden and intense aversion to the very woman he'd thought to share his life with. He swabbed shaving lather onto his face.

He had caught sight of Bass Young and One-Eyed Lester at the dance, and he knew that Lester Galt had seen him too.

Reluctance to confront Spearman gnawed at him. He supposed Long Tom had returned with news of the stampede, and if he was lucky, perhaps Poco Crawford was still scouting the canyons trying to round up the scattered horses and take them on into Fort McClaren.

Brady picked up the glass of rye Gunnar had poured and took a sip while waiting for the soap to soften his beard. In the mirror he noticed that the Swede remained at the window, looking out at the night. He noticed his swaying. Brady wondered if, for Hannah's sake, he could convince Gunnar that he'd had too much to drink and didn't need to return to the dance. He also knew that alcohol loosened the tongues of normally closemouthed men and turned lambs into lions.

He remembered the way Hannah's eyes had lit up when she spotted him and how beautiful she'd looked. It was as if he'd seen her for the first time all over again. Her hair had glinted like fire in the lanterns lighting the barn. She was rosy-cheeked and slightly freckled and feminine in her blue dress with the black velvet collar. She had an easy, friendly way that drew people to her, and she thought differently than any woman he knew.

Gunnar's shuffling away from the window broke his reverie. Brady finished shaving and rinsed the lather from his face.

The bedstead groaned in protest when Gunnar sat on the edge again. "Every time I look out at der boarded-up vindows and doors of mine office, I get mad all over again." He roared, "I should get mine gun and face Spearman like a man!"

"The alcohol has fuzzed your brain, my friend. You're not thinking straight," Brady reasoned.

Before he could say anything further, the door slammed back against the wall. Lester Galt entered, with Fiske Cooper and Willie Moon tagging behind him. Cooper smelled of horses, and Willie Moon reeked from his aversion to soap and water.

Lester said, "You going to the dance, Brady?"

Brady toweled his face dry and reached for the clean shirt lying on the chair.

Gunnar stepped to the middle of the room and halted on unsteady feet. He raised a hand and pointed a finger at Lester. His voice was thick with too much drink and fury. "I don't like you. I 'specially don't like you in my room. Take your two stinking curs and get out."

Lester regarded Gunnar and without a word took a step toward him and swung, landing a solid blow to the Swede's chin. Not expecting it, Gunnar fell like a piece of cordwood, hitting his head on a bedpost, knocking him out cold.

Brady lifted a fist, ready for a fight. Fiske Cooper pointed a revolver at Brady's belly and snarled, "Settle down, boy."

Lester placed a hand on the gun's barrel. "Put it away, Fiske. Brady won't give us any trouble."

Brady watched the hard, aggressive smile on Lester's face. "Long Tom brought your wagon in, Brady." He concentrated on a floorboard, scuffing it with the toe of one boot. "He used it to bring in Poco Crawford's body. You killed him in front of witnesses."

"Guess those witnesses forgot to tell you that Poco rammed his horse into mine. After we went down, I lost track of him. If he's dead, it's by his own stupidity and not my doing."

Lester flexed his shoulders and smirked. "I know. Trouble is, you're gonna have to explain to the sheriff and a jury how a bullet hole got into poor ol' Poco's chest. You've got a lot to answer for, my friend."

Brady puzzled over Lester's words. Willie Moon drew a knife, backing Brady against the washstand. "You kill Poco. Now I cut you up. Feed you to buzzards."

Lester gripped the man's wrist. He commanded, "Fiske, take this crazy Indian and get out. I'll handle this."

Fiske said, "Reckon I got a lot to tell the sheriff." He grinned at Brady, then said, "C'mon, Willie."

As the two men tramped out the door, Brady heard their boots heavy on the outside stairs. He felt an invisible noose tightening around his neck.

"What's Spearman want, Lester?"

The one-eyed man rubbed his chin as if contemplating. "You see, Spearman got a telegram from Sergeant Penn requesting remounts. You might say that Poco was on Army business, and the Army is honor bound to keep its contractors from being terrorized." He shrugged. "Once Spearman files a complaint"—Lester hesitated, a sardonic twist to his lips—"and tells them how you disguised yourself as a lieutenant to swindle ranchers, well, it's the Army's affair, and they'll bring in a United States Marshall."

Brady knew with bitter clarity that Lester was right. He didn't have to ask the price of Spearman's silence. He already knew, and he felt like a man in quicksand. The more he struggled, the deeper he sank, until he would finally meet his end.

His small triumph over delivering his horses to the Army and earning a tidy sum of money had become bittersweet and had given Spearman another weapon to use against him.

He thought of Kate, the only decent thing in his life. And he'd managed to mess that up too.

Lester's casual voice cut into his thoughts. "Fiske and Willie Moon are waiting to talk to the sheriff. What'll it be, Brady?"

Through gritted teeth, Brady said, "Whatever Spearman wants."

Lester looked at him and grunted. "All you gotta do is sign the deed making Lou partner in Anchor, Brady."

Lester lifted the bottle from the floor, uncorked it, and drew a long swig. He remained quiet while Brady finished buttoning the shirt and tucking it inside his jeans.

Brady picked up his hat and smoothed it onto his head as he headed for the stairs. Lester grabbed Brady's shoulder. "Where you going so fast?"

"Might as well get it over with. Judge Parker's at the dance. I'll tell him to expect Spearman and me Monday morning to draw up the papers." At the foot of the stairs Brady said, "Then it's with you to Bass Young's office so Fiske and Willie can spiel their trumped-up alibi." In a controlled voice he said, "How does Spearman know I won't change my mind, once Fiske has cleared me?"

"I think there's been a misunderstanding, Brady."

"What do you mean, a misunderstanding?"

"Ain't nobody cleared you of killing Poco, have they?"

It took no time to walk to the sheriff's office. Fiske, Long Tom, and Willie Moon loitered outside. Through the window Brady saw the sheriff sitting at his desk. "Let's get this over and done, Lester."

Bass Young looked up from a stack of papers. He greeted the men with a brisk nod. Fiske stepped forward. "Mr. Spearman said you wanted to talk to me."

"I do." Bass Young kept his voice tight and businesslike. "Where were you during the first nine days of May?"

Fiske filled his jaw with a plug of tobacco. He chewed for a moment with a thoughtful look on his face, then he stepped to the door and spat. Once back he said, "Was in jail the first five days."

"Where?" asked Bass.

"Bristol."

"What about on the sixth and seventh?"

Fiske scratched his head and laughed. "Got into a fight and landed back in jail."

The sheriff didn't share his humor. "And on the eighth and ninth?"

"Camped out with Brady."

The sheriff shifted his gaze to Brady. "That right, Brady? You were camped out with Fiske on the eighth and ninth?"

Much as he hated it, Brady had to play his part in this farce. "If I knew the date, Bass, I'd have told you."

The sheriff sat silently for a moment. He asked Fiske, "How'd you come to camp with Brady after you got out of jail, and especially on those particular dates?"

Fiske stepped to the door to let loose another spew of tobacco juice. He dragged his shirtsleeve across his mouth and grinned. "Me and Brady was supposed to be together the whole week, 'cept I had a little too much to drink and busted up the saloon in Bristol. Told Brady to go on with the horses and I'd catch up to him after I got outta the pokey."

"Why didn't you contact Lester or Spearman to pay your bail?"

"Hell, I'd rather sit in jail, have me three squares a day, and catch up on my sleep than risk losin' my job."

Brady saw how skillfully Spearman had orchestrated the alibi for him. True to his word, Fiske Cooper had been in the Bristol jail on those exact dates, and when Bass Young wired for the records, the alibi would be validated. The simplicity of it was final. The records would verify that it had been impossible for Brady to leave Colorado, arrive two days later, kill his stepfather, then ride back to Colorado.

The sheriff looked at Brady. "Is he lying?"

"Not this time."

Sheriff Young gave a curt nod. "It looks like you're off the hook for Hogue's murder, Brady."

Brady murmured his thanks, and the sheriff said, "Go on over to the dance, and have some fun."

By the time he arrived, the tables were lined with cakes and pies, boiled potatoes, and slabs of beef. All through supper with the judge and Lester, he tried to find a way to talk to Kate in private. Although stunned by her marriage, for some reason he wanted to let her know that men had come forward to provide him with a solid alibi for Hogue's death, and he could now accept Anchor with a clear conscience. The opportunity came at the end of supper and before the dancing resumed, while the judge was engaged in a discussion with his new son-in-law and Banker Hudson, which excluded Kate.

Kate fanned herself. "Mind escorting me outside, Brady, for a breath of air?"

He cupped her elbow and led her to where bales of hay had been set out for seats. The music started, and couples hurried back inside, leaving Brady alone with Kate.

He called himself every kind of fool. Disgusted that he'd ever been attracted to this deceitful piece of baggage, he closed his eyes tightly, breathing deeply to quell his anger.

"Why, Kate?" Contradictions raged within him, for her beautiful, innocent-looking face didn't coincide with her self-serving aims. When she didn't answer, he grabbed her arms and shook her. "Give me an honest answer—if you can."

She flung her arms around his neck and placed her lips against his.

"Enough, Kate." He shoved her away. "You're another man's wife now."

"Don't be hurt, Brady." Hers was a mirthless laugh. "You and I were never meant to be."

"How do you know? You didn't give us a chance."

Kate crossed her arms and released an exasperated sigh, a pout on her pink lips. "You're always running off. What would happen the first time we had cross words? You'd run off just like you did when things didn't go right between you and Hogue. I want more out of life than wasting away on a ranch or in a hick town like Willow Creek."

Brady stared through narrowed eyes at her as if seeing her

for the first time. "So the princess snagged herself a prince. Be careful, Kate. Fairy tales don't always have happy endings."

Not knowing what else to say, he remained silent for a moment. "I've decided to take on a partner at Anchor."

"Mr. Spearman. Yes, I know."

"How?"

"Daddy and Woodrow invited him for dinner to go over the legal aspects of the partnership."

"And you approve?"

"Well, of course, silly. Someone will need to manage the ranch next time you get a whimsy and run off."

Her words cut him to the core. "I'm not shiftless, Kate. I never could explain to you the reasons I'd leave."

She touched his face. "You are what you are, Brady, and you'll never change."

Spearman had been so sure of him, he had gone to the judge and paved the way for the deal. Worse, the judge and Kate had approved.

The irony of it formed a slow, stirring anger within him. Couldn't either of them see what Spearman was after?

When the music started again, Kate stood and tugged on his hand. "Let's celebrate, Brady."

"There isn't much to celebrate, Kate."

She gave him an impish smile. "Oh, yes, there is, Brady. I'm moving to Topeka, and you're taking on a partner."

"Go join your prince, Kate." He sent her a final glance and left her standing alone.

He danced with a few girls and with their mothers, talked ranching with their fathers, and found no pleasure in any of it.

It was much later that he caught sight of Hannah's blue dress. He walked through the crowd and took her away from three wranglers. "Gentlemen, if you'll excuse us."

He settled her in his arms and waltzed her around the floor to the music. It was disturbing to touch her, and they didn't speak for a while. He looked down and was surprised at the grave expression on her face as she watched the other dancers.

"What's wrong, Hannah? Not having fun?"

"I was until I saw Kate a few minutes ago. She told me you'd taken Mr. Spearman as a partner in Anchor."

Brady felt hot with embarrassment. He wanted to explain yet knew the time wasn't right. He intended to play out the hand that'd been dealt him—his way.

She looked away from him and in a soft voice said, "I wish you well, Brady."

The dance caller announced that the festivities were over and thanked everyone for a good turnout.

"Who escorted you to the dance, Hannah?"

"I came alone."

"Give me a second to get my hat. I'm walking you home."

In the darkness Hannah searched his face. "I'm sorry about you, Brady."

Bitterness welled up in him. "Hannah, I—" He fell silent, stopping short of sharing his plan with her. He looked into her eyes—eyes that admonished him. He studied her face a long while.

"Why, Brady? Have you become like your stepfather? Are you money-hungry?"

"Don't, Hannah." His voice was filled with misery.

"Brady, you know Mr. Spearman . . . you know he's not an honest man." She shook her head as if in disbelief.

"There are things you don't know. Things I can't explain. Things I have no control over." His eyes implored her to understand.

"Mr. Spearman is holding something over you, isn't he, Brady?" Her tone was bitter. "Tell me."

When he didn't answer, she said, "No one should ever be afraid or be a coward. It isn't a trait I admire in anyone, and I especially don't like it in you. Good night, Brady."

He held the door open and watched her hurry upstairs. He willed her to turn and come back down and tell him in her easy, friendly way that she understood and that they could figure it out together. It seemed the most important thing in the world to him.

But she didn't turn around.

He stood there for a full minute, hope draining from him, before he eased the door shut.

Chapter Sixteen

Gunnar lay awake in the darkness of his room, staring at the ceiling. His mind was fogged from too much imbibing, and his head felt as if a horse had kicked it. Lester's punch had driven his feet out from under him. Hitting his head on the bedpost had placed him in a state of semi-consciousness. He reasoned that what he'd heard before succumbing to darkness wasn't intended for his ears. He mulled the words over in his mind and wondered if he were mistaken in what he'd heard.

Gunnar rose to a sitting position and held his throbbing head between his hands until he felt steady enough to stand. He groped his way to the washstand. It took him a minute to remember why soapy water filled the basin.

Brady had washed in it earlier. Gunnar didn't care. He splashed the tepid liquid over his face and head. His eyes had adjusted to the dim light, and he walked to the outside stair landing and relieved his bladder.

He leaned his forehead against the doorjamb before stepping back inside. Every square inch of the small room was imprinted in his memory, and he didn't need a light to find the stove. His fingers found the box of matches, and he struck a sulfur tip on the side of the stove, lifted the lid, and lit the banked kindling.

He spooned coffee into the coffeepot and filled it with fresh water. Easing onto the bed, he lay down and waited until the brew cooked. In an effort to think, he reviewed Lester's words, trying to read meaning into them.

Brady had killed somebody named Pete . . . no, Poco . . . who worked for Spearman, and somebody named Fiske could clear Brady's name.

Poco?

He ticked off the names of Spearmen's men, and then it came to him. Poco Crawford, a man so loco, Spearman kept him away from Willow Creek.

Gunnar poured himself a cup of coffee and in the dark sat by the window, foreboding touching him. He liked Brady Wilkes, always had, and he found himself examining the reasons he did.

He accepted Brady's reckless ways. The boy was young and needed to sow a few wild oats. Most of the town's people liked Brady and his infectious humor. He'd never hurt anyone that Gunnar could remember. Brady knew horses and was honest in his dealings. He was the kind of man who could break a woman's heart but never know he did. He gave a willing hand and never asked for anything in return. And now Lou Spearman was stealing from Brady all the things the boy deserved to keep.

Gunnar cursed aloud. Spearman, One-Eyed Lester, and the men around him were blights, taking pleasure in destroying everything they touched.

He rose from the bed and paced about the room. "Sven and me must help our friend." Then he reasoned, "But murder is murder, even if it is a crazed lowlife like Poco Crawford."

He clasped the handle of the hot coffeepot and let out a yowl. He grabbed a towel and used it as a potholder as he filled a tin mug.

The sensible part of Gunnar told him that this wasn't his business and to stay out of it.

The more he thought, the more he knew he didn't want any part of whatever Spearman's plans were for Brady. "The thing to do is to ride out to the Slash T tomorrow, join Sven, and put this affair behind me."

He'd keep quiet so Lester wouldn't know he'd overheard the conversation.

Setting his cup on the windowsill, he climbed into bed and closed his eyes. His stomach soured, and he was overcome with guilt. "Brady is in trouble. He needs my help." Gunnar flopped over onto his belly and punched the feather pillow. "And I'm not man enough to help him."

It was all too confusing. His head hurt, and he berated himself for drinking too much. Before an avalanche of sleep fell on him, he wondered if he'd embarrassed himself at the dance.

Sunlight filled the room. A bright beam settled on Gunnar's face. He groaned and covered his head with the pillow.

Slowly last night's events came back to him. Pushing against a wave of nausea, he rose and doused his face in cold water, then stripped out of his clothes. He lathered his face and lifted the razor. He winced at a nick and decided to skip the shave for fear of cutting his own throat. Instead, he wiped his face dry and put on a worn pair of denim pants and a chambray shirt. Today he would ride out to the Slash T and tomorrow begin punching cows.

He stuffed his meager belongings into a wooden crate to store in Miss Emma's attic, as there would be no need for them in a bunkhouse.

He felt as if a drum banged inside his head. He placed his hands on both temples and squeezed, wishing the steady beating would stop.

His mind returned to Brady.

Was someone blackmailing Brady? If so, then may be it meant he had murdered Poco Crawford.

What can I do? Gunnar's broad shoulders slumped. He knew there was nothing he could do to help Brady.

Once he settled this in his mind, he decided to see Hannah. He wanted to make sure he'd not embarrassed her at the dance or given away their secret. He feared what Spearman might do to Hannah if he got wind of her collusion against him.

Gunnar picked up his hat and went out. At the foot of the stairs he paused and looked over at the freight yard with its boarded windows and doors. The sight of it brought a curse to his lips.

He strode over to the Silver Spoon and ordered breakfast. Church bells pealed, signifying the Sunday service was over. He pushed aside the plate of grease-congealed eggs.

When the waitress walked over to refill his coffee cup, Gunnar placed a hand over the top.

"Say, looks like you're off your feed today. You ain't comin' down with something, are you?"

Gunnar accepted the bill. He touched his hand to his heart. "I tink maybe I am sick in here."

"I never heard of such a thing. Hope it ain't catching." The waitress stepped back as if Gunnar were contagious.

Without bothering to explain, he paid his bill and lumbered over to the boardinghouse.

"Miss Hannah in her room?"

The clerk nodded his response.

Gunnar climbed the stairs and trudged down the hall to Hannah's room. Her door stood open, and he saw her leaning against the window, staring out. The fawn-colored day coat over a dark brown dress was too old for a girl with such a vivacious character. He thought her beautiful but knew she was not for him.

He tapped softly and, thinking she hadn't heard him, stepped into the room. "Hannah?"

She turned and offered a smile before looking back out the window. "There's a hint of fall in the air. Come smell it."

"If I look at the sky, Hannah, mine head vill fall from mine shoulders."

"You did tip the ladle a little too much at the dance." Her voice held a slight chastisement.

Gunnar was contrite. "Did I act foolish last night? I am very sorry to embarrass you."

She walked from the window and with a sweep of her

hand indicated he should take the only chair in the room. She sat on the edge of the bed. "There's no need to fret. You were the perfect gentleman."

"I am no gentleman vat didn't valk you home. I just vent to my room, and sleep came on top of me."

Hannah laughed at the expression.

"How did you get home?" He slanted a glance at her.

"Brady. Although I didn't need an escort."

"Did Brady have fun at der dance?"

"He was . . . celebrating," Hannah said with a catch in her voice.

The Swede eyed her with curiosity, and Hannah offered an explanation. "He was celebrating his new partnership."

"I don't understand. Partnership in vat?"

"I guess it's no secret. Brady was celebrating his partnership in Anchor . . . with Lou Spearman."

Gunnar sat motionless.

His silence disturbed Hannah. "Well, doesn't that mean anything to you, Gunnar?"

His words came slow and measured. "Vhy should it?" He knew now what Brady had meant last night when he'd used the word *blackmail*.

Hannah paced about the room. She stopped in front of Gunnar, her hands clasped together. "Don't you see? With Spearman as his partner, Brady is bound to tell him our plans to freeze him out."

"You are wrong, Hannah. Very wrong." He stood and punched a fist into the palm of his other hand. "Don't you believe it."

The strange bitterness in her voice surprised him. "I do

believe it. Brady is afraid of something," she said, "and frightened people can't be trusted."

"Who said he vas afraid?"

Hannah again heard the curiosity in Gunnar's voice. "I do. It's written in his face and his actions. You can't hate a man one day and then take him in as a partner the next unless you're afraid of him. Or unless he's holding something over your head."

Gunnar's glance slid away from her face, and he studied the pattern in the carpet. Without knowing it, she had almost guessed the truth. Perhaps there was a truth in women's intuition.

He considered telling Hannah about One-Eyed Lester's visit to his room and the threats he made toward Brady. Perhaps he and Hannah could put their heads together and come up with a plan to help Brady. But there was a flaw in his idea. Only Brady could help himself.

Gunnar knew the stakes in this game were high, and for all concerned he had to remain silent until the right time presented itself.

His expression and words were definite. "Brady vill not tell Spearman about our plans. You know how you can prove it, Hannah?"

She stood with her hands on her hips and determination on her face. "Of course. If I still have a job at the end of the week, and if Spearman hasn't ordered one of his 'associates' to flog me."

Gunnar nodded. He picked up his hat and walked to the door. As an afterthought he said, "How is der freighting business going, Hannah?"

"Not well." She offered a faint smile. "I wish you had stayed in business long enough to haul a two-ton pump up to the mines. It's a killer."

It was Gunnar's turn to smile. "It's easy, Hannah. All you have to do is—"

Hannah placed her hands over her ears. "Ssh. No more, Gunnar."

"Ja. I see. Vat you don't know, you can't be held responsible for."

She released a huge breath. Gunnar smiled and offered his hand. "Vell, I vish you bad luck in your freighting business. Vhen it gets so bad it looks good for me and Sven, you know vhere to find us, Hannah."

When he left, she pulled the chair to the window, sat with her elbows propped on the sill, and looked pensively down the street. The Bjorns' freight yard was a graveyard of inactivity. She wished she shared Gunnar's confidence in Brady.

Brady's face loomed in front of her, and her words to him haunted her. She would never forget the tortured shame on his face as she left him last night. Fear didn't fit Brady, nor did inarticulate apologies.

She fumed, "Oh, why do I care?" And why did she?

Brady would no longer be happy-go-lucky, nor wear his infectious winning smile. She would miss his careless friendliness. She felt her hands clench into fists, every muscle in her body tense.

Close to tears, she decided there was nothing she could do except to go about her Sunday routine. She grabbed her shawl and ambled downstairs to the dining room.

The waitress approached her. "You want the Sunday special, Hannah?"

"To tell you the truth, Sally, I'm not really hungry. Will you send a fried egg sandwich up to my room?"

"You got it, honey. I'll bring it myself."

Hannah watched the waitress walk toward the kitchen.

Afterward, she wrote a few letters, darned a pair of stockings, and mended a strip of torn lace on her chemise.

In the late afternoon dark clouds blotted out the sun, and thunder rumbled distantly in the hills. She decided a walk would cure her restlessness.

Outside she strolled toward the river and past the Bjorns' empty freight yard. As she followed the stream, she thought again of Brady. Tomorrow he would become Spearman's partner. She wondered if the partnership would be mutual and include any of Spearman's holdings.

At dusk she retraced her steps back to the boardinghouse. Full darkness had descended as she followed the cinder road behind the Bjorns' lot. She stopped and leaned against the heavy chained gate. Was it her imagination? She peered through the dark. A small light flickered between the cracks in the stable wall.

She strained to see through the darkness. Perhaps it was a lantern. She stood there, puzzled. It could be that kids, knowing the Bjorns had abandoned the building, had decided to play there. A careless lantern, she knew, amid dry hay and weather-worn wood spelled disaster. With Sven and Gunnar at the Slash T, she was more or less responsible to protect their interests.

There was enough tomboy left in Hannah to climb over the fence. She landed lightly on her feet and ran on tiptoe to the corner of the stable, then followed the fence until she came to a stack of empty crates piled against the side of the barn. Careful to steady herself, she climbed to the top and stood on tiptoe to peer through a crack in the wall. She could see the glow of dim light but nothing more.

She eased her way down the crates and then dropped softly to the ground. Cautious but unafraid, she made her way across the open wagon shed. Whoever those kids were, she intended to surprise them.

As she crept along stealthily, she realized that the voices she heard were not those of children. Bending down, she found a knothole to peek through.

A lantern sat on a barrel with its wick turned down. Sam Copeland sat on the floor with his back against a stall, his legs stretched straight. She watched him tilt a bottle to his mouth. As her eyes adjusted to the dim light, she noticed a stack of dirty dishes scattered about him.

Sam was about to lift the bottle again when a voice croaked, "Gimme a drink, you ol' coot. My shoulder feels like somebody stuck me with a hot poker."

"Now you know how a hoss feels when you slap a brandin' iron to its rump." The old man expelled a raspy cackle.

She looked beyond Sam and saw a man lying on a bed of straw. His shirt was off one shoulder, and his arm was bound to his chest with a dirty bandage.

The man groaned as he attempted to sit up. "I said, gimme that bottle."

"Nope. Your already meaner'n a rabid coyote, Poco, and likker makes you more loco." Sam strangled on the last swig. He wheezed until Hannah feared he might choke to death.

"If I could get off this bed, I'd cut your gizzard out and eat it, old man. Dammit. Gimme a drink."

Sam laughed and hugged the bottle to his chest. "Not until Spearman says so." He picked up the dirty plates and the lantern.

"Leave the light, Sam."

"What's the matter? 'Fraid of the dark?" Sam slurred the words and shuffled down a dirt aisle.

Hannah backed away and slowly retraced her steps. When she heard the door creak open, she froze. The hairs on the back of her neck prickled until Sam moved out of sight.

Once she was over the fence and on the ground again, she lifted her skirt and ran to the boardinghouse. She knew of Poco Crawford's reputation and had seen firsthand how he liked to carve on both women and men with his knife.

He was hurt. Why would Spearman hide him in the Bjorns' stable?

Once in her room, she jammed the bolt into place. She leaned against the door, taking a moment to catch her breath. She turned up the wick on the lantern, gathered pen and paper and wrote:

Gunnar:
Poco Crawford is hurt, and Spearman is hiding him in your stable. What should I do?

She addressed it to Gunnar Bjorn and sealed the envelope. Downstairs she gave it, along with instructions, to the desk clerk.

"Charlie, one of the Slash T riders always comes in for

supper. It's important you give this note to him and tell him with the utmost urgency that Gunnar Bjorn must receive it tonight."

The clerk laid the letter on the shelf under the counter. "You can count on me, Miss Hannah."

She walked to the kitchen for a bowl of beef stew and a slice of cornbread, and while she ate she made idle conversation with Ma Smalley to make the time pass.

"Delicious as always, Mrs. Smalley," Hannah told her.

"You seem a little preoccupied tonight. Anything wrong, Hannah?" Without waiting for an answer she prattled on. "Lou Spearman's freight drivers aren't hassling you, are they?"

"I suppose I'm a little tired." Hannah searched for a way to discourage further questions. "I haven't had a day off in years."

Ma Smalley patted Hannah's hand. "If I were you, I'd march right into Lou Spearman's office and demand a vacation—with pay."

Hannah smiled. "It's an idea worth consideration. I'll give it some serious thought." And then she bade her landlady good night.

As she passed the front desk, the desk clerk said, "Slash T rider was here. I gave him the note, Hannah."

She offered him a dimpled smile and trudged up the stairs toward her room.

In all the time she'd worked for Spearman, Hannah had enjoyed her job. This morning she had given the teamsters their assignments and sat writing out bills of lading when

Emmett Morton dumped a burlap sack filled with mail onto her desk.

"Body'd think it was Christmas with all these letters, Hannah. What's going on?"

Her eyes widened. For a second she remained speechless. "I don't know, Emmett."

She bade the postman a good day and set about opening mail. By lunchtime, she wished Spearman would fire her. The torrent of letters held abusive complaints of freight's not being delivered on time, or not delivered at all, demands for payment of merchandise damaged by drunken teamsters, and a scrawled note from a teamster sitting by the wayside with a busted wheel, delivered by a passing team.

She spent the rest of the day answering letters and working on new delivery schedules for the coming week.

She hadn't expected her plan to ruin Spearman's freighting business to work so soon.

Working past her quitting time, she glanced up when a Slash T rider came in and handed her an envelope.

"Evening, Miss Hannah." He touched his hat and left without stopping to socialize.

Though only her name was written on the outside, she recognized the neatly formed letters and knew the message was from Gunnar. Her heart raced, and she pushed aside a pang of conscience as she removed the note from the wrinkled envelope.

Tell Brady. This must be wat he is afraid of.
If he knows, he won't sign the papers.

A wild elation filled her as she reread the words. A frantic urgency caused her to rise and grab her shawl, and then she sat down heavily.

It was too late.

The agreement had been signed that morning. She'd known by the smile on Spearman's usual dour face when he'd come in late. He'd doffed his hat and said, "Now that young Brady Wilkes has made me an equal partner in his vast holdings, I'm a rich man. And rich men should spread their wealth." He'd chuckled. "Give yourself a nickel raise, Hannah. You deserve it." He'd whistled as he ambled to his office.

Recalling the sinister sound of his laughter, she felt as if the emotions she'd held in since the time of her father's death crashed in on her. Suddenly feeling like a lost child, she buried her face in her hands and wept.

Chapter Seventeen

Rain fell steadily for the sixth day. Brady shivered under his slicker as much from the September cold as from the knot of dread in the pit of his belly. He reined in his horse and paused on the grassy rise overlooking Anchor. In the early-morning haze, a curtain of low smoke hung over the ranch buildings.

A burden weighed on him as he sat slouched in the saddle, once again recalling the day he'd signed the papers in Judge Parker's office, when Spearman had clapped him on the back.

"Go fishing for a few days, Brady. I'll take care of telling the Anchor crew about our partnership," Spearman had said.

He'd been glad enough to have Spearman break the news and pay off the crew with the promise of a five-dollar bonus per man.

In the rifle scabbard under his leg he felt the faint ridges of his fishing rod. He'd gone fishing, and for the past five days he'd paced the wooden floor of the hunting shack while the rain turned the river muddy and wild.

Spearman had generously written into the partnership agreement a clause stating that Brady would oversee the cattle operations. Skeptical curiosity and the need to meet Anchor's new crew now drove him home.

When the sorrel beneath him quivered, Brady patted the animal's neck. "Guess you're eager for a warm stall and a good rubdown, huh?"

He urged the horse forward and into a canter. At the main barn he unsaddled the gelding and, after giving it a rubdown, forked a generous amount of hay into the stall.

Reaching into his shirt pocket, he drew out his tobacco pouch and rolled a cigarette while standing at the barn door looking over the ranch yard.

"How could I let the likes of Lou Spearman spoil this place?" he berated himself.

A pair of wranglers lounged in the doorway of the bunkhouse, watching him. These were new faces, men Brady didn't recognize.

Slipping the rain slicker over his head, he gathered his rod and reel and, dodging mud puddles, sprinted toward the main house. He nodded to the two men, who regarded him with little interest.

No smoke came from the office stove, and he wondered where Clem Garrett was at this time of morning. "Spearman probably paid him off too."

He wondered if the foreman had left of his own volition, not wanting to work for the likes of Lou Spearman.

Once in his room, Brady changed into a clean shirt and work pants. Sitting on the edge of the bed and tugging on a pair of dry boots, he pondered his next move. He'd never seen Spearman's entire crew, and he wanted a look at them. They would, he was certain, be a crew of hired gunmen, some of whose faces were likely on WANTED posters. Part of the bargain, he reckoned. He thought of one of his stepfather's favorite sayings: *Lay down with dogs, and get infested with fleas.*

Brady tugged on a boot. "Yeah, old man, you had sayings for just about everything."

Staying out of the cold, wet weather, he ambled to his stepfather's bedroom, a room that had always been off-limits to him. With Hogue dead, Brady decided to see what grand mystery lay behind the forbidden doors.

The arteries in his neck pulsed as he gripped the doorknob. Only once had he dared venture into this room. Hogue had whipped him with a leather strop, with the admonishment that *"Curiosity killed the cat, boy."*

Brady lit the lantern and turned up the wick. The room didn't seem as large as it had when he was a frightened nine-year-old.

A massive bed for a larger-than-life man nearly filled the room. An arsenal of rifles and shotguns lined one wall. A chiffonier graced the opposite wall, and a writing table stood next to a window. At the end of the bed sat a padlocked steamer truck. He nudged the lock with the toe of one boot before sifting through the desk drawer until he found a key.

"Well, old man, what secrets did you keep locked up in

here?" He inserted the key, and the lock fell open, revealing a stack of neatly folded women's apparel. It riled Brady. "Certainly not the kind of attire decent women would wear." These were the dresses Hogue had kept for the bawdy women he often brought to the ranch to keep him entertained, until he sent them packing with only the clothes on their backs.

He tossed the garish silk dresses and filmy peignoirs to the floor. A hatbox held the Stetson Hogue had reserved for special occasions, and wrapped in oilcloth was a Union Army uniform. "Never knew the old man was patriotic."

The clothes meant nothing to Brady. He rocked back on his heels, wondering at the lack of important items he'd discovered. "Why would Hogue keep the trunk locked if he wasn't hiding something of importance?"

His stepfather had never talked about his life, and after a while Brady had stopped asking questions. For reasons he couldn't fathom, his heart stumbled on itself, and the palms of his hands felt clammy as he lifted the corner of a striped horse blanket to reveal a wooden horse carved to fit a toddler's hand. He folded back the blanket to find a pair of baby shoes and a blue knitted blanket. He didn't dare imagine these items had once belonged to him.

The last surprise was a locked metal box. Brady held it to his ear and shook it. Nothing rattled. He walked back to the desk and, finding no key, used his pocket knife to break the lock.

The box held an assortment of deeds to land Hogue had purchased, mining shares, and a savings book from a San

Francisco bank. Brady released a long whistle. "Hellfire and six ways to Monday . . . fifty thousand dollars."

He tossed the bankbook back into the box and lifted out a Bible. He'd never had occasion to hold the Good Book and opened it with reverence. He read the name written in a neat hand: *Victoria, beloved daughter of Reverend Thaddeus Brady of Cape Hope, New England.*

Brady? He was taken aback at the name.

Wondering if the names were a coincidence, he used his thumb to fan through the pages. The Bible fell open to a place that caused him to ease down on the edge of the bed.

Printed in scroll were the words, *Certificate of Wedlock.* A flush of anger filled him when he read aloud, "Joined together as one this holy day of matrimony, May 15, 1853, Hogue Wilkes, beloved husband, and Victoria Brady Wilkes, beloved wife."

His hands trembled as he turned to the page of births, and his unbelieving eyes saw, written in the same delicate hand, *Brady Hogue Wilkes, born February 11, 1854.*

Agitation refused to allow him to sit still. He wanted to hit something . . . someone . . . anything, as he did a quick calculation and reasoned that this was no mere coincidence.

He tried to recall the day he'd come home from school stating that the teacher needed to know his birthday. Hogue had said, "Well, boy, I found you on the eleventh day of February, so I reckon that's as good a day as any."

Hogue hadn't believed in holidays—not Christmas and certainly not birthdays—a fact Brady had accepted.

He kicked the end of the trunk. "Hogue, you old buzzard.

If you were alive, so help me, I'd peel your sorry hide with a horsewhip."

He'd found the missing links to his life, and the last one was the daguerreotype of a young couple. The woman cradled a baby in her arms. There was no mistaking Hogue as the man. Brady reasoned that the woman was Victoria—his mother.

Raw anger seared his throat. "Why did Hogue lie about you?"

A more realistic thought entered Brady's head. Because of Hogue's cruelty, women didn't hang around the ranch for very long before they up and left or before he booted them out.

"Why did *you* leave?" Brady sorted through the stack of envelopes he had strewn across the bed and found his answer.

He slipped the yellowed paper from its envelope, and a gold band clattered to the floor. Picking it up, he tried to slip it onto his pinkie finger, finding the ring far too small.

The handwriting on the paper had faded with time, and he went to sit by the lantern to read. He drew in a deep breath and released it, wanting to know and yet almost afraid of the letter's contents. His breath burst from his lungs as if the wind had been knocked out of him. And as he read aloud, it seemed as if Victoria's voice spoke over his own.

"Hogue,
I do not know what happened in the war to change you into the monster you have become, but you are not the man I married. Your drinking and carousing with saloon

girls is abominable, and the men you bring into our home are disrespectful ruffians.

I have prayed and tried to understand why you call me the lowliest of names, only to find no answer. As your wife, it is my burden to bear when you strike me and leave bruises on my body, but to force our three-year-old son to stand outside in the cold for forgetting to refer to you as Sir is intolerable and unforgivable. I fear for the life of our son and what he will become if I stay. By the time you read this, Brady and I will be well on our way to New England, where I will raise him among civilized people. Goodbye, Hogue."

The letter was signed: *Victoria Brady Wilkes.*

Brady gently folded the letter back inside its envelope and placed it along with the gold wedding band between the pages of the Bible.

He lifted the daguerreotype and peered closely at the images, then closed his eyes and tried to recall the face of his mother, only to find that the memory, like her handwriting, had faded. Yet he seemed to remember her tucking him in at night and kissing him on the cheek. Gently slipping the picture back into its resting place among the Bible's pages, he turned back to the front.

"Thaddeus Brady." Brady repeated the name. "My mother's father." He swallowed hard and vowed that once he'd settled with Lou Spearman, he'd add a new chapter to his life. He'd travel to Cape Hope, New England, and locate his grandfather.

Brady situated Hogue's Stetson on his head and, finding it

too large, scooped it and all the gaudy women's clothing into his arms. He marched to the kitchen, grabbed a can of coal oil, and stepped out the back door.

He tossed the garments into a heap on the sodden ground, doused them with the oil, and then tossed a lit match onto the pile. The burst of flames caused him to step back and shield his eyes from the sting of black smoke. He watched flames lick the air while the clothing and years of angry memories burned to ash.

The rain had stopped. Brady pulled his collar up around his neck and hunched his shoulders against the chill as he walked to the cookshack, where the men gathered for noon chow. Now was as good a time as any to size up the crew Spearman had hired.

Not bothering to stamp the mud from his boots, he stepped inside. Seated on benches along the long table were eight men, and at a round table six more sat playing a desultory game of poker. Overhead, kerosene lanterns cast gray shadows against the rough-hewn walls. The men regarded him with silent indifference.

He'd seen most of these men before but knew the names of only three of them: Billy Jack, Fiske Cooper, and Stan Peters. Fiske stood outside the circle of men with one shoulder propped against a wall. He rubbed the barrel of his Colt revolver with a dirty rag. A small, wiry man, Fiske had viciousness stamped on every line of his sun-darkened face. His eyes glinted with malice at the sight of Brady.

Wearing a greasy apron tied around his large paunch, Stan Peters stirred a cast-iron pot of beans.

"You the new cook?"

Stan rubbed his jaw as he pointed the wooden ladle at Brady. "I owe you for bustin' me in the jaw."

Billy Jack sat at the round table with his back against a wall, a greasy deck of cards in his hand. His sallow, taciturn face was expressionless.

Brady drew a deep breath. "Howdy, Billy Jack."

The gunman grunted a greeting without looking up to acknowledge Brady.

"Where's Lester?" Brady stepped farther into the room.

"On an errand."

"What kind of errand?"

"Ain't nothing to concern yourself about. He'll be back in a couple of days."

"He take a crew with him?"

The gunman chewed on the end of a matchstick, rolling it from one side of his mouth to the other. He took his time answering. "Mebbe . . . mebbe not."

Brady nodded. He sized up the rest of the crew with a slow, searching stare, gauging each man's temperament.

"Did Lester assign me a crew?"

Billy Jack looked around at the others, who shrugged, and then he glanced at Brady. It was Fiske who answered in an aggressive voice, "He weren't 'spectin' you back so soon from your fishin' trip."

Brady eyed Billy Jack carefully and then looked at Fiske. He pointed at two other men whose names he didn't know. "All right. The four of you ride out with me tomorrow, daybreak."

Billy Jack reared his chair back against the wall. "First, you're disturbing my poker game." He slapped the cards down onto the table. "Second, we take orders from Lester, and he told us to stick here."

"And do what?"

"Wait for him and the boys to bring in the horses."

Temper edged up on Brady, but he checked his black mood, knowing he'd lose the battle if he pushed this sorry crew into a quarrel. It was plain whom the men considered boss of this outfit.

Remembering the last fight he'd been in inside this room, he took a cautious step backward and then stepped out the door into the misting rain. He buttoned his jacket and moved off through the drizzle toward the main barn.

Inside the tack room he studied the gear lying scattered in heaps. It seemed apparent that the old crew had had to sort the ranch stuff from their personal items. His lips curled in contempt to think that good men who'd worked for Anchor for years—for some the only home they'd ever known—had been replaced with riffraff loyal to Spearman and Lester Galt.

He kicked a saddle with a broken singletree. "Wonder what kind of errand would take One-Eyed Lester out in this kind of weather?" he murmured. And he wondered why the men had avoided answering that question.

Meandering to the blacksmith shop, he noted that most of the good tools were missing. He held no ill feelings toward Rube Winters. "Reckon I'd do the same in your place, Rube. Five dollars isn't much of a bonus for fifteen years of loyal service."

A clap of thunder echoed through the mountains, and jagged fingers of lightning rent the sky. The drizzle had turned to a deluge. He stood at the door, squinting through the curtain of gray toward the bunkhouse. Two men wearing black slickers lounged in the open doorway, and two more men stood in the barn's doorway.

He ascertained that someone had given orders to watch him, and he wondered if it were Billy Jack or Fiske. Brady turned that over in his mind, recalling the belligerence with which the men had greeted him and also pondering Fiske's announcement that Lester hadn't expected him back at the ranch so soon.

Wishing he'd worn his slicker, he walked back to the tack room and lifted an oilskin he'd spotted earlier off a peg. He walked down the wide aisle of the barn, listening to the nickers of horses, and stopped to look at the rumps of several geldings. He noticed they wore the Trident brand.

At the end of the barn's wide rear doors, wagon tracks mired deeply in mud stirred his curiosity. Stepping back inside, he noticed two supply wagons missing and decided to follow the muddied ruts. A closer look showed that the stalls of the horses used for pulling the wagons were empty, and he didn't see the animals in the small corral adjacent to the barn.

Lowering his head against the pelting rain, Brady raced toward the house. In no mood for beans and fried fatback, he decided to cook his own meal.

After supper, he stood at the window and rolled a cigarette, again pondering the wagon tracks. Two men watched the house from the barn. They weren't going to let him out of their sight.

He hadn't heard any horses leaving, and he decided no one was worried enough about him to send a rider out telling Lester that he'd returned from his fishing trip early. He'd use this to his advantage.

Chapter Eighteen

Hours before dawn and not bothering to light a lantern, Brady dressed against the cold. He listened to the pelting rain against the roof and cursed. Tracking wagon ruts in the dark would be difficult at best. He knew the possibility existed that the tracks had been washed smooth during the night.

Knowing every inch of the ranch like the back of his hand, he didn't need a lantern to make his way to the barn. He'd purposely stabled his sorrel in the last stall next to the rear door. Not wanting to startle the animal, he spoke gently. "It's okay, ol' son. We're going for a little ride."

He heard the animal shift inside the stall. Brady lifted the saddle and blanket onto the sorrel's back, speaking softly to the horse while tightening the girth. By now Brady's eyes had fully adjusted to the darkness. After bridling the horse, he led it from the stall and several yards from the house before stepping into the stirrup and swinging into the saddle.

He hadn't given much thought to the old ranch dog until now, and he was glad no shrill yips sent up warnings to the sleeping men in the bunkhouse. He wondered which of Anchor's former ranch hands the dog had laid claim to.

Nudging the horse forward, he put as much distance between himself and the ranch as he could before daylight. Using what Billy Jack and Fiske had said the night before about bringing in horses, Brady had a hunch where to find Lester and his crew. He cut a wide swath and rode toward the holding pens in the hidden canyon thirty miles northeast of the ranch.

At midmorning he stopped at a high meadow stream to give his horse a breather. Allowing the animal a few minutes to water, Brady followed the stream's bank, watching for wagon tracks. Figuring it a lost cause, he was about to give up when he spotted a clear path cut through grass in the meadow.

He reined in and folded his arms over the saddle horn as he examined the deep gouges in the earth. "Wonder what Lester's hauling?"

The horse under him grunted and flicked its ears back and forth as if understanding the question. Brady reached forward and patted its neck. "Yeah, I figure it's sacks of grain too."

Ten miles ahead, a canyon lay in a hidden corner of the ranch. Poor grass with a tangle of brush and little water made it the kind of place Lester would choose to hide a herd of horses.

Brady rode on, climbing the sharp switchbacks back down into the meadow. He spotted where the wagon had crossed a stream and labored across boulders and flinty ridges and slid down a rocky wash.

Around noontime he heard the chunking of an axe. He hauled up on the reins and listened until he discerned the direction of the sound. A second axe sounded, and that puzzled him.

Putting his horse into motion, he rode away from and around the sound, wanting to come up from behind. He rode until the brush broke away from a steep cliff. Dismounting, he dropped the reins, knowing the gelding would stand ground-tied, and then he belly-crawled to the edge of the cliff for a look-see.

Lester Galt wore a yellow slicker. Water poured from the brim of his hat. He stood propped against the wagon's wheel while watching two soaked crewmen swinging axes. Two more were hauling a fresh-cut pine tree across his view.

Lester yelled, "Carry that one to the mouth of the canyon!"

One of the men answered with a curse. "How much longer we gonna be out here? I'm soaked to the bone and ready for a cup of coffee laced with tarantula juice and some hot chow."

Still another man complained, "I didn't hire on to cut wood and build fences."

"Quit your bellyachin'." Lester's voice held a hard edge.

Mud splattered when the man threw down the log. He took a menacing step forward.

Lester pushed away from the wagon and reached under his slicker to wield his pistol at any man who dared challenge him.

Brady scooted forward for a better look and in moving sent a rock tumbling over the edge. Lester's head went up, and he searched the rimrock.

A wet slicker and muddy elbows kept Brady from scooting back fast enough before being recognized.

"You spying on us, Brady?" Lester called out.

Brady pushed up from the ground, mud and grass clinging to his black oilskin. "Guess it looks that way."

"Who sent you?"

"Why should anyone send me? I own Anchor, remember?"

The two men glared at each other. Even with the patch, Brady read the wrath in Lester's one good eye.

"I thought Spearman sent you on a fishing trip." Lester's voice sounded almost normal.

"Can't fish in the rain." Brady tried to sound indifferent. He shifted his glance to the pole fence strung halfway across the canyon.

The crew stood silently, drenched and muddy, waiting for Lester's orders. Lester called to them, "Watcha gawking at?"

"You want me to go up there and haul him down?"

"Leave Wilkes to me," Lester called back. "Go ahead and take a break. Grab some chow, but lay off the whiskey." He looked back up at Brady. His anger contained, he smiled. "Anything special on your mind?"

"Yeah. You didn't assign me a crew. The men back at the ranch made it clear they didn't work for me. I can't round up cattle single-handed."

"And you rode all the way out here to tell me that?"

"I came out to get a crew."

A tarpaulin stretched over one end of a wagon's end gate

provided little shelter from the elements, but Brady watched a man build a small fire beneath the sodden canvas, while others stood around stamping their feet against the cold drizzle.

Lester scowled up at him. "Can't do it. Need every man I got for the next few days. Didn't count on your getting back so soon."

"You think Spearman's going to like it when I tell him you didn't leave a crew, and that's the reason I don't have steers to drive to the railhead?"

"That a threat?"

"Nope. Business."

Lester's scowl deepened. "There's some loose ends need tying up at the horse lot in town. Come on down, have some coffee, and once you've warmed your belly, ride on into town and take care of things for me. When you get back to the ranch, I'll have a crew assigned to you."

Brady nodded. It was plain he'd stumbled on to something he wasn't supposed to know about, and Lester's excuse to send him on an errand in town was a ploy to get him out of the way.

"Reckon I'll take you up on the coffee." The cold shivers under his slicker were real enough. Brady grasped the reins and led his horse down the slippery embankment.

Five men huddled around the fire's stingy heat. They greeted him with indifferent stares and nods. Like those back at the ranch, these were strangers who wore their gun belts low on their hips and holsters tied down with rawhide strips— a sign of men more adept at wielding a six-shooter than an axe.

He knew if he didn't handle this situation with caution, it

would leave him a dead man. He accepted a cup of half-warmed coffee and grimaced at its bitter bite.

"If this business at the horse lot is important, I'll stick here while you ride in and take care of it." Though his body hummed with tension, Brady kept his voice relaxed. "As owner of this ranch, I have a say in what the men do."

Lester tossed the contents of his cup to the ground. "Stuff tastes like croton oil." He balled his hands together and blew on his fists as if to warm them against the cold. "*Part* owner, Brady. As I was saying, ride on into town and tell Hannah not to accept any more hay from Sorrenson's up at Starke, and if she's taken delivery, not to pay the bill. And while you're there, burn the bales."

"What's wrong with the hay?"

"Batch we hauled up here was filled with jimsonweed."

Brady was certain this was a fabrication and an excuse to get him away from the camp. "Jimsonweed, huh? Bad stuff."

Lester nodded. "You can also tell Hannah any horses destined for Fort McClaren are to be shod before delivery—you can help with that too."

"Anything else?"

He watched Lester scrub his chin as if thinking. "Yeah, make sure the Bjorn brothers aren't hauling freight behind our back. Spearman wouldn't be pleased if they were."

"If I didn't know better, I might get the impression you're trying to keep me away from the ranch."

Lester dismissed the remark with a shrug. "Once we get the horses moved, I'll have a crew ready for you soon as you get back to the ranch. Don't worry about the men. They'll go along with you."

Brady offered the one-eyed man a *yeah, right* look. He stepped from under the makeshift shelter, walked toward his horse, and swung into the saddle.

He looked from Lester to the crew of men, then back again, nodded, and turned his horse away from the camp.

When he'd ridden a few yards, he heard the heavy chunking of axes again. Lester was driving the crew, but why? And why build a corral large enough to hold a hundred fifty horses?

Unless . . .

By the time Brady reached Silver Creek, he'd made up his mind. Instead of taking the shortcut to the ranch, he crossed the meadow and rode steadily. The rain had stopped, and the sun warmed him. His stomach signaled it was past noon, and he considered taking a break to chew on a strip of jerky when he came across a crew pushing a hundred or more horses.

He rode toward the only man he recognized. "Howdy, Joe. You and the crew got your hands full with a bunch this size. How many?"

"Hundred thirty, more or less."

Brady let loose a long, low whistle. "Need help?"

"Naw. Where you headed?"

"Was looking for Lester . . . found him." He watched the man carefully. "On my way to town now."

He lifted a hand to signal his departure and rode on past the herd. He rode some distance before he turned in the saddle to look back at them and counted the men to make sure Joe hadn't dropped a man out to follow him. Satisfied, he pushed his sorrel into a gallop, putting distance between himself and the herd and Joe Tunney's crew. He'd purposely made himself visible to the wranglers and had established his errand for One-Eyed Lester.

Cutting toward the trail he'd followed earlier in the morning, and to put himself ahead of the herd, he circled around until he came to a stand of cottonwood. He didn't expect to find anyone at one of his old campsites. Using the trees as cover, Brady dismounted and backstepped into the shadows to wait and to watch the restless man camped there. He tramped back and forth like a caged cougar. He squatted, rolled a cigarette, then restlessness drove him back to his feet.

Brady hunkered down to wait, his back against a tree. Sleep lay heavily on his eyelids. Shrill whistles jerked him alert. He rose to his feet, eyes searching.

The first of the horses came into sight, and the point rider pushed them toward the corral. Brady did a mental count— the usual fifty. Once the animals were secured, the riders collected under the trees.

A fire was built, and the men settled around it as if waiting. Brady waited too. He shifted his position, seeking a drier spot. There was a reason Spearman wanted him away from the ranch, and why Lester wanted him away from the new corral, and he intended to find out if it took all night.

Clouds passed over, blocking the sun and sending more misting rain. Brady cursed the weather. Water trickled from the brim of his hat, water soaked through his boots, and the cold wet numbed his feet. Still, he bided his time.

He figured an hour had passed when a man stood and ran toward the corral. Others followed with questioning voices. The man raised a hand to signal for silence, and Brady knew he was listening. The wranglers waited, cautious and alert.

In minutes a band of horses broke out of the trail and crossed the meadow in scattered formation. Some of them stopped to graze, some lay down to roll in the wet grass, and some blew from the hard run. All were caked with mud from legs up to their bellies.

Brady spotted four riders galloping across the meadow on muddied, trail-weary horses. They rode straight for the waiting men and dismounted. After exchanging a few words, the four riders dropped to the ground, and from the loudly-spoken words Brady gathered they were as travel-beaten as the horses they brought in.

"Coffee ain't much, but it's hot. You boys help yerselves."

" 'Preciate it, Whitey. Got anything to make it go down smoother?"

"Nope," Whitey Ford said, "Boys an' me'll take over while you fellers rest your hindsides."

The crew mounted fresh horses and started bunching up the new herd that was scattered across the meadow. Too far away, Brady strained to see their brands. It took a while for the drovers to herd the horses into the pen, giving Brady time to count. He roughly calculated more than two hundred. He noticed that the animals were footsore, their tails burred, and though they were solid horseflesh, they were trail-weary.

He wondered where the animals had come from and from how far. Clearly Lester had expected these horses, and that was why he was in such a hurry to finish the corral.

Brady watched the men divide the herd. Half of the horses were released from the corral. Without allowing them to rest, the horses were driven back and forth across the meadow at a relentless pace.

He watched the drovers repeat the process time and again, dividing the corralled horses into two bunches and then driving without mercy back and forth until the exhausted animals stood with drooped heads and quivering muscles.

That baffled Brady. He wondered about the purpose of punishing these animals. And then it came to him—an old outlaw trick use by rustlers to cover tracks.

It made sense.

He'd bet his life that these were stolen horses, and anyone tracking this herd over the mountains would come to the meadow and find thousands of blurred tracks going in all directions, and the horses wearing Spearman's Trident brand would be placidly grazing here. It was a perfect plan. Spearman was smart.

Brady watched the men divide the horses into four groups and then herd them in the direction of Lester's camp.

Settling back on his heels, Brady slowly rubbed a hand over his face. He had partnered himself with a liar and a swindling horse thief. With Anchor's vast range, his ranch was a perfect place to alter brands and hide horses and cattle until fire-burned brands healed. No one would question the Trident or the Anchor brand. A disgusted chuckle rose from his lips. No wonder Spearman had wanted him to go on a fishing trip.

In deep thought, Brady lost track of time. He didn't hear the footsteps behind him until the voice said, "Gettin' an eyeful?"

Even before he rose to his feet and turned, he recognized the hard-bitten voice of Willie Moon. The renegade was sopping wet; he'd taken off his slicker so its rustling wouldn't give him away.

Brady eased to a standing position, his hands at his sides. As he turned, he saw the vicious jubilation in the Kiowa's eyes.

"Push ponies hard to get here." Willie's hand rested on the hilt of his skinning knife.

Brady remained quiet.

Willie pulled the knife. "Told you once I gonna cut off your ears," he jeered. "Too bad you poked your nose where it don't belong."

"Who sent for you?"

"Fiske . . . when you didn't show for morning chow."

Where he'd been cold before, now Brady was sweating. He beat his mind for a way out of this. He'd witnessed Willie's skill with a knife.

"Shoulda stayed dumb."

"Yeah, why is that, Willie?" Brady played for time. If he could shoot before being stabbed, it would bring the crew from the meadow here in minutes. And then it came to him. He didn't have to like what he was about to do—his life depended on it.

Willie's hooded eyes reminded Brady of a rattler ready to strike. "Cause now you gonna die." The man played the knife back and forth in his hands.

A cold, swift fear touched Brady. Once he'd figured out Spearman's business, he was dead. And sooner or later, with Spearman now half owner of Anchor, he'd arrange for Brady's untimely death.

"You the one who killed Hogue?"

Willie grinned. "Did what the boss said."

"And the boss is Spearman?"

"Smart, ain't you?"

Brady smiled with more confidence than he felt, one hand extended while the other pushed his hat off his forehead. He looked beyond Willie, waved his hat in the air, and yelled, "Over here, Lester! We're over here!"

The moment Willie turned to look over his shoulder, Brady lunged for the knife. His grip loosened on skin slick with rain and bear grease. Willie slashed at Brady's face, slicing clean to the cheekbone.

Infused with adrenaline, Brady was oblivious to the pain. He head-butted Willie's chest with the strength of a bull. The move took the Indian by surprise, and he went down cursing wildly. The knife had slipped from his hand. Willie scrabbled for it, Brady kicked it away, and the wiry man sprang to his feet with the agility of a cat and body-slammed Brady, knocking him to the ground.

The two wrestled, rolling in the wet grass. Brady searched for his pistol butt, his fingers wrapped around it, and he pulled it from his holster. The two fought with a wild and vicious tenacity.

Willie knocked the gun from Brady's hand, it skidded in the mud, and both lunged for it. Frenetic hands grabbed it.

Willie gripped the barrel while kicking Brady in the knee, sending him to the ground. In the frenzy, Brady didn't remember pulling the trigger until the blast echoed in his ears and Willie Moon's body fell limp, pinning him to the ground.

Dazed and winded, Brady sucked air into his lungs. It took several seconds to realize he was alive. With a grunt, he shoved the lifeless Moon aside. Blood spread out from the gaping wound in Willie's side.

On bended knees, Brady hovered over the man. He placed an ear to Willie's chest. "Don't you go and die on me."

The Kiowa's chest heaved, and Willie Moon's eyes fluttered opened. "You done gone and kilt me."

"You're an Indian—tell me what to use to stop the bleeding."

Willie choked on his own laughter. "Half-white part don't know Indian medicine. Half-Indian part don't know white man's healing." He lifted his head to look at his bloodied shirt, and as if understanding the seriousness of his wound, he lay back, his face a mask of pain. "Spiderweb."

Brady glanced around. There was no time to search for spiderwebs—not if he hoped to get Willie to the sheriff's office alive. He snatched off his rain gear and, shrugging off his jacket, impatiently popped the snaps on his shirt. Using Willie's knife, he cut the garment into strips. Shivering with cold, he bound the gaping hole in Willie's side.

"Why you try save my mangy hide?"

Brady tied a knot in the makeshift bandage. "You killed Hogue and admitted it was Spearman who gave the order. I need you alive to clear my name."

Oblivious to the pain from the deep wound in his cheek, Brady went to catch up the horses. Knowing that carrying double would tire his horse on the long ride to Willow Creek, he tied the reins of Willie Moon's pinto to the pommel of his saddle. This would leave his own hands free to keep the wounded man from falling out of the saddle and also give him a fresh horse when the sorrel tired.

He hefted Willie to his feet. "Wrap your hands around the saddle horn, and put your foot in the stirrup." Brady gave a boost, and the wounded man grunted in pain as he settled onto the saddle.

Brady situated himself behind Moon. The rump of a horse wasn't the most comfortable position for a long ride. Brady gathered the reins and kneed the sorrel into action. He figured a steady gallop, stopping once to change horses, would put them in Willow Creek by sunup the next morning. He knew the odds of getting Willie Moon to town alive were slim to none.

Chapter Nineteen

The first fingers of dawn crept across the gray and pink sky. A half mile from town and dizzy with fatigue, Brady ached from supporting the weight of Willie Moon's body.

Speaking soft words, Brady urged the tired pinto across the creek. "Don't give up on me, horse."

A spasm wracked the Kiowa. He lifted his head. "How far?"

"We're at the edge of town."

Willie's head lolled forward. His shallow breathing concerned Brady. Thinking to keep him alert, he decided to talk. "Good pony you have, Willie."

"You betcha. Damn good."

"He for sale?"

Willie's chuckle sounded more like a watery rasp. "You're a damn fool."

"Yeah, why's that?"

"Offering to buy a dead man's horse."

"You're still breathing."

"Brady?"

"Yeah?"

"If I tell Bass Young truth . . . you do me big favor?"

Not trusting the outlaw's devious mind, Brady hesitated. "If it's within my power."

"Bury me in Kiowa way—not like a white man."

"You have my word."

"Good. I give you pinto—damn fine horse."

Hannah clutched the warm shawl around her as she stood on the sidewalk in front of the boardinghouse. She'd lain awake night after night regretting her last words to Brady. He was her friend, and she'd let him down—scolded him on the very night he'd learned his fiancée had married another man, and had also accused Brady of being a coward.

She was glad she'd had the courage to tell Bass Young about discovering Poco Crawford alive and hiding in the Bjorn brothers' barn. But the satisfaction of knowing that Poco's was one murder the sheriff couldn't pin on Brady didn't help her guilt much. Though she couldn't prove it, she felt certain that Lou Spearman had orchestrated Brady's other troubles.

If only Brady had confided in me. Frowning, she chastised herself, "I wouldn't trust a friend like me, either."

A breeze kicked up a swirl of dust devils, and she watched them spin playfully down Main Street. Through the rising sand she spotted a pinto pony, not giving it much thought until she realized there were two riders, one slumped over, almost touching the horse's neck.

The way the animal shuffled along with its head drooped, she surmised it had come a long way. As the pinto drew closer, her throat muscles knotted. Wind caught her shawl, twirling it high as she ran to meet the riders.

"Brady, you're hurt!"

"Never mind me. Get Doc Bell, and meet me at the sheriff's office."

"But, Brady . . ."

"Do it, Hannah!"

With a quick nod and without further questions, she lifted her skirt and raced toward the end of the block.

Brady halted the pinto at the hitching rail in front of the sheriff's office. Afraid to slide off the horse's rump and let go of Willie Moon, lest he fall out of the saddle, Brady yelled, "Bass Young!"

In spite of the cold, sweat beaded his forehead, and the deep gash in his cheek throbbed. His garments were soaked through, and rain had left his hat limp.

"Bass Young!" His voice seemed to echo inside his own head.

The sheriff opened the door and stuck his head out. "Brady? What the—"

"Willie Moon is almost done for. I shot him." Brady's voice came in an exhausted clip. "Sent Hannah for Doc Bell. He confessed."

"I don't understand. Just what is it Doc is supposed to have done?"

"Not Doc. Willie." Weary exasperation filled Brady's voice.

"Then I reckon we'd better hope Willie Moon lives until Doc gets here." Bass reached up and grabbed hold of the unconscious man.

Brady helped hand the wounded man down to the sheriff and watched as Young lifted Willie Moon into his arms and toted him into the office.

Brady's legs buckled when he slid from the horse. He clung to the stirrup strap to keep from collapsing to the ground. His mind challenged his legs to move.

Hannah matched Doc Bell's quick strides as they hastened toward Bass Young's office. The flush on her cheeks had more to do with her thoughts about Brady than keeping up with the doctor's brisk pace.

She regretted again the cavalier way she had treated Brady and recalled the haunted expression in his eyes when he'd stood at the bottom of the staircase looking up at her. He had needed a friend, and she'd let him down. She wiped the tears that stung her eyes.

She knew of Brady's childhood, growing up with a domineering stepfather too self-involved with running his vast empire to take an interest in the son he'd committed to raise. She knew too of the cruel accusations Hogue Wilkes often made against Brady's mother. It was no small wonder that Brady had developed the habit of running away from his problems rather than facing them. What was remarkable was that he hadn't turned out more like Hogue, and surely a more selfish and evil-minded person than Hogue Wilkes had never walked the earth. On second thought, maybe she should include Lou Spearman.

Seeing Brady slumped against the pinto, Hannah hastened across the street. "Brady—" She stopped abruptly, not sure what she wanted to say, not sure what she felt other than sudden confusion at the wild thumping of her heart.

She gathered him into her arms, heedless of the blood and dirt that stained her dark wool dress. She grimaced at the frightful gash that had missed his eye by inches.

"You're hurt." She held on to him and felt such an all-consuming protectiveness that she found it difficult to breathe.

He straightened and squeezed her shoulders lightly. "I'm more tired than hurt."

Doc Bell huffed up and, with the critical eye of his profession, looked at the flap of laid-open flesh on Brady's cheek. "Nasty cut—needs stitching."

Brady, tired, chilled to the bone, and dusty from travel, winced when Doc touched the wound. "Willie Moon is hurt bad, Doc. He needs you more than me."

With Hannah on one side and flanked by the doctor, Brady said, "I'm all done in, Hannah. Would you mind writing down everything Willie Moon says and get him to either sign it or make his mark?"

She nodded and followed him into the sheriff's office. The trio walked through the doorway leading to the jail cells. Bass pulled a blanket over his prisoner.

"He's alive. Don't know if he's unconscious or asleep." Bass young offered a worried glance to Brady.

Doc Belle sat down on a wooden stool and rummaged inside his black physician's bag. He removed a pair of scissors and snipped away the makeshift bandages Brady had placed over Willie's wound.

"Willie told me to find spiderwebs to stop the bleeding, but there wasn't time, Doc. I did what I thought was right."

"You did fine, Brady, just fine." Doc reached into his bag again and pulled out a bottle of tincture of iodine. Without looking up, he said, "Hannah, get me a basin of water."

Doc reached under Willie Moon's back, feeling on one side and then the other. "Bullet didn't go all the way through. With the amount of blood he's lost, I'm surprised he's still alive."

He removed a stethoscope from his bag and listened to Willie's heart.

"Will he live?" Bass wanted to know.

Doc simply pursed his lips. "I'll bring him around with some ammonia. He's not long for this earth."

Hannah returned and sat a ewer of water and a basin at the end of Willie's cot. She glanced over at Brady, who leaned against the cell bars. "Let me clean your wound while Doc is tending to Willie."

To Hannah, he said, "Not yet." To the sheriff, he said, "Bass, you have pencil and paper? I want Hannah to write down everything Willie says."

The sheriff nodded his understanding. "In my desk drawer, Hannah."

She returned within seconds and seated herself on a stool brought from the adjoining cell.

Anxiety showed on Brady's face. Not only did his life

depend on Willie Moon's testimony, it would also serve as Brady's ultimate revenge on Lou Spearman, One-eyed Lester, and all of Spearman's crew.

Doc Bell broke an ammonia capsule and waved it under Willie's nose. The Indian grimaced, then coughed as he inhaled, and his eyes fluttered open. He glanced around at each face, his gaze landing on Brady.

"Reckon I ain't dead."

"I lived up to my end of the bargain, Willie. I got you here." Brady offered a thin smile. He kept his voice low and even. "What about you—ready to tell Bass Young what you told me?"

The wounded man's eyes fluttered, and Doc gave him another whiff of ammonia. Willie coughed, and a trickle of blood ran from the corner of his mouth.

Hannah wet a cloth and wiped Willie's mouth. She folded the cloth and laid it across his forehead.

Willie sucked in a ragged breath and exhaled. He turned his gazed toward the sheriff. "Me kill Hogue Wilkes."

Hannah set pencil to paper and wrote.

Bass said, "Tell us all of it, Willie. If you live, I'll see what I can do to make things go easier for you."

Willie's attempted laugh caused him to grimace. "Don't 'spect no favors."

A knot of tension gripped Brady. What if the man died without telling enough details to hang Lou Spearman?

Doc Bell spoke up. "Willie Moon, you don't have long for this earth. Whatever you've got to say, you need to get on with the telling of it."

Willie nodded. "Spearman and Brady's ol' man argument—

bad'un. Him want Hogue to make him pardner in ranch, and Hogue refuse."

Willie drew a breath and closed his eyes for a moment as if to rest.

"What else did they argue over?" Brady was burning with curiosity.

"'bout you . . . Spearman thought he could blackmail Hogue. He tell the ol' man 'bout you wearin' soldier-boy uniform and said if Hogue didn't go to the judge and sign papers, Spearman said he'd go to quartermaster at fort and get him to swear you were workin' on your own and cheatin' ranchers out of their horse money, pretending you work for Army."

"What did Hogue say?" Brady knelt next to the cot.

"Told Spearman to go to hell. Said he wasn't paying no blackmail money."

Now it was the sheriff's turn to ask a question. "Were there any witnesses to this besides yourself?"

"Yeah. Long Tom. Him there, and so was One-Eye hisself."

"You mean Lester?" Bass asked for clarification.

Willie nodded.

Bass looked at Hannah. "Are you getting all this down?"

She flexed her hand to ease a cramp. "Yes."

"Willie . . ." Whether from fatigue or from tension, Brady's voice trembled. "You mentioned the judge. Was he . . ."

"Yeah, all of 'em—the judge, the quartermaster, Spearman . . . in cahoots."

Brady felt as if a mule had kicked him in the stomach. "Hannah's written it all down. To make it legal, I need you to sign the paper."

Willie shoved the pencil away. "No can write name. Hold paper." He dipped his finger in his wound and as he crossed the X, his hand went limp, leaving a bloody trail down the paper. His eyes glazed over, giving them the look of two shiny black marbles.

Doc Bell placed the stethoscope to the Willie Moon's chest and then reached up and closed the staring eyes.

Chapter Twenty

Sun rays peeked through the jail cell's bars, disturbing Brady's sleep. There was a kind of numbness in his mind when he awoke, and his body protested when he shifted on the sparse cot. Shoving himself to a sitting position, he reached up and touched the bandage on his cheek.

His tongue felt as if it had fur growing on it, and he remembered Doc's handing him a cup of whiskey. His own wry chuckle echoed inside his aching head. "Doc, you sly old codger."

The acrid-sweet taste of laudanum lingered. He'd had it once before when he'd broken his leg; the doctor had given him a spoonful to ease the pain. This time he'd evidently laced it with whiskey.

Struggling to his feet, Brady bent over the basin and sloshed cold water over his face and hair. He smiled at the neatly folded towel. "Hannah."

He stretched and yawned. The cell door stood open. After Willie Moon's confession and the telling of Brady's impersonating an Army officer, he was surprised Bass hadn't locked the cell door and thrown away the key.

He tried the handle on the massive wooden door separating the sheriff's office from the prisoners' cells. It opened, and he stepped into the office.

"Morning."

Bass looked up and nodded toward the potbellied stove. "Coffee's hot. Hannah brought over a basket of biscuits and fried ham."

Brady's stomach grumbled at the food's aroma. "Can't remember the last time I ate."

He pulled a biscuit apart and placed a slice of ham between the layers. Pouring a cup of coffee, he carried the plate to a chair in front of the sheriff's desk. He wolfed down the biscuit before wrapping his hands around the coffee mug to slake his thirst. Then he drew a sleeve across his mouth and sighed.

"You arresting me, Bass?"

The sheriff thrummed his fingers on the desk and took his time answering. He rose from his chair and refilled his own mug, sat down, and leaned forward on his elbows while peering over the cup's rim.

"I know about Spearman's double-dealing scam, and I know your part in it. I also know that you tried to break away from Spearman and about his threatening to turn you over to the Army if you didn't continue posing as Lieutenant Hasting."

Brady stood. He shoved his hands into his pockets and

paced across the room and back. He leaned on the desk with his fingers splayed. "How?"

"Had another prisoner a few days ago. Poco Crawford."

Bass related how Hannah had seen a light in the Bjorn brothers' barn and had gone to investigate.

"She recognized Poco from the few times he'd slipped in to see Spearman, and she immediately came and got me. Poco was busted up pretty bad.

"She told me something else—Spearman's scheme to bankrupt the Bjorn brothers' freight business."

"I didn't see Poco in a cell last night."

"Nope. Doc figured he had a punctured lung—patched him up best he could. Me and a deputy escorted Poco up to Hayes. He won't last long enough to hang."

"Did he talk?"

Bass harrumphed. "Must've had a pint of rotgut hidden in his boot. We camped one night, and danged if he didn't stare into the fire and jabber all night long. Told me more'n I wanted to know."

Brady felt oddly calm. "I have a lot of misdeeds to account for, but if you'll hold off on arresting me, I can lead you to where Lester and his crew are holding a herd of more than two hundred horses. I'll wager they're stolen and Lester is altering brands so he can sell them to the Army. If we catch him, we catch Spearman."

"How many in his crew?"

Brady did a quick calculation. "At least six hired guns."

Bass recognized most of the names Brady spieled off. "Yep. Got WANTED posters on all of 'em.

"Sent my deputy to haul Willie Moon's body down to the

Indian Agency—let it be their responsibility to get him to the reservation so he can be buried like a Kiowa."

Bass was solemn. "That leaves just me against a bunch of good-for-nothings, and the town's men are mostly too old to risk their lives acting as a posse."

Brady's face was serious. "Sven and Gunnar work for the Slash T. Spearman fired Anchor's entire crew. I think I know where to find most of them. They've all got a grudge to settle."

"You'd better hope it's not with you."

Bass grabbed his hat, checked the cylinder on his Colt, and lifted a scatter gun, two rifles, and a box of shells from the gun rack. He tossed a Winchester to Brady. "Raise your right hand."

"For what?"

Bass reached into his desk drawer and tossed a badge to him. "Until all of this is over, I duly deputize you."

"I won't let you down, Bass."

Bass opened the office door. "We're burning daylight. Good Luck gettin' a few ol' boys to ride with us. I'll meet you at the livery. By the time you get there, I'll have a horse saddled for you."

Brady squared his shoulders and without hesitation headed for the saloon.

Three days later the sun was setting behind the western horizon as Brady, the sheriff, the Bjorn brothers, and ten of Anchor's ranch hands and a mule laden with supplies halted in a cottonwood grove.

"This is where Clarence Poe and his bunch brought the

big herd and where Willie Moon got the jump on me." Brady dismounted and pointed toward the makeshift pen. "We can corral the horses in there and make camp for the night."

"How much farther?" Bass Young stamped his feet as if to get the circulation going. "Been a long time since I rode this far this fast."

One of the ranch hands said, "Sittin' behind a desk done made you go soft, Bass?"

A round of good-natured guffaws filtered through the group of trail-weary men.

"Lester and his crew are camped over the rise. Thirty minutes more or less." Brady loosened the girth and slid the saddle off his horse.

"Reckon you've lost track of time, Brady. Between the two days it took you to ride in with Willie Moon and us riding hard for three days, most of a week's passed. Lester and his men are probably long gone by now."

Brady looked over at Anchor's foreman. "Clem, how long you figure it'll take to put an iron to about three hundred horses?"

The older man scratched his chin. "My best guess is a month, and that's if he's working several crews at the same time."

"What about guards, Brady? You think Lester will have any posted?" The sheriff's voice was terse.

"Not likely. We're miles from civilization and on Anchor land."

"Good. We'll take 'em by surprise."

After seeing to the care of their horses, the men gravitated to the campfire.

Murmuring broke out among the men and then silence. Tension rippled through the camp, and Brady waited. Sooner or later the questions were bound to come. A tide of thoughts flooded his head. What could he say to these men he'd let down and yet who chose to remain loyal to Anchor's brand?

He looked up at the cold blue sky with its three-quarter moon, trying to judge the time. Weariness throbbed in him, and he rolled his shoulders for comfort.

In the darkness polite coughs were expelled, feet shuffled, and one of the men stood and poured a round of coffee.

Clem Garrett flicked a spent cigarette into the fire. He coughed as if to clear his throat. "Brady, me and the boys, here . . . well . . ."

Brady sat up. At this moment, he figured that he and Anchor's ex-foreman were on equal terms of discomfort. "Whatever's on your mind, Clem, go ahead and spit it out."

The foreman cleared his throat again. "All right. Anchor's been home to most of us 'round this here campfire for more years than we can remember. Not pointing any fingers, but ain't too many ranches want to hire men who're betwixt young and old." He shifted his stance. "Reckon what I'm saying is, what are your plans for Anchor when all this is over?"

Brady stood. "Fair question, that's for sure. I've owned up to my crimes, and if I come out of this alive, I'll serve whatever punishment the law deems fit to hand down."

He scanned the expectant faces of the men he'd known most of his life and those he'd known a few months. "I'll hire a lawyer to find a legal loophole in the papers Judge

Parker drew up to break the partnership between me and Spearman, then with Bass' help, I'll rid Anchor of Spearman and the men he hired. Afterward, I plan a few changes."

An expectant quiet fell over the men, causing Brady to hasten on. "I'll need a ranch manager, a foreman, a couple of top hands, and a good crew to help me run the ranch."

Brady held out his hands to the fire's warmth and offered an unflinching gaze to each man.

"Brady Wilkes, ve help you get rid of Spearman, and ve get our freighting business back. Ja. Vhat you say, brother Sven?" said Gunnar Bjorn.

Sven stood and pounded a beefy fist into his other hand. "I'd like to break Spearman's head. He's a no-güt man vat takes away people's lives." In a more serious tone, he said, "Vhat about Hannah? Vhat vill happen to her in all of dis?"

"Hannah is smart girl, and she knows freighting from one end to the other. Ve hire her to run der office, ve buy horses from Brady, and ve drive our own freight wagons. Ja. Güt plan," Gunnar's said.

Bass spoke up. "I plan to catch those thieving galoots with their britches down. Have your weapons ready, but no shooting unless I signal otherwise."

He glanced at Brady. "I want One-eyed Lester alive."

"His testimony will put Spearman away for a long time." Brady crossed his arms over his chest. "What about his collusion with the quartermaster at Fort McClaren? And what about Judge Parker?"

He'd known Kate's father had regarded him as a shiftless good-for-nothing not fit to wed his daughter. But not once had he suspected the judge of colluding with Spearman.

Bass' voice pierced Brady's thoughts. "We'll worry about what comes next after we have Lester and his men behind bars."

Bass sat down and laid back against his saddle, pulling a blanket over him. "Gonna be a long day tomorrow. I suggest we all get some shut-eye."

Snores mingled with the songs of night creatures. Brady lay awake, his hands folded behind his head. With all the recent events in his life, he hadn't given much thought to Kate's unexpected marriage and how it felt to be a jilted man.

He flinched under his blanket. A small part of his pride still stung. As he lay there beneath the stars, he realized he'd never truly given his heart to Kate.

Instead of fearing tomorrow's dangers and the possibility of getting killed, he felt a sense of relief.

Chapter Twenty-one

Brady tamped down his impatience as he led the sheriff and the posse. With the crisp air and a night's rest, the horses stepped lively with heads held high.

The men rode toward a long, swollen ridge stretching out across the flatland.

At the middle of the ridge, Brady signaled for the men to halt. With barely the jingle of bridle chains, the posse dismounted, leaving their horses ground-hitched.

Bass removed his watch from its pocket and through the early-morning darkness held up fingers on one hand to indicate five o'clock.

Approaching the land swell on foot, the men fanned out and bellied down to the ground, their weapons aimed at the sleeping figures below.

Brady hoped the element of surprise would work as he

and the sheriff and the Bjorn brothers dug their heels in to keep from sliding as they descended the slope on foot.

Cold embers lay in fire rings. Men wrapped in gray blankets reminded Brady of cocoons. His eyes scanned the group for a quick count. He held up eight fingers—two more men than he'd figured. Bass and the Bjorns nodded their understanding.

Bass walked over to a sleeping form and, using the tip of his shotgun barrel, eased the man's sweat-stained hat up far enough to show a black patch that had slipped out of place to reveal scar tissue where once there had been an eye.

He flipped the hat off and placed the shotgun barrel under One-eyed Lester's nose. "Morning, Lester. Now that you've had your beauty sleep, you're under arrest."

"What—what the—" The expression on Lester's face was one of outrage and disbelief. He reached up and adjusted his eye patch. "Brady, what the hell's going on?"

"I'm a duly deputized officer of the law. You and your crew are going to jail for stealing horses and changing their brands as well as selling stolen horses to the United States Army."

Bass' loud voice boomed. "All you scudders are under arrest! Throw your weapons out from them blankets nice and easy-like."

Brady stood, legs wide, with the Winchester braced against his shoulder while Sven and Gunnar went about kicking the boots of sleep-bewildered men.

Lester shrugged off his blanket. He grabbed the handle of his Colt.

Bass cocked both shotgun barrels. "Nice and easy, friend. At this range, this here scatter gun'll make a mess of you."

Lester tossed the pistol at the sheriff's feet and then turned an angry eye toward Brady. "My, my, my. Brady Wilkes, hiding behind a badge. You think a tin star will protect you from Spearman? His power stretches all the way to Topeka."

Brady knew he was referring to Spearman's connection with Judge Parker. "Bass knows everything. Willie Moon confessed before he died, and Poco Crawford is awaiting trial in Hayes—if he's still alive. I'll take my licks, Lester. I'm not running anymore."

Someone shouted encouragement from the corral less than fifty feet away. A pistol spat, and dirt kicked up at Brady's feet.

A deputy from the rimrock returned fire, driving Fiske Cooper backward. For an instant he held his pistol in the air before he crumpled into a lifeless heap.

Men with faces filled with sleep and hate lunged for Sven and Gunnar. In a bold move, Lester tackled Brady, driving him to the ground.

Bass held his shotgun in the air and squeezed off both barrels. "All you sons of Satan, freeze!"

Gritting his teeth, Brady shoved hard, pushing Lester to one side. Brady drew back his right arm and sent a powerful haymaker to the one-eyed man's jaw, stunning him. Grabbing him by the shirt with both hands, he hauled Lester to his feet.

Eyeing Brady with a venomous glare, Lester curled his lip and snarled, "I'll dance on your grave before this is over, Wilkes."

Brady's slow smile was filled with contempt. "Shut up. Put your hands behind your back."

After Bass placed handcuffs on Lester, he pointed toward the freight wagon. "Get on up in there."

Bass looked up at the ridge. "Four of you boys bring rope and help us hog-tie this crew. The rest of you bring the horses."

He looked at Brady. "What's the best way to get the horses here?"

Brady pointed and yelled up, "Follow the rimrock for a half mile. There's a natural opening."

The prisoners' feet were hobbled, and the men were tied to each other.

Long Tom bellyached, "How come I gotta be tied to Billy Jack?"

Bass said, "If he decides to bail out of this wagon, he's taking you with him—right under the moving wheels."

Long Tom snarled his discontent.

"Listen up," Bass said to the prisoners. "It's a long ride back to Willow Creek. We'll feed you and allow time for when nature calls." He offered a thin smile. "Heed my word, boys, I won't object to any one of my deputies pluggin' you if you try to escape."

After settling the outlaws with coffee and a thrown-together breakfast of fried fatback and skillet bread, Brady, the sheriff, and Clem Garrett rode to the canyon where, days earlier, Brady had first spotted Lester and his crew building corrals.

Sliding from the saddle and stepping up onto the bottom rail of the rough poles, Clem blew a long, low whistle. "Fine-looking bunch of horseflesh."

He climbed down into the pen with Brady, and the sheriff followed.

Sleek and well fed, these were no ordinary range mustangs. Brady moved among the bunch. "Look at this, Clem." He rubbed his hand across the flank of a well-muscled dun gelding. "Sure would take a good eye to spot the change."

"Yep. By the time the hair grows in, it'll look like an old Trident brand."

Clem and Brady moved among the bunch, checking the brands before moving on to another pen. Clem said, "Looks like every last pony is wearing an altered brand."

"Four pens of fifty and one pen to hold the culls." Bass harrumphed. "Lester, Long Tom, and Fiske Cooper sure know their business."

Clem glanced at the sheriff. "What do you propose we do with those wearing altered brands? We can't turn them loose, and we can't sell 'em to the Army, and there's no way of knowing who they belong to."

Bass scratched his head. "Danged if I know. It's a dilemma, that's for sure."

Brady moved on to the other three pens. "These and the culls are still wearing their originals brands." He chuckled. "Slapping a hot iron on a horse isn't quite as easy as roping and throwing a steer." He stepped up onto the rail, swung a long leg over, and jumped to the ground.

"You know, Bass, there's plenty of feed and fresh water for the horses, and from the amount of beans and bacon, I'd say there's enough supplies in camp to last a month. We could leave a couple of men here to take care of the horses until we get the prisoners back to town."

"Still don't answer the question about how to get these animals back to their rightful owners."

"Mind if I make a suggestion?"

"I'm listening."

Facing the sheriff, Brady said, "Chances are most of the horses came from Colorado and Wyoming, maybe even Idaho. You might ask Mr. Pierce at the newspaper to write an article about stolen horses and wire it to surrounding newspapers, inviting the owners to come claim their stock—with proof, of course."

"Smart thinking, son. I'll have Pierce add that any horses not claimed by their rightful owners within sixty days will become property of Willow Creek's sheriff's office and sold at auction."

"Good. I've got plenty of corrals at the ranch. As soon as we rid Anchor of Spearman's henchmen, Clem can send a crew to bring the horses in."

"Reckon that means I can trust you not to hightail it over the mountains." Bass squinted hard at Brady.

Brady fixed an unwavering stare on the sheriff's face. "My running-away days are over, and whatever the law says I'm guilty of, I'll serve my time. You can trust me on that."

With a look of silent approval, Bass patted Brady on the shoulder. "Sooner we get this gang of misfits into my jail, the better I'll like it."

Full darkness covered Willow Creek as the posse reached the edge of town. According to plan, Clem Garrett clucked the horses and headed the freight-wagon load of prisoners down a back alley leading to the sheriff's office.

None of the group was aware of the lone figure watching from a darkened boardinghouse window. As she'd done every night since Brady and the sheriff had left, Hannah sat in her room and watched and waited until sleep drove her to bed.

Tonight she rested her chin on folded hands. She resisted a yawn as her eyes searched in the direction of Bass Young's office. With no prisoners to guard, the office was locked for the night.

Hannah couldn't help feeling a certain despair. All she'd ever wanted was to be loved by a man the way Brady had loved Kate Parker. Instead she'd settled for independence. *So be it.* She sighed heavily. *I've made my bed, and now I must lie in it.*

Against her will, her eyes fluttered shut. The moment her chin touched her chest, she jerked them open again. When she spotted the light in Bass Young's office, she jumped up so fast, she bumped her head on the windowsill.

Grabbing her cloak and fastening the hood in place, she eased the door open a mere crack and peeked outside before stepping into the hall. Glad the hall was empty and not wanting to draw attention to herself, she decided to use the back stairs.

Once outside, she crossed where shadows from the street lamps were deepest and, lifting her skirts, ran on tiptoe to keep the heels of her shoes from clacking on the board-walk.

Standing in front of a thick wooden door, she knocked and called out, "Sheriff Young, are you in there? It's me, Hannah Osterhaus."

As soon as the door opened, Hannah slipped inside and stood where she wouldn't be seen from a window. She stared at Brady, thinking for one idiotic moment that she'd conjured him out of thin air.

"Something wrong, Hannah?" Brady offered her a chair.

She stared at him. Her heart raced from hustling to bring her news and from something she couldn't define.

"Brady, Mr. Spearman came in on the afternoon stage from Topeka. About an hour later, he rode out to Anchor."

Brady glanced over his shoulder as Bass Young, Clem Garrett, and the Bjorn brothers entered the office.

Both Sven and Gunnar snatched off their hats and chimed in unison, "Evenin', Hannah."

She greeted each man with a fretful smile.

Bass Young said, "Well, we got the prisoners bedded down for the night."

Brady leaned against the desk and crossed his legs. "Bass, Hannah was telling me Spearman's back in town. He's already at the ranch."

The sheriff walked to the windows and pulled down the shades. "When?"

"He came to the office and gathered some papers, then said he was riding to Anchor as soon as he'd had supper." She turned back to Brady. "He said he needed to check on Lester and the horses."

"This isn't good, Bass." Clem Garrett paced about the office. "He'll gun down the men we left to look after the horses without the blink of an eye."

Bass Young heaved a weary sigh. "Too late to do anything about it tonight." He looked at Brady. "How long a ride from the ranch to the hideout canyon?"

"At a fast gallop, two hours. Spearman's gone soft sitting behind a desk. I don't see him pushing himself."

Hannah said, "Tomorrow is Saturday. It's the only day Mr. Spearman allows himself to sleep past seven o'clock, and he never goes anywhere without a large breakfast."

Brady offered her a grateful nod. "I think Mr. Louis Spearman is about to get the surprise of his life."

Clem Garrett said, "You can count on me and the boys to back you up, Brady."

"Ve too." Sven Bjorn glanced over at his brother, who nodded in agreement.

Gunnar placed his hands over his stomach when it grumbled. "Been long time for vhen I eat plenty güt."

By now the remaining posse had filed into the office. Wally Sims said, "Did I hear somebody mention food?"

Bass scratched the three-day-old bristles on his face. "Hannah, you run on over and let Ma Smalley know the sheriff's office is paying for these fellers' meals. Ask her to keep it quiet. Then I'd like for you to fix two plates and bring them back to the jail. Can you do that for me?"

"Oh, you can count on me."

"I'll go with you." Brady pushed away from the desk and stepped to the door.

"No, you mustn't. It's too risky." Her eyes pleaded with him not to follow. "Mr. Spearman said he had hired a few more men and told them to hang around town." She shrugged. "Though he didn't say why, I knew he meant for them to keep an eye out for you."

"I suppose he's planning another 'accident'—the way he planned Hogue's." Brady snorted with anger.

Without a word, he opened the door and watched her dash down the boardwalk until she disappeared into the shadows.

Before the men left the office, Bass Young said, "Clem, you and the men have rooms at the boardinghouse?"

Clem Garrett looked down at the floor. "No, sir. Those of us with no jobs are camped down by the river."

"That's about to change." Brady placed a hand on his foreman's shoulder. "As soon as we rid Anchor of Spearman and his scum, all you boys have your jobs back—if you're willing to work for me. If not, no hard feelings."

He was met with a hearty round of appreciation.

"We'll ride out together in the morning." Brady hesitated before he added, "With all the cells full, we need a warm place for the men to bed down. Got any suggestions, Bass?"

Gunnar Bjorn answered for the sheriff. "Ve haf room in our barn and der hay for bedding—a stove and plenty vood too."

"Good." The sheriff sighed. "Before you men go on and have your supper, a word of caution. Eat your meal, and don't discuss anything about where we've been or who we've got behind bars." He issued another warning. "Stay out of the saloon. Whiskey loosens a man's tongue. Right now we have the element of surprise, and I'd like to keep it that way."

Clem inquired, "What time do we ride, Bass?"

"Before dawn." Bass Young added, "Use the side door. No sense calling attention to ourselves."

An hour later Hannah arrived with a large basket dangling from her right arm, a smaller one on her left arm and a coffeepot wrapped in a towel. She rapped on the locked door. "Sheriff Young?"

Brady opened the door wide enough for her to scoot inside.

"Looks like you brought the whole kitchen." He took the coffeepot from her hands and set it on the desk in front of the sheriff.

She placed both baskets on the desk and removed the checkered napkin covering the food. "Beef stew, boiled potatoes, biscuits, and apple dumplings."

Bass Young slapped his hands against his belly. "I'm so hungry, I could eat Brady's share."

Brady laughed as he accepted the plate Hannah handed him. "What's in the little basket?"

"I was afraid you wouldn't take time for breakfast before riding out to Anchor, so I brought boiled eggs, more biscuits, and a crock of Ma Smalley's homemade jam. There's enough for all your men."

Brady flashed a weary smile and held out his hand to her. "You shouldn't be alone on the streets this late at night. Stay until I finish my dinner so I can walk you home."

She looked into his eyes and felt warmth flood through her body. Her heart said one thing—good sense said another. "The answer is still no and for the same reason—you need to stay out of sight."

"You're a good friend, Hannah. I won't forget what

you've done for us." Brady opened the door and watched her leave.

When he turned the key in the lock and again took up his plate, Bass Young said, "Son, you're a dang fool if you don't go after that girl when this is all over."

"Nope. Can't do it."

Bass shoveled another spoonful of stew into his mouth. "Why not?"

"I've got no right to ask her to wait while I'm serving time in prison for horse stealing. Besides, impersonating an Army lieutenant is still a hanging offense, isn't it?"

"Who said you were going to prison or getting your neck into a noose?"

"Come on, Bass." Brady didn't try to hide the exasperation in his voice. "You know Spearman and Lester aren't going to let me get away clean. Not with prison hanging over their heads."

The sheriff seemed to ponder Brady's statement. He washed his last bite of biscuit down with coffee. "Here's the way I see it. You were duly employed by Lou Spearman to buy horses—true?"

"True."

"Okay. Who set the prices for those horses?

"Spearman."

"All right, then. An employee can't go against his boss, no matter how raw a deal is dealt the rancher. Ranchers aren't obliged to sell their horseflesh cheap—true?"

"You got me on that one, Bass. But it still doesn't clear me of wearing the uniform."

The sheriff slammed his cup onto the desk. "Dagnabit, boy. I'm trying to help you out here. You got a death wish?"

"I don't think any man would wish such a thing on himself."

"And I don't think," said Bass, "whether you did or didn't wear a uniform will come out in the trial because it will definitely point fingers back at Spearman and maybe even Judge Parker."

The sheriff exhaled noisily. "Which would open a whole 'nother can of worms about Spearman's contracts with the Army, which would point fingers at the quartermaster, all of which would reflect very badly on the United States Army, and what with Judge Parker now living in Topeka with a son-in-law who is aide to the governor . . ." He spread his hands wide and smiled as he reached into the basket and pulled out the tin of apple dumplings. As he spooned a large portion onto his plate, he said, "You get where I'm going with this, Brady?"

"I do. It's just . . . well, I did wrong, and I feel—"

Waving a fork in the air, Bass said, "Yeah, I know. You feel guilty. Well, don't. I'm not saying falling in with Spearman was right. No, sirree."

He chewed appreciatively on a dumpling. "Here's the way I see it. You grew up with no ma, you had a pa who rode you hard and didn't mind puttin' the spurs to you—we all know how Hogue treated you.

"You've tried to put things right, son. I'll speak up for you, and, whether you know it or not, you've got a lot of friends here in Willow Creek who'll speak on your behalf in front of a judge—if it comes to that."

Brady supposed he'd become reconciled to the idea of going to prison. He glanced at the sheriff with a neutral expression, and though he cleared his throat, words refused to come out.

He touched the bandage on his cheek. "Think I'll head over to the Bjorns' barn and try to get a little shut-eye."

Chapter Twenty-two

Stars littered the morning sky as Bass Young and his posse rode toward Anchor. Brady knew an accounting would come at the ranch and that Spearman and his gang would spare no mercy. The one thing he was certain of was where to find his enemy. Spearman would set himself up in the main house, away from the crew in the bunkhouse.

Only the jingle of bridle chains, the creak of saddle leather, and the thud of hooves on packed dirt sounded in the darkness.

Brady thought about the letter he'd written the night before, before he'd turn off the lantern and hunkered down in a bed of moldy hay. His hand went automatically to his coat pocket, where he'd tucked the envelope. If things went wrong, he'd left instructions on how to dispose of the ranch, and he'd amply provided for the men who'd remained loyal to him, as well as his grandfather in the East, and especially Hannah.

Before leaving town, Brady had instructed the men to halt their mounts at the arched entrance to the ranch. Only the lone stamp of a horse's hoof sounded in the early dawn.

Gradually the lights of Anchor winked on. Brady watched the house until the dim glow of the office window was visible. He whispered, "Nice and quiet, boys."

On the dew-soaked earth, the posse and their horses made little sound as they entered the ranch yard. Skirting the wagon shed, the men dismounted behind the main barn. Without a word, all of them followed Clem Garrett to position themselves strategically around the bunkhouse and the cookshack while Brady and Bass Young strode to the house.

Easing up onto the stoop, Brady raised a fist and knocked on the outside office door.

Spearman called out, "That you, Stan?"

Brady slipped into the room while Bass Young stood guard outside to listen to Spearman hang himself.

Spearman sat at the desk, hunched over a stack of papers. Without turning around, he said, "I'll need a man to show me the way to Lester and the boys. They ought to have enough horses branded and ready for sale by now."

When nothing but silence answered him, Spearman swung around. "Dammit, man, cat got your tongue?"

When he saw Brady, he straightened and sat back in the chair. He removed the toothpick from a corner of his mouth and waved it idly at Brady in greeting. "How was the fishing? Catch any whoppers?"

"A few." Brady offered a wry grin. He flexed his gun hand.

"Glad you're back. Need you to ride with me to Lester's camp." No suspicion showed in Spearman's eyes.

"Willie Moon is dead. He told quite a story before he died."

Spearman tilted his head. "What kind of story?"

"He confessed to killing Hogue."

"Now, ain't that something? And all this time we suspected it was you."

Brady flexed his fingers again. "He said *you* gave him the order."

"Hope you didn't believe him. You know Willie Moon and Long Tom are both liars."

Brady didn't miss the way Spearman's hand inched downward. "Don't do it. Keep your hands where I can see them."

"You're a sniveling coward, Brady Wilkes. What're you gonna do—shoot me?" Spearman threw back his head and laughed at his own joke.

"Only if you push me. I'm no murderer." Though he didn't feel calm, Brady kept his voice mild. "Sit back and relax. I've got a story to tell you."

Spearman gave the appearance of a self-assured man as he interlaced his fingers across his ample belly. "I'm listening."

"Rain drove me back to the ranch—can't fish in the rain. So I took a little side trip instead. I know all about your operation of altering brands on stolen horses."

Spearman sat up straighter in the chair. "What're you trying to say, Brady? Go on, spit it out."

Although Spearman wore a smug grin, Brady didn't miss the faint line of perspiration on the big man's forehead.

"Bass knows I wore the Army uniform. I told him. Just as soon as I settle with you, he'll contact Major Erlich at Fort McClaren and fill him in on your and Sergeant Penn's scheme to keep out the other horse contractors. That's a Federal offense that reaches all the way to Judge Parker's accepting bribes from you." Brady pulled his Colt . 45. He motioned for his enemy to stand.

"Don't matter none." Spearman heaved himself to his feet. "If I go to prison, I'll still own half of Anchor. Watch your back, kid. I can always arrange for you to have an untimely . . . accident."

Before Brady answered, a flurry of shots rang out.

Bass Young yelled, "Sounds like all hell's brought loose at the bunkhouse! Grab Spearman and come on!"

The moment Brady glanced over his shoulder to look out the door, Spearman snatched the opportunity and leaped away from the desk. Using his massive hulk, he body-slammed Brady.

The two men tumbled out the door and down the steps, knocking the weapon from Brady's hand. Brady rolled to one side and grabbed for the pistol.

With the ferocity of a wounded bear, Spearman kicked the gun aside, and, pulling his own weapon, fired as he sprinted toward the barn.

Pain seared Brady's temple.

Continued gunfire splintered the morning. Shots sounded in every direction.

Brady knew he had to move—to help his men, to catch

Spearman—but an unrelieved blackness seemed to breathe all around him. A faint chill touched his back, and his mind jerked to his father's cruel punishments when he was a child and the hateful memory of being forced to stand outside the house for several hours on a frigid wintry day when he forgot to address his father as *Sir*.

He tried to lift his head. That was long ago. Another world. Another lifetime. Then he saw his father slap his mother across the face. Twice. Three times. Blood crept from the corner of her lip. She'd said nothing. Not a whimper.

He wanted to erase the memory. Moving his head brought pain, and he felt more tired than he'd ever felt in his life. Memory relinquished its hold on him, and he faded into a swirl of darkness.

Bass Young snarled as Brady's body jerked from the impact of Spearman's shot. Bass raised his weapon and pulled the trigger.

The empty chamber's click seemed to echo in the air.

With an angry growl, he holstered the empty pistol and raced through the barn to catch Spearman before he escaped on one of the saddled horses.

No longer a young man, Bass felt his lungs sear with the need for air as he lunged, grabbing Spearman around the waist and hauling him from the saddle.

The two men grappled, rolling under the hooves of startled horses that sidestepped, whinnied, and reared against reins wrapped around the hitching post.

Both men huffed as they rolled clear of the hooves. Fists tightly clutched shirtfronts as they both struggled to stand.

Spearman crashed Bass Young's body into the water trough. Bass struggled against hands that felt like steel traps around his throat.

Bass held his breath, clawing at the clutches that imprisoned him in what he was certain was about to be a watery grave.

The water muffled the shout, "Let go, Lou! It's over!"

A shot rang out, and Spearman released his hands from around Bass' throat. Bass guessed someone had fired a warning shot into the air.

Water dragged at his body as he fought to crawl out of the trough. He blinked to clear his eyes in time to see Spearman whip out his Colt and turn to face the voice.

Spearman squeezed off a shot before his massive body was slammed by two bullets in the chest. He staggered backward, dropped to his knees, then fell facedown in the mud.

A great, ragged gash angled across Brady's temple. The whole front of his shirt was stained with blood. Slowly he lowered the smoking gun.

He labored to where Bass stood bent double and gagging to clear his lungs of water.

Brady looked down at the massive, still form of Lou Spearman. Gunshots at the bunkhouse had stopped, and it was quiet.

Streaks of dawn cut brilliant strips of gold through the sky.

Chapter Twenty-three

November brought a dusting of snow to Willow Creek. After several months Brady's headaches were almost gone. He had invited Hannah to dine with him at the boarding-house restaurant. He sat back in his chair as Ma Smalley approached the table.

"Glad to see you up and about, Brady."

"Thank you, ma'am."

"Was a nice thing you did, giving Judge Parker's house to Gunnar and Sven Bjorn."

Brady picked up his napkin and wiped his mouth. "After the way Lou Spearman ruined their freighting business, it was the least I could do. Terms of my 'partnership' with Spearman stated that if either partner became deceased, the other gained legal ownership of all properties. Since the judge had sold his house to Spearman, it was mine to give away."

"The whole town's talking about the trial. Those boys of Lou's were sentenced fair and square—got what they deserved."

"Yes, ma'am. I'm glad it came out the way it did."

"How's it feel now that you're a free man?"

"I'm breathing a lot easier these days."

Ma Smalley patted Brady on the shoulder. "You and Hannah enjoy your dinner. I'll send over two extra-large slices of apple pie."

A faint smile curved Brady's mouth. He was scarcely able to believe that the circuit judge had exonerated him of all charges. Sometimes miracles did happen.

"Your long silence and brooding stare can only mean you've got something on your mind." Hannah gazed at Brady with the beginnings of a frown puckering her brow.

"Am I so easy to read?"

That made her smile. She shoved her food aside. "I can't eat another bite."

Brady pushed from his chair and offered his hand. "Hannah, is there a quiet place where we can talk?"

"My room."

"Not there—it wouldn't look right."

"I don't think Ma Smalley would object if we used her private parlor. I'll ask."

Without giving him a chance to answer, Hannah whisked herself away from the dining room. At the front desk she asked, "Is Ma Smalley in her office?"

The clerk merely nodded and went back to his paperwork.

Brady ambled to the lobby. He held his Stetson in one hand.

Hannah approached him with a smile. "Ma said it was okay." She reached out to him. "This way."

The parlor was a pleasant room with floral wallpaper and white lace curtains. Brady sat in a wing chair across from Hannah.

"What's this all about, Brady?"

He pulled the yellowed envelope from the inside pocket of his jacket and explained about the day he'd discovered the letter.

Hannah clasped her hands together in glee. "It must gratify you to know that your mother and Hogue were married. But why did he lie about finding you and most especially what he said about your mother being a . . . you know?"

"A fallen woman?" Brady shrugged. "Hogue was a hard man. Too hard."

Brady slipped the letter from the envelope. "I found this when I was going through an old steamer trunk in Hogue's bedroom. It explains why she left."

"If it isn't too personal, will you read it to me?"

Brady swallowed to clear the lump in his throat. He drew in a deep breath and held it a second. His voice was soft as he began, "Hogue . . ."

After Brady finished reading, he looked at Hannah. "My mother's name was Victoria Brady."

He went on to explain about finding the name of his grandfather written in the front of his mother's Bible.

Hannah pulled a hankie from the sleeve of her dress and dabbed at the tears on her lashes. "Then the story about you being the only survivor of a wagon train was a lie too."

Brady handed Hannah a news clipping. "This was tucked inside the letter. It says the driver of the stagecoach was trying to outrun a gang of outlaws, and the coach turned over when rounding a sharp curve. I was the only survivor. Hogue apparently went after my mother . . . for whatever reason—pride, perhaps."

"I don't understand why there's no one in Willow Creek who would remember your mother."

"The clipping is from a Topeka newspaper. I guess Hogue moved to Willow Springs after her death."

Hannah gave a little sob and dabbed the corner of her eyes with a hankie. "It's all so sad. What do you plan to do now?"

"I wired my grandfather and will leave for New England in two weeks."

When her brow puckered, Brady said, "I'm not running away, if that's what you're thinking. Visiting him will help me learn about myself."

She leaned forward, took his hands, and looked deep into his slate blue eyes. "I wasn't doubting you. Honest. I was just wondering about the ranch."

"Until I return, Anchor is in good hands. I've promoted Clem Garrett to ranch manager, and Wally Sims is now foreman, with Acosta and Meade working together as top hands."

She gave a little squeal. "I'm happy for you, Brady."

He liked the warmth of her hands. He regarded Hannah

with a look that might have been interpreted as indulgent. She was different from Kate. She was fresh and pretty, and she enjoyed a challenge, and he liked the way she accepted him for who he was.

"You once told me you wanted to know what was on the other side of the mountain. Still curious?"

Hannah laughed. "How will I ever earn enough money for such an adventure?"

Brady again reached into his coat pocket.

Her eyes widened when she looked into the envelope he handed her. "I . . . I don't understand?"

"It's a train ticket to San Francisco."

"Brady, this bank draft is for *five hundred dollars.*"

When he didn't answer, she asked, "Why?" Words seemed to escape her.

"You've been more than a good friend, Hannah. You stood by me during the trial. You rode out to the ranch to doctor my head wound." He shrugged. "A good friend deserves a reward. Travel wherever you wish and for as long as you desire. When you run out of money, I'll wire more to the nearest bank."

Her voice trembled when she spoke. "I don't know what to say."

"Say you'll have a wonderful adventure."

Lamplight from the overhead lanterns fell across her face in a gentle glow, and the rich sheen of her hair gleamed in shades of copper. When she looked up with a smile, he felt as if he had been hit in the pit of his stomach with a sledgehammer. It was the most unsettling thing that had ever happened to him.

He leaned forward and kissed her on the cheek. "Good night, Hannah."

Loneliness ate away at Brady as he sat next to the window, waiting for the train to leave Willow Creek Station. The warmth of his breath fogged the window. Using his bandana, he wiped a large circle and looked out at the thick copse of trees beyond the railroad tracks. Clem Garrett had driven him to town in the buckboard and had assured him not to worry about the ranch.

The conductor called, "All aboard!"

The train lurched forward, and Brady settled in the seat, sliding his Stetson down over his forehead and closing his eyes.

A soft voice interrupted his impending nap. "Excuse me. Is this seat taken?"

"No, of course not. Please, sit down." His voice trailed off as he sat up and snatched the hat from his head. "Hannah?"

"Hello, Brady." She tossed her valise onto the seat.

"This train isn't going to San Francisco."

"I know. I changed my ticket." She grinned at him as she slid into the seat and faced him.

His heart thumped wildly as he stared at her. She wore a stylish frock and a smart new bonnet. He sat with an open mouth, then he asked, "Where are you going?"

A soft smile flickered on her lips as she looked at him, and Brady swore he detected a hint of mischief when she said, "I thought I might like to begin my travels in New England."

Laughter burst from his throat, and she offered him an

impish smile. He reached forward and clasped her hands in his. This trip would certainly not be boring with Hannah along, and Brady suddenly knew he wouldn't have things any other way.

09/10/09